The BETELNUT KILLERS

The BETELNUT KILLERS

Manisha Lakhe

RANDOM HOUSE INDIA

Published by Random House India in 2010
13579108642

Copyright © Manisha Lakhe 2010

Random House Publishers India Private Limited
MindMill Corporate Tower, 2nd Floor, Plot No 24A
Sector 16A, Noida 201301, UP

Random House Group Limited
20 Vauxhall Bridge Road
London SW1V 2SA
United Kingdom

978 81 8400 106 8

This book is sold subject to the condition that it shall not, by way of trade or otherwise, be lent, resold, hired out, or otherwise circulated without the publisher's prior consent in any form of binding or cover other than that in which it is published and without a similar condition including this condition being imposed on the subsequent purchaser.

Typeset in Sabon by Inosoft Systems, Noida

Printed and bound in India by Replika Press

To Masho

ONE

'On a motherfuckin' day of the Lord...the bastards!' Detective Franklin D Wade muttered under his breath as he negotiated the fir-lined curves to the sanatorium located by the woods along the Willamette. 'Bugger the IA!' he muttered under his breath again. Wade turned down the radio and turned up the volume of his favourite FM station. 'I don't know what waits but I'm not afraid.' Randy Travis had just started singing.

'Yeah, motherfuckers!' Wade appreciated the sentiment. He waved his badge at the sleepy guard as he drove into St Vincent's Hospital and Sanatorium. The Sierra squealed as he pulled into the parking lot. He waited to hear 'I'll just make my own sweet way around the bend, here I go' before switching off the radio. The bastards had made him drive out on a Sunday. It better be worth it...

'I'm Dr Anjali,' she said needlessly. 'Damn! She is beautiful,' Wade thought, as he remembered the faint smell of spices in her hair when he had first met her at Harry's Bar. She had told him she was a doctor and he had not cared. She looked great in a miniskirt and that was all he had seen. And now he was following her white-coat-covered tush down the cold corridor of the asylum.

'That's your man,' she said. 'Mr Chiman Shah.'

The glass window in the door was fogged by her breath.

'Why is he tied to the bed?' asked Wade, inhaling Crest as he peered through the window.

'His blood pressure has been 149/99 but we have been asked not to give him any medicine until after you have spoken with him. You were supposed to be here two hours ago.' She looked at him squarely in the eye, making him stare right back into her own brown pools of honey. There was no fear in them, Wade noticed. She hadn't been afraid of him that night either. Wade was a big guy and his size could intimidate just about anybody. Immigrants, anyway, were easy to scare. They were usually physically small, and mostly lived frightened lives.

'Since we could not sedate him, we strapped him down. It's a standard precaution; makes it easier for the staff to undertake routine examination.'

And before he could say anything she added, 'Your department made a special request so we have not given him anything. They said you needed to see him in the same state as he was when he was found. We've had to clean him up, of course, and have clothed him, but there are photographs.'

Wade stared through the little glass window. So this was the little bastard who could be responsible for that unholy mess! He had read the report and then driven past what could only be described as a disaster zone. The explosion must have been quite powerful. The neighbours had called 911 and the $250,000 home had been reduced to ashes even before the firefighters had reached the damned gates. They had found Chimanbhai with clothes ripped to shreds, naked for all practical purposes, incoherent to boot, shivering from the cold and the shock, and hiding in the woods adjacent to the once beautiful home. Yet here he was now, dressed in an incongruous blue hospital gown with pink flowers, strapped to a grey bed in a grey and cold room. The room was so devoid of personality that it could have been anywhere, any place. As Wade looked on, he could almost smell the discomfort the 'patient' was feeling.

It was a damned stupid question to ask a man whose house had blown up, perhaps with all the occupants burnt to cinders. But who could tell? There were no apparent signs of any body parts left. No, nothing. This man was the only witness. And Wade was here to make him talk.

'They brought him here in an extremely agitated state,' the doctor was saying.

'Hmm...I am sure you can fix that. After I find out why and what got him so agitated.'

'They'll bring him to you.'

As she shook her head to point to an adjoining room, her dark hair escaped the severe coil at the back of her head. Wade had not noticed the two burly men who had followed them quietly. He was slipping. He was trained to notice everything, miss nothing. Maybe it was because it was a damned Sunday. Or maybe it was the faint smell of spices that surrounded her like a damned halo.

The next hour and forty-five minutes were spent in a barrage of questions. Wade was one of the 5th Precinct's best. He could get the toughest cookie to crumble. This puny Indian in a straitjacket was nothing.

'So Chee-man Shah, what do you have to say for yourself?'

Nothing. Not even an eyeball twitch.

'Don't fuck with me, Shah. How did your $250,000 home blow up?' Wade wished he could smash that bald head against the walls. 'What's the matter with him, doc?'

'Detective, he's already agitated. You have to calm down.'

'I am calm dammit!' He said and turning back to the patient he barked, 'Shah! Tell me. What happened?'

Not a fucking thing if his silence was anything to go by.

'Doc, he's glassy eyed. Are you sure you guys haven't given him something?'

'Detective!'

He pulled up a chair and sat down in front of the patient. Wade opened the file with all the pictures that the firemen and the police team that answered the 911 had taken of the rubble that was the Shah home. He showed each picture, and asked the same question over and over again, patiently this time, enunciating each word as if talking to someone who did not understand English.

'You are Chee-man Shah, right? Then this is your ho-muh. What happened to your home?'

'Did you blow up your home? You understand "blow up"?' Wade was beginning to count to ten in his head. 'See this picture.' He pointed to a burning hole in the house. 'What happened? Why did the house go kaboom?'

The vacant look from Shah was getting Wade more and more frustrated. 'Shah! Look at me. You must tell me what happened. You understand? I am the po-lees,' he emphasized. 'Po-lees! I am here to help you. H-E-L-P. But you must talk to me.'

Chiman Shah didn't stir. Agitated, Wade dumped the file on the floor. He leaned forward. 'What happened to your family? Fa-mee-lee? Where did they disappear?'

Nothing. The bastard wasn't going to answer. Turning to the doctor, he asked, 'Look, you belong to the same community, eh? Are you sure he speaks English? Maybe you can talk Indian to him. Do you know anything about him?'

'Bob! There are more than 2,000 Indian families in the Greater Portland area. And over 1,500 in the Beaverton area alone. You think I know them all? And yes, I should think he speaks English. He used to run the grocery store down at the Beaverton Mall.'

Wade stared at the man. He didn't look like he

could run anything. Unless...unless he was pretending all this time... A sudden urge to hit the man with the chair crossed his mind. Of course Anjolie was not helping him. She was pretending to be all cool and professional.

'A store at the mall? And he made enough money to live in a swank place like that? Something's not right about this Paki bastard...' Wade was thinking aloud.

And the moment he said it, the incident at Harry's flashed through his head. Wade had been out celebrating a marijuana haul with the boys when he spotted Anjolie dancing with a couple of other Indian girls in the corner. He had danced with her that night. She had looked so hot in that miniskirt. Wade had made a pass at her in front of the boys. The boys had jeered at her and he had been too drunk to notice any racial slur. She had walked out and he hadn't apologized. He knew she was a doctor, but...

'Paki? I can't believe you're saying this!'

The doctor flounced off. God! Nothing was going right! He stared at Chimanbhai Shah who was staring blankly at nothing. Wade felt a need to do something so that he would stop feeling like a bloody upcountry white boy. He was not a racist, but the niggling thought that these bloody outsiders were making so much more money than him kept coming back. He was living in a Northeast apartment whereas the grocery store guy was rich enough to live...Wade turned to Shah again.

'Shah, let's try this one last time,' he said, his

voice raised a trifle higher. 'Your Winderly Heights home...do you remember what happened to it?'

Mr No Expression just sat there on the chair, without blinking his big brown eyes.

'If you're having me on, I'll make sure you're put away for many lifetimes. I'll make sure you'll regret sitting on your fanny and not sayin' a thing.'

Not a muscle twitched on the bastard's face. A slap across his little brown cheeks was what he needed, Wade thought. But he would save it for when they had him in custody. He did not want to create a scene in front of the two guards standing discreetly at the door.

'Detective.' She was back, the guardian angel of madmen.

Wade was sure she could feel his frustration.

She did. Because she was extending a slender arm that held a cup. 'Chai latte?' she offered.

'Chai? Hmm...thank you.' He extended his hand for the styrofoam cup. Their fingers touched briefly.

'Chai it is. With two sugars!'

'I like this chai.'

'CHAIEEEEEEGAAAAAAHHHHHHH EEEEEEEYAAAAAAAAIIIIIIOOOOOOO-OOOOMAAAAAAIREEEEEEEEEEE...'

He had just raised the cup to his lips when Shah started wailing on top of his lungs. Stunned, Wade dropped the hot chai latte on the floor. 'Fucccck!' he yelled, as the hot chai scalded his hand and splashed on his trousers.

'KALEEEEEEEEE! OH MAAAAAAA AAAAAAAAAAAAAA MAAAAAAAAA... KALEEEEEEEEEEEE!'

It was as if Shah was possessed. That yell was unreal! And Shah's eyes were rolling with such ferocity that they could pop out of their sockets any moment.

The two silent helpers had come barging into the room and were now trying to hold the thin, geeky man down. It took an old-fashioned restraining with duct tape to keep Shah from kicking. But the screaming continued.

'AIMAAAAAAAAAA! KALEEEEEE EEEEEEEEEEEEEEEEEEEE MAAAAAAAAAA OOOOOOO MAAAA KALEEEEE!'

Wade stared at the doctor and then at Shah. Now, he was used to sirens and loud noises, but this was something out of the world. It made his skin crawl, and the hair on the back of his neck bristle. Anjali looked as though she had been gobsmacked. It seemed she knew exactly what the man was saying.

'What is he saying?'

'I...I'm not sure,' Anjali said hesistatingly.

So she wasn't going to tell him. Pretty women were all the same: difficult. Wade wanted to wring her neck for being so fucking...

'AAAAAAAA KALEEEEEEEEEEE!'

Wade did just what he had been itching to do since he had started asking Shah his simple questions. The slap resounded in his ears, and his hand stung like a bitch. But it felt so good. And it worked too. Shah stopped wailing. He was now rocking back and forth in his chair, mumbling.

Wade watched the man. He realized that he was not going to be an easy nut to crack. He looked at Anjali. She was not about to say anything either. And he couldn't force her to tell him anything. At least not with those two men watching silently.

'I don't see any point talking to this man right now. If there's any change in his condition, call me. The rooms are being monitored, right? I shall have someone collect the tapes. Thanks.'

He opened the door and marched down the corridor to the elevator. He knew she was following him, but he did not break his stride.

Once outside, he wanted to turn around and confirm if she had followed him. The breeze that had sent a chill down his spine when he had arrived at the hospital, was not shuffling through the large Douglas firs in the parking lot of the hospital any more. Instead there seemed to be a strange eerie silence everywhere as though it were imitating the patient he had just left. Had Wade studied Shakespeare, he would have understood.

He stopped walking only to unlock the door of his truck, and that's when he saw Anjali running towards him.

'Detective! Robert!'

He paused. So she remembered his name. His eyes were covered by standard issue sunglasses, otherwise she would have noticed his irritation melt away at the sight of her breasts. 'He was saying "Kali" repeatedly. Now Kali is the Mother Goddess. When she's...erm... pissed off, she destroys everything that's in her way. But that's Hindu mythology...' she said, making an effort to get her breath back to an even keel.

So she had finally decided to help with some mumbo-jumbo religious shit? And she expected him to believe it? Heaving breasts or not, he was still a bit pissed at her.

'Sure. A rampaging goddess blew up his house. With what? A couple of sticks of dynamite? I believe ya, doc. I'll write that in my report. It'll look pretty darned credible in my report, Anjolie. Thanks.'

Anjali corrected him instinctively, but chose to ignore the sarcasm. 'It's An-ja-li. But you heard him too, right? But there's something odd here. Chiman Shah is Gujarati. Now these people don't say "Kali". They believe in "Amba"—the calm goddess. Kali is the one who destroys.'

'Oh! There's more than one now?'

'No! I mean yes. He said "Kali", right? But why would he repeatedly call on Kali? And did you realize he went berserk when you mentioned "chai"? Why?' She was looking away from him, genuinely puzzled.

'Yeah, I said chai, but you brought me that chai. You leave the investigation to me, doc, okay? You just fix him so that he can talk.'

'He said Kali destroyed...'

'Enough of the bullshit, An-jali! You know that

man was wailing. Maybe you just heard "Kali". Now why would an Indian goddess show up in the US and destroy his home? God doesn't destroy, evil does. And that man looked pretty evil, wailing like that. So don't. Don't take me for a fool, all right?'

Wade turned on the ignition and drove away, his truck leaving a spray of gravel.

As the truck disappeared from view, Anjali noticed a sticker at the back of it which said, 'Jesus saves'.

'No wonder he did not believe the story.' She giggled hysterically.

* * *

Back in the makeshift interrogation room, the wailing had stopped. Chimanbhai was staring at the floor as the nursing assistant cleaned up the mess left by the detective's tea. He swayed his head from side to side, imitating the movement of the mop. The two burly helpers had seen it all. But this man was clearly demented. The doctor returned, and asked them to move the patient back to his room. The two men carried the straitjacketed Mr Shah, legs duct-taped to the chair, back to his room, and dumped him there. The lone camera on the ceiling was on, recording Mr Shah mumbling to himself.

TWO

Ever since Californians discovered the joys of living in the Pacific northwest, the population had grown and Portland had expanded right up to Vancouver, Washington, in the north, and Salem in the east. Now there were stories of murder and marijuana where the governor's missing cat had once made headlines.

However, the governor's planners kept the tree huggers in the news by creating one more ugly mall down by the southern plains, not twenty-five miles from the city centre. Off the I-5, this new Beaverton Mall was an eyesore to one and all. But the planners were one step ahead. The governor announced and created—to the joy of all those who had planned to boycott the mall—an artificial lake and woods. Under the expert supervision of the tree huggers, fully grown trees were transplanted and a lake created by tapping into the rich water table. The result was fantastic.

Funds for such fabulous public facilities came from yet another crafty venture. Affordable luxurious housing at mortgages one could only dream about.

Anyone who wanted to be someone bought a home there. The politicians even had the police chief's granddaughter name it. And she was so darned cute when she said, 'It's so winderly out here, Grandpa.' And so it was named 'Winderly', Winderly Heights for the ambitious Oregonians. The row and the hatred for the ugly mall soon faded from public memory.

Developed in the prettiest corner of Beaverton and Tigard, the houses in Winderly did not resemble any of the cookie-cutter houses of the rest of the suburb. This development was special. The woods shielded the $200,000–300,000 homes from the row houses and the apartment complexes that dotted the rest of the landscape. The lake offered the residents a place to walk or jog. Each home was designed to have a landscaped garden in front and a beautiful yard at the back. The garages were created with a workshop room above them, and the rooms were spacious. Only a few who could afford such luxury could make these their home.

Chimanbhai was the proprietor and entrepreneur of Indian Groceries in the Beaverton Mall. The fact was that he could not really afford to pay the $1,700-per-month mortgage, and that he had actually bought the place because of Radhika, his wife. Radhika, the matriarch and chief nag, had persuaded him to invest in this beautiful but overpriced home. Radhika knew a Winderly home would make her the object of envy among all the Indian women. She had taken great pains to furnish the house, filling it with knick-knacks from India. She had sent for the best velvet curtains from Ahmedabad, and there were vases strategically placed with matching silk roses, carefully covered in polythene to keep the dust away. The furniture was American, markdowns from the Sears catalogue, but cleverly disguised by the crochet and embroidery covers from India. But the pride of place was occupied by not one, not two, but four Lazyboys.

No matter how hard Radhikaben and Chimanbhai tried to remain Indian in an alien country, their two kids Maya, the older one, and Suraj, the younger, were very, very American. They were brought up on daal dhokli, but if given a choice, they would happily exchange these for cheeseburgers and fries. Radhika was happy with Maya's explanation: 'Cheeseburgers are made from cheese, Ma, and hamburgers from ham. Suraj and I don't eat hamburgers, so don't worry. We are Indians after all.' She didn't understand why Maya and Suraj had laughed hysterically at this. She blamed it on the company of white kids her wonderful children were keeping, but she could fix that.

Suraj was going to grow up and look like Chimanbhai. Radhika was happy with that. She knew that Suraj would inherit the receding hairline, but that was okay for a man. At least he had a nice straight nose and her colouring. As for Maya, she thanked her stars that they were in foreign lands. If they had been in India they would have had to collect dowry for her since her birth. However, why

Maya had to inherit Chiman's dark colour Radhika failed to understand. Fate played such games! Chaalo! She thanked the gods every day that they were far away from the matchmaking mausis, who would have disapproved of Maya's complexion. She tried her best to get Maya to put all kinds of fairness creams for that milky whiteness but the stubborn girl insisted she was not dark but dusky. 'Duskee? Aajkaal ni chokri...' Radhikaben sighed. 'They will never understand a mother's worries!'

In spite of Radhika's many trivial concerns, the Shah family was doing all right.

Today Chimanbhai was in a good mood. He was wearing his favourite pair of track pants and his lucky Mount Hood sweatshirt. Four years ago the children had insisted that the parents accompany them to Mount Hood. That show-off Mehta had challenged Chimanbhai into learning skiing, and had bet that Chimanbhai would fall more times than him. But Chimanbhai had won and by twelve falls. Mehta had to reluctantly buy the $150 sweatshirt from the gift shop for Chimanbhai.

Chimanbhai wore the sweatshirt carefully. He was feeling lucky again today. A second store was certainly a good thing, and perfectly fit his expansion plans.

'Dhando badhee gyo! Suraj ki ma! The shop is the beginning of our empire! Soon Bill Gates will call us to his home for chai. You make some for me now, Radhika?'

'You also, na! Calling me by my name in front of

the kids. We left country but we still have culture. Take chai. I put extra milk. Because you bring good news. I am telling you now, my papads and chutneys we will keep in separate section in the nava store.'

'You promised me a new car, Puppa!' That was from Maya.

Chimanbhai looked at the girl at the dining table from over his glasses. She was dressed in short black clothes, and her hair always looked like she had not combed it for years. Her lipstick was bright red. And, except when she was eating the chewing gum, was a constant companion. As were the many rings, bracelets and chains of skulls and daggers that jangled as she walked. Chimanbhai often wondered how this vision of what the Americans called punk was actually the fruit of his desi loins.

'Maya! Go change your blouse. I can see through to your navel! Ambe! When will this girl learn!'

Radhika had encouraged Maya to become American, but she herself was still a Gujarati mom. Thank god for the little mercies! Chimanbhai knew there was no point in him trying to discipline Maya. She would just stare and stare at him until Chimanbhai walked away in despair.

'What's wrong with my blouse?'

'Everything, Didi!' piped up Suraj.

Chimanbhai saw in his son a lot of himself. And a bit of what the Americans called 'geek'.

'Shut up, Suraj! You retard! Shut up or I'll tell Dad you've been surfing for porn.'

'Bhawani Ma! Ab yeh porn kya hai? Maya! Don't laugh like that!'

'Neeraj, you've been looking at my blouse, ne? Tell Ma there's nothing wrong with it!'

Neeraj was Chimanbhai's second cousin's son who lived in Surat and had married a tart, Sumati, from Mumbai. Neeraj looked handsome, just like Himesh Reshammiya. Although he had the same eyes, he could not sing at all. He was trained for computers. Neeraj had moved from India a couple of years ago, stayed in a bachelor pad somewhere in the hippy northwest part of town. Chimanbhai knew Neeraj had a job in a computer company but he had never seen him dressed up to go to work. Every time he walked into their home (for food mostly), along came a funny smoky headache-inducing smell.

'Heh, heh, heh! Raadha…er, Chachi…the blouse is…'

'Papa, I will computerize the system in the new shop!'

'Leave it, Suraj. I don't need your computer and your fancy system. I trust my chopdo and my brain.'

'Maya! Go change your blouse now!' shouted Radhika.

'Ma! You are so unfair!'

Maya's complaints at the breakfast table were suddenly interrupted by the shrill ring of the telephone. Chimanbhai picked up the phone and with a wave of his hand asked them to stop arguing. As he turned to the big bay window with the phone, Suraj busied himself with a comic book, Radhikaben started clearing the table. Neeraj resumed ogling at Maya, and Maya playfully pulled the neckline of her blouse down and sat provocatively across him at the table to make his jaw drop.

* * *

It was drizzling again. More than forty years had passed since he had left his hometown in Gujarat. He was only a young chhadaa when Motiben and Bapu sent him to America for 'bhaag khulwanu'. Chiman's heart was broken when his Meenakshi was married off to some rich trader. He had worked damned hard at his uncle's grocery store, dreaming of meeting Meenakshi once again. But America was big and it had swallowed him. And with the passing of years Meenakshi had become an almost forgotten fading photograph hidden behind Bhawani Ma's picture in Chimanbhai's wallet. His uncle had not left him a fortune, but it was enough for young Chiman. He had persevered to make the store work. More and more Indians, Bangladeshis and Pakistanis were moving to Portland, and his was the only store that brought the authentic tastes of home to this country of cold, grey rain. 'Bas!' Chiman said to himself. He switched on the light in the temple and bowed to Devi's photo. 'Tamaru pariksha ma saru likhiyu, Ma! Now you just give me good marks for my effort. A new store would be perfect pass marks for the exams.' He trusted Devi Ma to look after him, but had worn the lucky sweatshirt just in case.

The little 'ding' of the bell announced an arrival. Had Devi Ma answered his prayers so quickly? 'Jai Ma Ambe!' Chimanbhai exclaimed and turned to the arrival. It was Mr Menon.

'How you are doing, Mr Menon? Kem cho?'

'I am fine, Mr Shah. You have done well. I remember when your uncle used to run this place. It used to be smaller then, no?'

'Very right, Menonji. I bought two shops next to the old shop and made them into one. And that too all by myself. Chachaji would be happy, no? Business is good now. But it is time to branch out. Portland is becoming bigger. I want to reach out to more and more people. Maybe start home delivery like back home. Expand on videotape business. Children now want only DVDs. We have to cater to young people, no?'

Mr Menon was shaking his head. Chimanbhai remembered Maya call it the Indian yes and no. 'Ambe Ma!' he prayed in his head. Let it be a yes. Just then he noticed that Mr Menon had not brought any papers with him. 'You did not bring the papers for the shop?'

'Rahu kalam, Rahu kalam,' muttered Menon.

'So we wait until the planets are right. But we need to sign the papers today. The bank will need it by 10 am tomorrow.'

'Listen to me, Chimanbhai. There is a slight problem. Only slight, but still a problem.'

Chimanbhai touched his lucky sweatshirt involuntarily. 'Whaaat? What are you saying?

Everything from my side is done. You agreed to the price. The cheque will be in your hand tomorrow at 10 am, just as we had planned. How can there be a problem now?'

'I cannot give you the shop,' blurted Mr Menon.

'You cannot say that! Why you backing off? You got a new buyer? Who else can handle this area? All are my customers. Everybody knows I am opening a branch.'

'Please listen to me, Mr Shah. I am most embarrassed about this. I am a man of my word. But...'

'But what, Mr Menon? You sold your honour to some Punjabi fellow? I know that Singh from Seattle has been travelling around Beaverton. You sold him for better price, haan?'

'No, Chimanbhai, it's nothing like that. I am really ashamed to say no to you. It's actually my niece Supriya. She's a modern young girl, studying sports at the university and recovering from an accident. Doctors say that she needs a quiet job. No more active sports or rock climbing. It is the family's decision. We have to let her handle the shop.'

'Your niece? What does she know of handling shop?'

'We were hoping you will be her guiding light. Teach her.'

'She wants job, she can work in the store. In any case, she has already worked here before in the summer. Why you are not selling me the shop?'

'It's not possible, Chimanbhai. She's very proud

and wants to handle store by herself. Her father, that is my elder brother, helped me when I left home to come here. It is only right that I help his daughter. You understand, no?'

Chiman Shah stood staring at the achaar counter and his brains felt pickled suddenly. He could not even begin to imagine how this man who smelled of coconut oil had turned his whole life upside down in one minute.

'Okay, Mr Shah. I am sorry, so sorry. But you understand.'

That bichchhoo ni aulad! He stabbed me in the back, and slimed out like a true scorpion, scurrying out after stinging me...

'Hey Ma! Su thai karochyo! What did I do to deserve this?' Chiman Shah's dreams had crashed to the ground. His heart was beating like a dholak as he stood there with his mouth open.

'How am I going to break this news to the family?'

Menon tricked me! He asked me if his niece could do a summer job with me. No salary, she needed to show work experience on her résumé. Who knew that a girl who did not have a job was going to turn out to be such a snake!'

He sat down in his chair. It rains two hundred days in a year in Portland. It is mostly a drizzle, but today, the whole sky threatened to come down. Chiman Shah felt the burden of the sky like no one else had.

* * *

'Su kayocho? What you are saying, Chiman! How can you work for a chokri? It was supposed to be our shop. Not her shop with you working under her! Our shop, no one else's.'

'How did you even agree to such a thing, Dad?' asked Maya in disbelief.

'You must've heard it wrong, Dad. You never listen to anyone correctly anyway,' said Suraj.

'What heard wrong heard wrong you are doing, Suraj! If I had heard wrong, then where are the papers? Hey Mata! Babaji is also coming. I have told everyone we are going to have new shop. What all I will have to hear! Babaji was going to bless the shop!'

'Who is the girl, Dad?'

'Arre, that Menon's niece. Her name is Supriya. He wanted me to "mentor" her, show her how to run the shop! Mhari mat maree gayee hai ke? I will not teach my competition how to run shop!'

'Yes dad. That's a bad idea!'

'Maya didi! Feed that damned cat of yours. She has been mewing for the past hour,' said Suraj.

'How many times I said that cat is not good omen. Bad for house. Now see! Bad news come about shop. But go feed it. If she is hungry, she will bring more bad luck.'

'Caligula! Caligula! Here puss, puss, puss!' Maya called, stepping away from the table, and then sauntered off to feed her cat.

THREE

It had been only three months and Chimanbhai was already feeling the pinch. This morning had been somewhat okay, considering Chimanbhai had two customers, both women, who hated the new store as much as they hated the new owner, the sexy Supriya. She had managed to take away so much of his business that at one point he was considering shutting shop and going back to India. The day he refused to drink tea is when Radhika decided to take charge. She would not allow Chiman to think about India. She stopped watching the Indian TV channels, she even made pasta at home to remind him that his kids were American, and that he had to stop listening to 'Dukhi man mere' on his iPod again and again and psyche himself into believing all was lost. Although the kids had claimed that jeera and heeng tadka in pasta was a disaster, Chiman had cheered up a bit. He had called her Mother India and had promised her that he would not give up the shop so easily.

Suraj had created a wonderful poster showing Chimanbhai as Clint Eastwood and had named the scheme 'A Few Dollars Less'. Customers had not exactly poured in, but for four days, the forever broke Intel chaps had come in to buy bread and other items. Just when Chimanbhai had decided that he would take Suraj's help and make more posters from the Internet from here on, he spotted Supriya calmly walking up to him. He was talking to that good Bengali boy Tapas and handing over the change.

'Hello Tapas boy! You forgot something...' Supriya was pouting at his customer! Chimanbhai saw red.

'Ei! Kya karti hai! What are you doing in my store?' Chimanbhai bristled, then sputtered because he had noticed her very short skirt and her very long legs and her cowboy boots.

'You talkin' to me?' Supriya was batting her eyelashes at him! The cheek! Then she looked at Tapas and imitated Chimanbhai, 'And what are you doing in *this* store, my roshogolla boy? Haven't you forgotten something?'

Tapas had not stopped staring at the girl's cleavage. Chimanbhai understood this typical Indian male fancy with things mammary. Thank goodness he was a leg man. He liked generous thighs. But he needed to concentrate. Get this...this harpy out of his store! Right in front of his eyes she was seducing his customers! She was extending one red-tipped finger towards Tapas's chin and tipping it so he was now making eye contact with her. 'Naughty Tapas! Have you finished being a typical miserly little Indian and buying discounted foods? Then come over to my store. I have got the DVD you wanted...'

Tapas muttered, 'I'm coming now, I'm coming now.'

Supriya burst into laughter that reminded Chimanbhai of Kaikeyi and other vengeful women in all the stories he had heard growing up.

In spite of knowing that it was a pointless exercise Chimanbhai yelled, 'Get out of here! He's my customer!' She had come into his store to steal his customer who was looking very uncomfortable now as he stared at Supriya standing right next to the Clint Eastwood poster. 'Very cute, Chimanbhai! More for less?' Then she looked at Tapas and said, 'In my case, less is always more, no?' Tapas said nothing. He was staring at her short skirt, her short tee and her cowboy boots that offered him so much more...

'Get away from my poster! Get away from my shop!'

As Maya and Radhika drove past the mall, they spotted a group of two to three young Indian men walking with dazed expressions towards their cars. Radhika started sniffling. Tears came easily to her.

'Ma!' Radhika called for divine intervention. 'How long do we need to suffer the insults?'

'Mom! What good is it praying to some god? Dad needs to do something instead of taking longer and longer siestas, and shutting the shop in the afternoon.'

'Don't say anything about Chiman! He is doing

his best. It's that…that waidi… What's her name? Menon ki saali…'

'Saali naheen, niece.' Maya giggled at her own joke.

'Chup! That vanari is showing her true colours now! Chhote chhote kapde pehen kar choron ke aage yeh aise, aise jhuk jaati hai! Ab aisee kootri ke saamne Chiman kya karega bechara!'

'Mom! Can you imagine Dad putting it all out for Mrs Mehta? She has the hots for him, you know!'

'Chup reh! Bahut bakwaas karne lagee hai! You think I am your equal, ne? We are Indian parents, remember. You don't talk about your father like that. Show some respect! It is my fault only…'

'Ma!'

'Don't interrupt! Totally my fault. I only told Chiman. We are in new country, we must bring our children up like American children. No beating. Now I regret it much. Chiman was always telling me, inside the house we are Indian, outside we can be all American. I am only at fault.'

'Mommm! Cut it out. You just rant away, don't you? From Supriya to Dad to me and upbringing! Really now! Get a grip.'

'Just take me back home now. I don't feel like shopping.'

The Nissan Sentra took a neat turn and Maya took her mum back home. Kishore Kumar's CD playing 'Koi humdum na raha…' did not help. Radhika sniffled all the way back home.

***

The days were passing too fast for Radhika. And every new day brought fewer customers for Chimanbhai, and more domestic troubles for her. That morning it started with Maya. Again.

'What is that you are ironing, Maya?'

'This? It's a skirt, Ma.'

'Skirt? Hey Ma! Chiman, maybe Maya could help you in the store!'

'Radhika! What is happened to you? You think I should ask my daughter and her legs to bring in customers? Chi-chi, Radhika! Just listen to yourself. As if I am not trying my best already.'

'Discount, discount, discount! What else can you give at the store? What did you get? You forgot how that kootri shamed you?'

'What happened, Ma?'

'Arre, just last afternoon it happened. Your father and I were shutting the store for lunch. That...that waaghrail was coming with the two lafangas from Intel, you know, the one that has that mooch like a brush, and that other who is just a haddion ka dhaancha. They were carrying bags for her as though she were some queen of Bikaner.'

'Mom! You're digressing. What did Supriya do?'

'That kootri! She walks like Helen. Such heels. So she walks up to Chiman and me and begins to giggle.'

'She giggled?'

'Shamelessly she says, "Cho chweet, Chimanbhai, how is your discount store going? Is the little wife helping out?"'

'What did you say to that, Dad?'

'"Discount store?" Your dad says, "This is not a discount store, beta!" He called her beta!'

'Arre, what else could I say?'

'Mom, get on with the story!'

'So she says, "But look, you are offering so many discounts! But I take your word for it. Maybe you should sell the store to me. I have not needed to sell anything at a discounted price. These boys love my new store. Maybe you should come see it sometime. I have installed a new slush machine. The boys like that, no?" The stupid boys just laughed like heheh-hehh. I was so mad. I said, "My Chiman has been selling daals and papads before you were wearing diapers. He doesn't need your advice."'

'Good for you, Mum!' Maya said.

'Arre, aur naheen toh kya! She has some cheek! I gave her my best evil eye. Just like Bindu in the movies. She just shrugged her shoulders and walked off! What else could she say! I stopped her stupid mouth. And what colour lipstick was that! Red! I feel so angry just thinking about it.'

'Arre, just listening to this again is giving me a headache. Please Radhika, make me a cup of your lovely milky chai.'

'Ugh, chai latte!' Maya said, shuddering dramatically.

'What ugh? Only poor people drink chai that is more like paani. We Gujaratis prefer tea that is made with proper time given for tea leaves to boil with the milk. Lots of sugar needs to be put otherwise it tastes bitter. And in my mother's side, we put ginger. Chimanbhai likes cloves and cardamom. I, too, have started liking tea like that.'

'Arre baba, are you going to only talk about chai or make us some?' asked Chimanbhai, a tad impatiently.

'Going, baba, going.'

***

A flash of irritation crossed Maya's face as she spotted the teal-coloured Honda Civic sputtering to a stop in the driveway. The dashboard was filled with junk mail, and the car rattled with the empty beer cans that were meant to be taken to the recycling centre at five cents a can. Neeraj! Ugh! He was like the lowest form of life. You could smell his stink a mile away. He reeked of stale beer, rain-drenched newspapers, marijuana and sluts. He stepped out of the car. His hair was tousled, his T-shirt an unremarkable green, the grey flannel shirt and cargoes he wore were so crumpled that there was no doubt he had just stumbled out of bed. He spat out a ball of tobacco on Radhika's beloved hydrangeas and stretched. Maya shuddered in disgust before stepping away from the window. She did not want to be noticed by him. It was all right to flirt with him when he was eating at their table, but he was mostly revolting. Radhika had spotted her visitor from the living room. He was not civilized, this man. But Radhika also knew that they needed some radical solution for their dilemma. After quickly scanning her living room for any small but expensive object that this man was quite capable of stealing (she was sure the last time he came he had stolen the silver supari box), she put on a perfect hostess smile and opened the door. Only to spot the man spitting something largish into her hydrangeas. How delightfully Indian he was. She walked up to him and stopped short of hugging him. He smelled like her nani's blanket that she had inherited upon her death, which was soaked in her sweat and tobacco that she was so fond of chewing.

'Sexy Indian lady!' he said coming towards her.

The way he looked at her, Radhika suddenly felt dirty and took refuge in a namaste which she usually considered very middle class. 'Namaste, Neeraj beta.'

The chap knew why she had said namaste, but he came over and hugged her instead, saying, 'Auntyji' in a way you'd be embarrassed to admit, planting a sticky wet kiss on her cheek, and wiping his hand on her butt. She wanted to hit him. But they needed him. For Chiman's sake, she extricated herself from the hug and said, 'Come in please, Chimanbhai is waiting for you.'

'You call him Chimanbhai? Your bhai?' Neeraj said and laughed pointedly.

Radhika ignored the man and led him inside, keeping enough distance between them.

Ever since Chiman had confessed to Neeraj about Meenakshi one drunken night, Neeraj had called Radhika 'second best ben' and 'sexy second option' all the time. Radhika had wanted to put Neeraj's head in a khandni and pound it to a pulp. But she had hated Chiman more for hankering after some woman from his past.

Radhika understood that now was not the time for hatred. It was crisis time. And only when the family was together, could they solve this problem. And whether she liked it or not, Neeraj was family.

***

He was eating parathas with both hands. Radhika noticed his nails were outlined by dirt. He would break off the aloo paratha, make a quick little cup with the piece, and dip it first in the yogurt, then the achaar, then put it in his mouth. Oh his teeth! Radhika remembered Tauji's tobacco-stained teeth. This boy's mouth was fouler than that. He was dribbling the yogurt all the way to the mouth. Then licking his fingers.

He saw Radhika stare at him with a fascination that one has for snakes. He hadn't missed that look.

'Chimanbhai,' said Neeraj, emphasizing the 'bhai' again and looking at Radhika, 'I understand the situation. It is very clear. That south Indian bitch is encroaching on our territory. We Gujaratis must stick together. We are family, after all.'

Maya and Suraj had been told to stay away. But they were wondering why their parents were entertaining an obviously creepy character.

Neeraj was still eating and talking, slurping and talking, smacking his lips and talking and rattling off details of Supriya's business. He looked like he never got out of bed. How then did he know so much?

'Chimanbhai, I know you are a gentleman and that in normal circumstances what I am about to suggest now I would not even dream of suggesting.'

Neeraj's face was intent with concentration, his forehead beaded with sweat. Radhika wondered why the boy sweated so much in spite of the temperature of the home being an even 68 degrees. He had stopped eating the mirchi chutney and had gulped down a large glass of Coke.

'Wait!' barked Chimanbhai, and got up to go towards the kitchen. Radhika was surprised at the usually mild-mannered Chimanbhai showing so much aggression. 'Ambe Ma! Mere Chiman ki madad kar!' Radhika prayed.

Chiman knew the two brats were listening to the conversation. It was his fault. Had they raised the kids like he was raised in India, they would not be peering from behind doors. In India, if kids were asked to stay away, they stayed away. They didn't skulk behind doors eavesdropping.

'What are you two doing here?' Chimanbhai hissed. 'I had told you na to stay away when we were talking? It was for your good. You don't need to hear this. You don't need to hear how difficult it has become for your father to make ends meet.'

Maya and Suraj stared at their father. They had not seen him this angry, ever. This was not the time to argue as they usually did. It was easy to step back and run upstairs. Chimanbhai was surprised. Maybe the children finally understood how much their father could be pushed. Maybe he was finally turning out to be as full of rubaab as his old man. He turned around and came right back.

'Okay now, continue.'

It took Maya and Suraj less than thirty seconds to realize that their old man was about to commit to something totally radical. They would not miss this for the world. They tiptoed right back downstairs.

Neeraj was a tad surprised at this new version of Chimanbhai. He did not look like his usual useless self. He took a deep breath and put forth his ultimate idea.

'Chimanbhai, you will need to get rid of this Supriya.'

Radhika's eyes were like saucers. Her voice seemed alien to her own ears when she said, 'Get rid of maane exactly what?'

Neeraj looked at both of them one by one, and then gravely uttered but one word, 'Osmanbhai.'

Chimanbhai looked suitably shocked. He had left India many many years ago, but everyone, and anyone worth their money hidden away in their mattresses, had heard that name. Behind the door in the kitchen, Maya and Suraj looked at each other puzzled. Who was Osmanbhai?

Fortunately for them, Radhika asked the question, 'Arre pan, Osmanbhai kaun che? Who is Osmanbhai?'

Neeraj was enjoying this drama. He stood up, and leaned on the dining table. Then dropping his voice a couple of decibels, he said, 'Osmanbhai is the best supari killer in the whole of Gujarat.'

Chimanbhai pulled his feet up to the chair and hugged himself. His heart was beating so hard he could feel it move to his legs. His hands felt clammy and he was horrified to see Neeraj take his forefinger, run it across his neck like one would a knife, and make that awful 'kerrraaccchh' sound with his tongue.

Radhika was taken aback at Neeraj's gesture as well. She had watched enough movies to know it meant 'khallas', 'khatam', 'finish'. Her sweet Chimanbhai was going to get Osmanbhai to finish that waid.

When? How? What would she need to do? Oh Ambe Ma! Osman might finish that waidi, but would he rape Maya! Maybe he would want Radhikaben too! Questions and fears filled her little head, and Radhika suddenly felt warm. Sweat was trickling down her back and the whole world seemed to be closing in on her. The ceiling seemed to be coming down on her. Radhika uttered an incoherent strangled 'Chi-man' and fell with a great big thud on the mustard yellow and brown carpet.

FOUR

Five thousand kilometres away in a muggy city by the sea, the temperatures soared. It was almost always summer here. Mumbai, the city of dreams, was reaching out for the skies. They were constantly building things here. The roads were perennially dug up, one would see 'Go slow, work in progress' signs on every other road. Billboards advertising new housing schemes promised bigger and better rooms and happier families. They were cutting down trees to occupy more of the skies, reaching higher and higher every year. And there was dust everywhere. Among the cement and iron bars and high cranes and hard-hatted people were four who did not belong.

The makeshift elevator made its way up to the twenty-second floor of a building still under construction. It would inevitably be named after an exotic flower, like tulip or frangipani or bougainvillea. But right now it was iron rods and cement and scaffolding. There were two men on the lift that made its rickety way to the top. They were propping a sack that looked like there was a man stuffed in it. There was no pretence to hide the shape or anything. They dragged the sack off the lift, and across the floor, without a care if the package was getting damaged in the process.

At the far corner of the open roof, there were two more people. One sitting on a cane chair, legs propped on a bag of cement. His eyes were closed, and he seemed to be enjoying the slight evening breeze that stirred up loose cement on the high floor, and the warm glow of the setting sun. He was listening to Mukesh on his iPod. The other man was standing nearby, hand resting on a bamboo danda, making sure he wasn't coming anywhere between the man's unrestricted view of Mumbai. A gun holster worn over his kurta and lungi showed he didn't care if anyone saw his gun or not.

'Salaam Osmanbhai!' One of the two men who had come up the elevator disturbed the perfect iPod moment.

The cane chair creaked, but the man said nothing. He waved a hand.

The two men sat down by the sack they had dumped. The sack wiggled a bit, one of the men hit it with a chappal. The next fifteen minutes were spent in silence. The tableau watched the sunset.

The moment the sun disappeared from sight, the chair creaked again. The man who stood up was a spitting image of Santana, the singer. Only he didn't know it. And neither did the people he usually associated with. If they did, they wouldn't dream of telling him. Osmanbhai would probably be seen with a ghoda rather than a guitar. This gaana bajana was good when Chandni was dancing to phoren music, then Osmanbhai would go phoren on her. But then here he was, dressed in a lungi and hawai chappals. He had witnessed one of the best sunsets there ever was under Allah's sky and he was happy. The evening air was so clean, he felt good to be far above the stifling heat of the kholi down in the slums. He knew that as long as he was living in Mumbai this was the only way he was going to breathe clean phoren-type air.

He flexed his neck muscles, and the two men who had brought the sack were standing at attention now, staring speechlessly at him. He didn't have to be a fortune teller to know that they were scared of him. He nodded. He liked that. He had spent years in the gallis, building that reputation.

All he had to do now is nod his head, and the two guys were scrambling to open the sack. They had finally found that bastard Kripalani. The crafty real estate agent had duped his last client. Normally Osmanbhai wouldn't have accepted a job to put a low life like Kripalani out of commission, but his head was buzzing with ideas and whatever money that dhanda brought him would just be a silver warq on his khubani ka meetha.

Kripalani had a rag around his mouth and he was hog-tied with cheap nylon string his wife used to dry clothes on. Fear was writ large in his eyes.

He knew what Osmanbhai was capable of. 'Kutte ke pille! Osmanbhai se bhaagta tha tu!' Osmanbhai had whipped out a sharp knife out of nowhere and had cut the rag binding his mouth. Kripalani was wincing in pain. The knife did not care what else it was cutting.

'Naheen Osmanbhai! Kasam se! I didn't know you were looking for me! I was not running. I was in the house when these...these bastards caught me.'

One of the two men who had carried Kripalani interrupted, 'Bhai! We found him in bed all right. With that Khurana's wife's sister.'

Osmanbhai merely raised his hand to stop his men from speaking. He didn't care where or how they found him. This snivelling had never bothered him. Ever. But he was okay if they grovelled a little. It amused him.

'So where do you want to die?'

'Bhai, what are you saying, bhai! I beg you to let me go!'

'Someone is very angry with you.'

'Bhai, I'll return all their money, bhai, I will give you everything I have, bhai. Just give me one chance, bhai.'

This was not the first time his victims offered him their everything.

'Where are the Firdausi papers, Kripalani?'

'I don't know what you are talking about! I have to look in my office...'

'Taang do saale ko. Ulta.'

Osmanbhai's instructions were drowned in Kripalani's scream, as he found himself hanging upside down from the edge of the building. Held only by the two goons. The crows that were returning home after sunset were forced to take flight and answer the scream with their own cacophony.

'Kidhar rakhele papers? Or do you want to die?'

'I'll tell you! I'll tell you! Don't kill me here. I always wanted to die among flowers, not concrete.'

The men who were holding him upside down started laughing. 'Saala!' one said. 'He's hanging at this height and wants to be taken to a garden!'

Osmanbhai ignored them. 'Where have you kept the papers? At Khurana's house?'

'Haan Osmanbhai, haan!' Kripalani agreed. 'Please, please let me go. I don't want to die like this!'

'Okay,' Osmanbhai agreed. 'Let him go!'

Before he knew it Kripalani was falling down twenty-two floors and on to the dug-up ground that would one day become the spot where the building gardens would be. Javed and his crew would be filling in the ground any day. Kripalani would have his last wish.

Osmanbhai turned away from the edge. He was smiling. 'Saala Kripalani. Wanted to die among flowers. Ab akkha garden will be growing on top of him.' Taking out a supari from his pocket he chucked it in the direction where Kripalani had fallen.

The three men who were with him laughed. It had

been a good day at work. Osmanbhai's cellphone began to ring. It was an unknown number. 'Kaun hai be!' Osmanbhai barked.

***

Neeraj lived like he had never left his chawl in Ghatkopar. Everything he owned was pushed and piled up against the walls. And everything was stuffed in cartons. His dealer had taught him that the best place for his work clothes (yes, he still had to report for work some days) was the refrigerator. The weed smell would not get into the clothes that way. Neeraj had a laptop and he worked on it by logging in to his neighbour's unprotected Wi-Fi. You'd think someone who was on the payroll of a software firm could afford to buy window blinds. But Neeraj had used old bedsheets as curtains for as long as he could remember, and if they allowed the occasional sun in and kept the nosey neighbours out, he didn't care. He used the cash on the finest weed in Oregon. The shabbiness of the room was hidden by a low cloud of stale air and cigarette smoke. He was sitting on the bed with his cellphone glued to his ear.

'What are you saying! You will come! Free?'

He could not believe what he was hearing. Not the right moment for Juanita to step out of the bathroom looking like the hottest thing in a thong but there she was distracting him from the call by wiggling her butt at him. The voice on the other side of the phone sounded irritated now. So he simply slapped Juanita's butt lightly and turned away from her. 'Haan, Osmanbhai. Bolo.'

Osmanbhai was clear about what he wanted. 'Apun bahut aadmi ko khallas kiya idhar. Now I take lessons. Speak dhaansu English. I come to Amrika, become bigger than Godfather. Saala uska record fod daalne ka. I will kill for you free, Neerajbhai. But you fix my visa. Agent say you can apply for me. I am happy to kill.'

Osmanbhai knew the Gujju would agree to anything if he added a 'free' to his offer. But just then the liver-spotted building supervisor burst into Neeraj's home with the spare key. 'You filthy pig! That's the last time I am going to warn you. Mrs Kowlaski is right. The stench is unbearable. And no whores! We are decent people here. Clean up or clear out! Bloody Asians!'

Juanita was laughing hysterically. He must remember to not let her drink gin so early in the afternoon. Neeraj gritted his teeth and went back to the call. He hated the supervisor. He smelled odd, like he had not seen sunshine for years.

'Osmanbhai, you might have to kill two here.'

***

The light filtered through the pink-and-blue acrylic sheets that masqueraded as glass panes on the eight tiny windows in her room. Only two opened out to the street view. The others were just like a movie set.

Because Chandni was like the star of this Kamatipura kothi. Whatever Chandni wanted, Chandni got. After all she had a big guy like Osmanbhai climbing up six flights to her third-floor kholi to feast on her night after night. He was her 'exclusive', so he didn't have to hurry. And she enjoyed seducing him and teasing him whenever he was out of breath.

She was dressed at her loudest best: gold and fuchsia pink. But Osman saala was in a hurry. Normally he would watch her dance, allow her to try out all her little tricks, laugh loudly in appreciation when she begged like film heroines, simpering and behaving as if she were coy. But not today. He had that look today. He was always like that whenever he snuffed out some lowlife. He had just lunged at her like some wild beast. No 'raani ke maafik jhakaas lagti tu apun ko', no singing 'Desi girl desi girl' in a voice that could drown the noise produced by the sugarcane juice machine installed on the road below. Osmanbhai had come charging in today, unwashed and unbathed, spread her legs apart and was thrusting himself with a savage force. At first she wanted to shout at him, ask him why, even turn on the coy heroine act which he loved. But there was one part of her that liked this savagery, this raw, forceful sex. One part of her wanted to punish him for simply using her. After all this time Chandni knew she had gone soft on Osmanbhai. So she just watched him with her kohl-lined eyes wide open, and mentally started counting the drops of sweat falling off his brow on to the bed and on her. He hadn't noticed a thing.

After what felt like an eternity, she decided she needed to start moaning and wiggling under him which would make him khush. Then he would talk and talk and talk, and Chandni would listen.

Men were predictable. He had started to talk.

'Tere yeh jo mamme hain na, unku yeh bade bade banwaatoon!' His hand gestures suggested how huge he wanted her breasts to be.

She hit him playfully. 'Kaise bante itte bade?'

'Amrika mein bante re! Main batana bhool gaya, jaan, tere ko! Mera pucca hua jaane ka.'

'You're going to Amrika? How? When?'

Chandni was sitting upright on the bed. She pushed his hands away from her breasts.

'I knew you would push me away! But listen, jaan. Apun ke paas ek plan hai. I go first. Then I take you there. Dekh, ek Neerajbhai hai. He looks like a perfect bakra. I got him to agree to help me get to Amrika. All I have to do there is kill someone. Bas! It's that simple.'

Chandni could not believe her ears. Osmanbhai was going international with his supari killings. And although he was saying he would take her there, she was realistic enough to know that the idea was simply far-fetched. So she pulled the hand she had brushed away not minutes before and placed it on her breast. 'And what about them?'

'Ohh! Chandni! How can I forget them? When

you come there we take you to the finest doctor and make them big...'

'Sachchee?'

'Of course! You think all the firangis in the videos are perfect like you? Udhar ke doctor ko plastic surgeon bolte hain. When you come there na, we will go to doctor and have you all fixed up. Bas in six weeks Chandni, cheh hafte! I will be gone! But if I am getting you there, I had better work a bit more so we can go to Amrika.'

Osmanbhai then lay on his back like a beached whale and with one hand on her thigh promptly fell asleep.

Chandni sighed. She was lying wide awake. She could not imagine her luck. America! She had watched all the Van Damme movies. She wanted to be in America where the men could kick butt just the way her Osmanbhai did, where they had big cars and big highways, and ate Kentucky Fried Chicken every day. And the girls all were...Oh Mata Rani! How will she live with big breasts that Osman was dreaming about? She tried to picture herself sitting down, standing up, walking, sleeping...it just seemed impossible. Maybe she would persuade him to think about it. For now she was just happy to go to America.

***

Chimanbhai was muttering the Hanuman Chalisa as he hastily brought down each blind in the living room. Then he sat down on his favourite single seater with both feet up, after covering himself up with the mirrorwork throw. He was rocking himself. But it wasn't working.

'Jai Hanuman gyan gun saagar! Arre! Bring chai now! Jai kapees tihu lok ujagar...My last cup! Sankat se Hanuman chhudaave! Haai! My head! I am so nervous I am forgetting the Hanuman Chalisa which I have recited all my life! I am forgetting the verses! Ambe Ma! Even God has left my side! What are we going to do! Why did I agree to join this awful plan! We're all going to jail! I cannot believe we did what we did today!'

'Chimanbhai, Chimanbhai! Stop! You must understand. This is going to be for the best. Did anything happen? Nothing, na? No demons came out from the grey walls of the Homeland Security Office, na? Everything was all right, na?' Neeraj tried to pacify him.

'Tha...that black lady at the counter was a witch, I tell you! She was glaring at us!'

'You don't look at people and say, "Baddho black che!" Uncleji! It's an insult! It's a good thing Auntyji asked her if we needed to fill the form in black ink or blue, otherwise they would have arrested you!'

'When I saw the men and women in uniform, mhari toh jaan hee nikal gayee thee! My heart was beating so fast I was sure they could hear it. They have cameras everywhere! Like eyes watching me sweat. Baap re! I am sure they have technology that reads thoughts. You think *X-Files* is just a story? It's true.'

'*X-Files*? The TV show? No, no. You are mistaken. They don't have mind-reading devices. Remember, they said that the papers looked in order? Why are you worried?'

Radhika wheeled a tea trolley from the kitchen. She knew Chiman was very wound up, he would be tossing and turning all night, disturbing her. She handed him a cup of hot masala chai. 'Chiman! How many years have you been in States? Why do you react like that when you see black people? It's terrible.' Turning to Neeraj she said, 'We used to have Susan who would come and clean up once every two weeks. She was poor, so she charged less than others. Usually she came when Chiman was gone to the shop. But one day when Chiman was in bed with fever, she went into our bedroom and Chiman came out screaming as though he had seen a ghost. After that day Susan never came back.'

'She was looking inside my head, Neeraj! I am not hating black people. I have that Drey working for me, ne? He is black. I am not afraid of them. But I don't want to go to jail! Dekhna all this we are going to do, you and my missej will be free, but I will end up going to jail.'

'Neeraj beta, let him be. I have been married to him for so many years, even I cannot stop him from thinking all these negative things. He will think and think and pace the whole room. Arre beta, when he has exhausted all the possibilities that will take him from one police car ride to the station to some maximum security prison in some remote corner of the country; from his family broken up and impoverished after he is sent to jail to everyone of the family dying long-drawn-out exaggerated deaths only then will he relax. Tere uncle is like that. Overactive imagination!'

Neeraj drank his cup of masala chai and decided that it was better to leave the subject alone. While Chimanbhai muttered away incoherently on his sofa, Neeraj thought about Osmanbhai and the effect he would have on Chimanbhai. But this was not the time to say anything. He then turned his attention to Mrs Shah. The effort of the day was telling on her as well. Her gorgeous large arse was emitting heat. He was that close to her. But it wasn't time to do anything about that either. He was content to hug her and feel the four-hook bra that she was wearing. Life had taken a good turn for Neeraj.

FIVE

If you travelled east and then south to Eugene, you would come across the biggest trailer park in the West— Hell's Park. And it attracted the lowest of the low, the weird, the shameless, and the misfits. The last time a priest visited the park he had ended up tied to a stake surrounded by cultists who wanted him to call upon Jesus, chanting 'save him now' until someone called the police to intervene. The police were busy with the rowdy students of the university to bother with the residents of Hell's Park.

Elmore and Dean fitted in perfectly. Their broken-down trailer occupied the corner of the hundred and eleventh and thirty-fourth East. It was not unlike others, but they had an advantage. Among the ignored, they occupied the lowest place. That was because Elmore was an African American from Pittsburgh and Dean was a white boy from the South. They didn't look right together. Even the twelve-member Stuggie family who lived in a trailer across theirs looked down upon the duo. Whoever heard of a black man and a white man living together? It wasn't the Lord's way. The Edsons were Mormons.

Bren Edson had stopped the white boy and told him so. But had received a black eye for his trouble. They had avoided eye contact with the two ever since. Not that either Elmore or Dean cared. Three years ago they were thrown together by circumstance and they had slowly formed an unlikely but steadfast friendship based on appreciation for each other's craft, respect for each other's intelligence and mutual suspicion.

How they came to be in the Pacific Northwest was a long story. But at this point their lives were in limbo, so it was easier to dwell upon the past as Elmore drank the home-brewed whiskey Dean had just distilled. Although Dean preferred to stay inside and watch TV, Elmore did not mind sitting out on the weather-beaten red velvet sofa that was parked outside their trailer. But the heat was getting to Elmore.

'What does the letter say, Dean?'

Dean was still fiddling with the pipes of the distillation contraption and cursing. After equalizing the pressure and switching it off he cursed again. Elmore's question was valid but he did not want to answer him yet. And his arm touched the overheated copper pot. He stumbled out of the trailer and sat down on the steps. He stared at Elmore. He wasn't ugly. But he was big. Dean didn't mind that. If anyone even thought of snooping into their trailer to steal, the very idea of having to deal with Elmore kept them away. Elmore was not exactly violent, but he had a short fuse. He had once strung a lost kitten simply because he couldn't deal with the bloody mewing. Anyway, his question was valid. So Dean took one swig from his cup and told him. 'We've gotta report to the parole office.'

Elmore reacted just as Dean knew he would. That was the last fucking glass they had and now it was lying shattered on the gravel.

'Dammit, Dean! Let's skip town. They will find the slightest excuse and dump us behind bars.'

'This is the easiest parole officer we've had, El. Why would we skip town?'

'Ever since the supervisor brought the letter, I've had a niggling feeling...'

Dean grinned. 'What the fuck! You turning into witchy Margot Stuggie?'

'Fuck you, Dean!'

'Think about it. They didn't say a thing when we picked up our dole check on Monday. Now unless you have gone and killed someone in the last three days, I think they can't do shit.'

'All fucking right.'

The parole office was located in the far corner of the nondescript social services building. The two walked in reluctantly, were frisked, and let inside. The parole officer looked at the duo. Tough nuts, she thought to herself. But she wasn't nicknamed 'Boots' for nothing. She could kick the hardest arse without looking like she was some kind of dyke. And although she had her auburn hair tied in a severe bun, she still looked like some TV star.

But the uniform and the steel in her eyes would stop even a die-hard ogler like Dean in his tracks. Dean would not have done anything. He was a coward, would look but had no balls to do anything. His excuse was that he had just not met anyone who would prompt him to drop his guard. Elmore watched Dean stare at her breasts and kicked him. She knew, but chose to ignore it.

'So you've been clean...'

Too normal. Elmore was still not willing to let go of that tiny niggle inside his head.

'This is Officer Hudson, from the Employment Office. She has a job for the two of you. Take it. If you know what's good for you. You're hanging by a thread here, let me tell you. Two strikes...'

Elmore and Dean turned around. Officer Hudson had materialized silently behind them. They stood up awkwardly and meekly followed the officer out. Officer Hudson waddled like a little duck. Elmore would've liked to skewer and cook her. A job? What was this? He looked at Dean, and Dean answered with a shrug. Hudson showed the two into another room.

The room was occupied by two men. Two Indian men. They were looking determinedly away and concentrated on Officer Hudson who had asked Elmore and Dean to take the other two chairs. As the officer read the file in front of him, the two Indian men surreptitiously looked at the two men. Elmore looked back directly. They looked as though they had just swallowed something nasty.

The older one looked nervous. The younger one looked determined.

'Mr Shah, will you explain what this job entails? We think we have found two candidates for you.'

'But...but...the job is clearly specialized skill for Indian. These are Americans. How will they...'

'Mr Elmore Sutloe and Mr Dean Stanton have a farming background, Mr Shah. I am sure you are willing to cooperate with the United States Government and give them both a month's trial. You will be paying the two minimum wages of course and deduct room and boarding costs. Sure appreciate your help.'

Mr Shah lapsed into his own language in a voice that sounded extremely panicky to Dean. Elmore was staring at the older man as well, the thought of wringing his neck running rapidly through his single-track mind. It was the younger guy who recovered first.

'Officer, the job is not easy. Handling betelnut involves fine work and years of practice. I don't think...'

'Stop thinking. These two men have handled hazelnuts. Hazelnut, betelnut. How difficult could it be?'

Neeraj swallowed a ball of spit and bile that had collected at the base of his tongue. 'One month?' he asked the officer.

Officer Hudson was looking at Mr Shah, who looked like he was about to collapse. 'Is he all right?'

'Ek gora che. Ek kaalia. Ma! Kai gayee tu?'

Neeraj had no answer but a hasty yes. Mr Shah signed on the papers in the same daze. Initialled each page and signed the first and the last.

The officer was handing over Mr Shah's address on a card. They were to report on Monday. 'Thirty days, boys. These guys are harmless. If you fuck with them, trust me you are fucking with me. I've seen grown men die horrible deaths when the injection spreads through their bodies. We don't want to waste government chemicals on lowlifes like you guys, so don't push it. Good luck.'

It was Dean who nodded a yes and Elmore who grunted. As the four men stood up to leave, a thought crossed Officer Hudson's head. The two Indians looked too darned tiny when compared with the big Elmore and tall, lanky Dean. He would have to make sure someone was keeping an eye on this situation.

***

Neeraj drove a stunned Chimanbhai back home to Winderly. He was glad Chimanbhai had not gone over the edge like the last time. He, too, was a jumble of thoughts. He had simply not anticipated this development. When he was working on the contract for manpower consultants, they always put in an ad in the local paper. It was worded just perfectly so that only the candidate they were pushing at the client got the job. This was a law and the agencies had found a watertight argument-proof way out. The ad was a minor hiccup for the agencies. Then why the heck had the ad Neeraj had so carefully worded been thrown back at their faces in the form of those two thugs?

Should they withdraw the application? He drove like a madman down I-5 but just past St Vincent's exit he spotted the red and blue lights behind him. Fuck, fuck, fuck! This was not turning out to be right. That bitch Juanita be cursed. She had stopped him from leaving the house muttering something about omens. All that Mexican mumbo-jumbo was fucking with his head. He was given a $125 dollar citation and a stern warning. The officer had heard all kinds of excuses from speeding assholes, but one look at the little Indian man sitting beside the driver, he was willing to believe that the two Indians were worried about someone who had suddenly taken ill.

Neeraj joined the traffic once again and drove in the slowest lane until he left the last speed trap at Tigard where he took the exit to Winderly.

In the confusion with Officer Hudson and then getting a ticket for speeding, Neeraj had not looked at his phone which had been on silent all this while. When he pulled into Chimanbhai's driveway, he looked at his phone lying in the back seat with horror. There were twenty-six calls from India. Bile rose up instantly and he had to, just had to upchuck into the nearest hydrangea. Osmanbhai! Fuck, fuck, fuck! He had forgotten all about Osmanbhai. Neeraj shuddered. Osmanbhai would not care how big Elmore was or how bad Dean was supposed to be.

He would kill Neeraj first.

Chimanbhai was still sitting stupefied in the car. He watched dispassionately as Neeraj puked all over Radhika's favourite hydrangeas. A wave of hysteria as thick as freshly churned butter rose up from recesses deep inside his stomach. He had been cornered, stunned, as though he were that deer in the headlight which he had hit three years ago when driving the kids and Radhika from a Mount Hood trip and had run without reporting the accident to the police.

The phone was buzzing again. Chimanbhai looked at Neeraj. He was still heaving. Chimanbhai leaned and reached out to the phone. 'Hello?'

The loud, angry voice from the other side of the phone was swearing at Neeraj in Hindi. Chimanbhai said again, 'Hello, kaun?'

'Neeraj! Kutte! Ab awaaj no recognyje? What meaning this? I will not listen to any bull from you. What is happening with my visa?'

At that moment Chimanbhai understood why they showed a light bulb over characters in cartoons. One such bulb must be shining over his head right now. 'Osmanbhai?'

'Yes, yes, Osman I am. Who did you think it waj, hain? Achcha Neeraj, you tell me when you fixing visa?'

'Mr Osmanbhai. Chimanbhai Shah this side. Neeraj is my nephew...my bhanja. We are coming from visa office only. There has been a little...'

'Dekho Chimanbhai! I am coming to Amrika, okay? You get me visa. And quick. You no fucking with Osmanbhai. If my bheja is turned no, then I am not thinking. My bheja gets fried very quick. And when I come there, that's it. Then you and me and my gun. We fix everything.'

'Arre, Osmanbhai. I am not saying "no". I am just informing you that Neeraj and I have just come back from the visa office only. You see, in America, they ask many questions, and we have to answer. If we want to get best supari man, then we have to answer question, samjhi gayo na? Baddho questions pooch rahe the woh. Now we want you to come here. Just give me some time. Everything will be good.'

He had lapsed into a mixture of Hindi and Gujarati the moment he figured out that Osmanbhai was struggling with English. Neeraj had recovered and was now frantically listening in because he had just realized that Chimanbhai was speaking with Osmanbhai. Osman was smarter than the two thought. He had bought Rapidex English Speaking Course and was already having a conversation with American people. He was getting the hang of it faster than he thought. Soon he would up his price because he would speak in English and would become the Indian Godfather in America. He decided that he was going to finish the book soon and then call up Chimanbhai again and threaten to break every haddi in his American body if he didn't fix the visa soon. Haddi. He made a mental note to find out what they called haddi in English.

***

Elmore and Dean could not guess that so much depended upon two little cups placed in front of them. The cups were small. Only as big as a newborn chick, Elmore thought. He could crush both the cups in one hand. But steam was rising from them. And every one of the Shah family was staring at them as though they were some circus act. Mrs Shah looked formidable; she was wearing red lipstick so early in the morning that it looked scary. She had the biggest fake smile Dean had ever encountered. Dean knew they were all nervous to have them in the house. It looked like it would be a cakewalk. If the family pushed them to doing any work, they would just threaten them and relax.

'Drink. It is tea. It is special.' The lady with the red lipstick was saying. Instinctively the two reached for the cups. Mr Chimanbhai was nodding his head in approval.

Elmore took a swig. It was too hot and too sweet and disgusting. 'I prefer beer,' he said.

But Dean looked like he had just tasted heaven. His eyes were glazed and he was savouring every sip. Mrs Shah looked at him with supreme approval. Mentally she had ticked him as the good guy. Anyone who appreciated her special masala tea could not be bad. She sniffed her nose at Elmore. She knew

Mr Shah reacted like a racist quite often so she knew she could not actively dislike Elmore. What if her husband's views were rubbing off on her? She had been brought up to believe in equality. Her dad worked with a lot of low-caste people who were the finest diamond cutters and did not mind sharing meals with them, and Radhika and her brothers were brought up to be Gandhians as well. She just watched Elmore as he drank from the cup rather tentatively now. He finished the tea and put the cup down. That was good enough for Radhika.

Maya had been sent off to check on breakfast. Now she was standing right there shamelessly in a sleeveless T-shirt and shorts, staring at the two. Hey Bhagwan! When was this girl going to see sense? Just because the two men were not staring back at her legs did not mean they had not noticed all that skin. And Neeraj was late. Otherwise he would be saying some flirty things to Maya hoping Radhika had not heard. Suraj deekro who was usually the smart studious one had decided to leave the computer and join them. But he too was behaving badly. He wanted to converse with them! He had read the papers that the Employment Office had sent for Chimanbhai and it seemed like he wanted to ask the two a few questions.

'We talk over breakfast, okay?' Radhika led them all to the dining table. Elmore and Dean gawped at the life-size portrait of Elvis hung on one wall. It was the cheesy velvet painting you bought as a tourist outside Graceland or something. On the opposite wall was a shrine of some sort, with pictures and statues of what must be Indian gods and goddesses, garlanded with plastic flowers. But dominating the multi-headed, multi-armed pantheon of gods were the garlanded portrait photographs of two very sad-looking people. Chimanbhai's parents. The woman looked constipated and the man looked exactly like Chimanbhai would look twenty years later: bald and sad.

The doorbell pealed loudly and Suraj was sent off to see if it was Neeraj. Maya had set the table so Radhika went to the kitchen and brought in the breakfast trolley. Elmore sniffed appreciatively. It wasn't bacon, but it was ages since he had eaten a hot breakfast. He sat down happily at the table next to Dean. Chimanbhai sat at the head of the table, with Elvis looking down on him. Maya sat across Elmore, adjusting and readjusting her bra, drawing needless attention to herself, and grinning widely when Dean glared at Elmore for staring. Suraj and Neeraj came in talking in Gujarati, obviously exchanging some rapid-fire insults because Radhika admonished both of them. Suraj sat down quietly at the table next to Maya and Neeraj took the last remaining seat under the gods.

Nobody got up to give Radhika a seat, and she went about serving food to everyone. She served Chimanbhai first. 'It is Spongebob!' Elmore thought. Served steaming hot on a breakfast plate! The

Spongebob song started playing in his head as he too was served one large cube. 'Absorbent and yellow and porous is he' played in his head as Elmore tentatively touched it with his fork. He had never liked Spongebob, so Elmore took great pleasure in stabbing his fork into that...that thing on the plate. He hadn't meant to say 'Die Spongebob!' out loud. But he had, and Maya and Suraj were now giggling and laughing out loudly, stabbing at the food just as Elmore had.

Elmore put in a mouthful of that spongy food. He did not need to chew it at all. It simply melted away in his mouth. 'Fantastic!' he said. 'What is this thing called?'

Suddenly Radhika had a smile for Elmore. It made her look so scary that Elmore did not know whether he liked her stony face or her smiling one. He looked at Dean. Dean looked unwell. He looked like he had tasted hell. He was frantically drinking water. Maya poured him another cup of tea and gave him a plate of biscuits and Dean accepted them gratefully. Elmore had demolished the dhokla on his plate and Mr Shah kindly offered him more. If only it weren't so sweet! There was a plate of green chillis that Mr Shah was helping himself to when he saw Elmore's expression. Elmore followed suit.

'Fuck! These things are lethal!'

'You don't know the half of it!' Maya added. 'We have many lethal things in this house.'

'Shut up, Maya! Go to your rooms. Both of you.'

Mrs Shah was not just serving food, she looked like she knew everything that was going on at the table.

Suraj protested loudly. 'What did I do? Why do I have to go upstairs? I want to talk to the killers.'

Mr Shah choked on Spongebob. Elmore and Dean looked puzzled. Did they hear right? Neeraj looked stunned. Mrs Shah looked like one of the goddesses, infuriated, and saucer eyed.

'Go!'

Suraj and Maya meekly left the table. But Maya being Maya, stopped at the foot of the stairs and looked over her shoulder. Then she sashayed upstairs swaying her hips as though she were filled with water and there was a tidal wave propelling her forward by illogically moving side to side. Neeraj was watching her and Elmore was watching Neeraj watching her.

Mrs Shah cleared Maya's and Suraj's plates and sat down. And then she took over.

'You stay here with us. There's room for you above the garage. You eat with us. We don't eat meat. I will send egg for breakfast only because Mr Shah says Americans eat eggs. That's room and board taken care of. Mr Shah will show you the work. He takes you, he brings you back. It's easy. So that is travel taken care of. And if you can do the job, after deducting all the expenses we incur, you get three dollars a day. Take it or leave it.'

Neeraj and Mr Shah gaped at Radhika admiringly. Elmore and Dean looked sucker punched.

'Three fuckin' dollars? Fuck that Officer Hudson! Fuck three strikes! I'm outta here!' Elmore pushed the chair back angrily and stood up.

Dean was angry too. But he had seen that self-satisfied smile appear on Mrs Shah's face. There was more to this than just a pathetic daily wage. And he would get to the bottom of this. If only he could get Elmore to see that the harmless little Indians wanted them to get pissed off and leave.

'May I have more of the excellent chai latte, Mrs Shah?' Dean was polite. Very polite.

Neeraj and Mr Shah, who had stood up in an instinctive reaction when Elmore had kicked back the chair violently, looked at Dean open mouthed. Mrs Shah looked bewildered. Elmore was the first to react.

'You shittin' me? She's probably going to cut dimes from that three-dollar deal to account for your extra cup of chai latte. The bitch!'

Dean smiled a smile that made him look like some enlightened white fakir. 'Sit down. All of you. Tea, if you please, madam?'

This was said so quietly that everyone simply obeyed. The fact that Elmore hadn't kicked the chair and walked off meant that he was intrigued. He was still glaring at Mrs Shah. Neeraj and Mr Shah were looking warily at Elmore. Only Mrs Shah was looking at Dean with narrowed eyes. Then just as suddenly, her expression changed to one that matched Dean's calm face.

'Of course! This tea is made from milk, a little water and boiled with the finest Assam tea dust. We add seven spices: ginger, black pepper, bay leaves, cardamom, cinnamon, cloves, and a little bit of dhania. Oi Neeraj, what do you say for dhania in English?'

Dean was holding the cup of milky tea as though it were some precious glass of wine and sniffing to discern the distinct taste of each spice.

Mrs Shah continued explaining, as though she was unaware how ridiculous the two of them looked to an outsider.

Chimanbhai was irritated. 'Radhika, I am sure Mr Dean doesn't want to know the recipe of your tea.'

'Yes,' Dean drawled. 'What is it do you think I want to know?'

Mrs Shah was sitting down. She was not about to say anything. This was turning out to be a very poor Mexican standoff.

Elmore was the first to blink. 'Oh fuck it!' You guys have a staring match for the rest of the day. Say nothing. I am outta here.'

Dean was still doing his Clint Eastwood act. 'They don't want us here, Elmore. And I sure would like to find out why.'

The chai cup in Mr Shah's hand shattered on the wooden floor. There was milky tea everywhere. He was staring aghast at Dean and not the tea. Mrs Shah looked irritatedly at Neeraj who was vehemently shaking his head in denial.

'Toh okay!' she said. 'I thought you would be too dim to figure that out. But now that you have, it is better to be open. We don't want you here. You were not part of our plans. In fact, you are just problems—two problems. But I am from Surat. We have faced more enemies than you can imagine! If you stay, you stay like I have just explained. But... of course you are free to go. We won't mind. You can tell Employment Office that you cannot deal with the Indian job. We won't say anything. Easy for you, easy for us.'

Elmore sputtered, 'You bitch! I will kill you!'

Dean had had enough. 'Am glad you make everything so clear, Mrs Shah. I don't think Elmore or I are afraid of you or your family. We won't be the ones going back to the Employment Office. If you think you are not happy, you go back. But it won't be us.'

Elmore and Mr Shah looked stunned although for different reasons. Neeraj was looking a little green around the mouth. 'In...in that case, let's show you your room, eh?'

***

The room was meant for midgets, or really small men to potter about on their knees. Neeraj just shrugged his shoulders when Dean entered almost half bent. Neeraj explained that the room was used to store things that the Shahs imported from India before stricter laws on foodstuffs were enforced. A food inspector's surprise weekly visit ensured that they gave the warning serious heed. The storage space was empty. No sooner than Neeraj confessed to that, Elmore had put a fist in the false ceiling to have it rain down on them all.

The noise brought Mr and Mrs Shah running out of the house only to see the three emerge coughing and spitting dust. Suraj appeared at a window upstairs. 'Mom, can I help break it all down? I'll clear it up too.'

Neeraj waved at him to come down. 'It was the false ceiling,' he explained to Mr and Mrs Shah needlessly. 'Now that it is broken, we might as well fix it, no?'

Suraj was down in a trice, running straight into the garage and bringing out shovels and a shabby chainsaw. The chainsaw was useless, so they chose a pick. It took them a good part of the morning to break the ceiling. It was too dusty for any conversation and the viciousness with which Elmore was attacking the ceiling eliminated any possibility of everyday civility. It was not easy for Suraj, who was adept at demotion derbies on the computer, but had never broken any more than a glass or two in real life.

Dean and Elmore dusted themselves off, and left Neeraj and Suraj to do the clean-up job. They went home to collect their belongings and lock up the trailer. On the way back they decided to park by at the truckers' stop. They were not going to taste meat for the next many days, so they spent eight dollars on their corned beef and rye sandwiches topped with sunny-side-up eggs, bacon and large glasses of iced tea on tap and topped their meal off with a jello pudding.

They ate in silence. The waitress was used to truckers who were silent because they were bushed from the driving or the garrulous ones who would not fail to pinch her butt after she had served them coffee. These two did not look like they were up to any good. But they were not up to any bad either. They were eating like this was going to be their last meal. She had seen desperate bastards like these as well. They either tipped her well, or barely had money to pay for the meals.

'Coffee?' She sauntered up to their table and asked.

The white boy said yes, but the big black guy just grunted.

'Milk?'

The black boy started laughing as though she had said something really funny. 'Weirdos,' she muttered under her breath and ignored them until they paid the bill. Men were so predictable. They had the exact change, but no tip. She should've listened to her instinct and spat into the corned beef. She sighed as she cleared the table. The two had left no crumbs. Not from the sandwich, not from the egg, not even from the jello. They must've been really hungry.

***

Mr Shah drove his Honda Civic back home. It had been the toughest day of his life. With two tired, bleeding and bandaged men sitting at the back of his car, not even the '108 Om Chants' tape helped. He pulled into Winderly and almost ran over the rheumatic Mrs Chopra out on her evening walk. Why couldn't she take the walkway built around the lake? wondered Chimanbhai. He dare not stop and apologize because she would peer into the back seat and wonder who his passengers were. She let out a yelp and stepped back in alarm. He could see her wave her walking stick at him, cursing. He didn't need any more curses. Eventually they would have to tell the Indians who lived in the neighbourhood. But hopefully the two asuras sitting in his car would leave much before the neighbourhood speculation brought nosey neighbours dropping in for a chat.

When he pulled into the driveway, he realized that the house was ablaze with lights. What the heck was going on? Maya was never at home at this time, Suraj ought to have been at his computer class, and Radhika should have been watching some Ekta Kapoor show on TV. So what the heck was going on? He tried to remember what day it was. No special occasion that he had forgotten. No invite had been issued to people for dinner. No visitors' cars parked nearby. Then why the heck was the whole house lit up?

Elmore groaned at the back. Chimanbhai hushed them both. 'Please, please stay quiet. I want to find out what is going on. Why the whole house is lit up like its Diwali...erm...like Christmas.'

Dean nodded. He was too tired to protest. He just wanted to hit the sack. Elmore had no energy left to grunt.

Chimanbhai tiptoed to the front door, then slapped his palm to his forehead when he realized that people inside would have already heard the car pulling into the driveway. He took one deep breath and rang the bell and counted. He didn't know why he was counting but he knew he was ready to flee if some stranger opened the door. And he didn't know why he expected a stranger to open the door to his own house. He had counted to twenty when he put his finger to the bell once again. This time Radhika opened the door.

'Why are you ringing the doorbell like some stranger? Why didn't you use your keys?' she asked. Radhika was dishevelled and dirty. 'Keys?' Chimanbhai slapped his head with his palm. Hey Bhagwan! What was wrong with him? But he asked Radhika, 'Su karoo choon? What have you done to yourself? Why you looking like this? Why are so many lights on?'

'I will tell you, come in, come in first.'

'And what should I do with the two bleeding men sitting in my car?' Chimanbhai stepped in and began turning off the lights, but stopped as he remembered Dean and Elmore groaning in the back seat of his car.

'Those two? Bleeding?' Radhika looked shocked. Then she looked towards the stairs and yelled, 'Neeraj betaaaa! Maya! Suraj! Come downstairs now! Now!'

When Radhika yelled like that, the gods would have come down from the heavens. Chimanbhai saw Maya, Neeraj, and Suraj come down clattering in their flip-flops. Ghastly fashion these flip-flops. Birkenstocks were bad enough, now young people wore them everywhere, as though it wasn't Portland but Goa. Yes, yes, this stupid trend had helped the sales of the ladies skin-coloured one-toe socks which he imported from India, but then again that Supriya had started selling those Bangkok five-toed socks and it had killed the chances of any more sales. And now he had the extra burden of the two men put on his shoulders by the Labour Department. What kind of divine tests were these!

Everyone trooped outside to Chimanbhai's Honda. The passenger doors were open and the two guys were still inside.

'What have you done to them?' Radhika whispered to Chimanbhai.

'I did nothing!' he hissed back. 'These two are crazy.'

Neeraj and Maya helped Elmore out first. He seemed to have come out of a fight. He was bleeding through the bandages. Suraj just had to help Dean get out of the car and then he walked in by himself. But Dean was looking so exhausted, he had only managed to step into the house when

Suraj, Radhika, and Chimanbhai came back inside after locking the car.

Neeraj and Maya had barely placed Elmore on the sofa when Chimanbhai's cellphone began to ring stridently. In the panic of taking the mobile out of his pocket and checking who had called, Chimanbhai dropped the phone. The battery separated from the phone and the phone stopped ringing.

'Hey Bhagwan!' Radhika yelled.

Suraj charged ahead and picked up the pieces. He put the phone back together, slapped the phone as if to fix any internal damage and switched it on again. The moment the Verizon logo popped up on the screen, the phone began to ring. Suraj looked at the screen. It was an unidentifiable +91 number.

'Puppa! Osmanbhai lage che!' Suraj announced.

Radhika glared at Neeraj. 'Why don't you tell that Osman jallad to stop calling? Each time the phone rings I jump out of my skin.'

Maya and Suraj giggled as they pictured the possibility. Radhika turned to the two. 'Instead of giggling like idiots, why don't you get the first aid box, Suraj? And Maya, get some warm water and your pedicure tub. We will need some old towels as well to wash their wounds.'

She then turned to Chimanbhai who was sitting down on the recliner heavily. 'How did they get hurt? You aren't strong enough to hurt anyone. Let alone these two chaps.'

Chimanbhai's already weary shoulders sagged even

further. 'Ae Radhika, ab bas bhi kar ne. Enough insults for today.'

But Radhika was on a roll. She found fault with the way he had tied the bandages. She found fault with how he had treated the wounds. She even found fault with the way he was sitting down now. It was Maya who suggested that she put turmeric on the wounds.

Suraj made a face as he was sent off to the kitchen to get the yellow powder.

'This will sting a bit,' Radhika said.

Elmore was too knackered to protest. His hands had gashes that looked like they needed stitches. But the turmeric would fill the gap nicely and when bound tightly, the gash would heal. But Elmore would have scars. Neeraj had made himself useful. He had made a huge pot of tea. Dean gratefully accepted a mug of the sweet milky tea. His hands were a bit wobbly though. Mrs Shah noticed it and held out her hand to steady the chap.

'Why are you being so nice?' he asked Radhika, with narrowed eyes.

'We *are* nice people. I don't know what you guys have been doing in the shop, but it looks like you two are not fit enough for this job. We had requested and requested that handling betelnuts is a specialist's job. Maybe after we go to the Labour Department tomorrow morning, this farce will end. You won't have to deal with us any more and we will be more than happy to get who we want.'

His hands were sore from the work, but Dean's brain was sharp again. The milky tea was something.

Chimanbhai could not take it any more. The tea had burnt his tongue and that was the last straw. 'Neeraj beta, I hope the room above the garage is clean now and the beds have been made. Take these two there. Stop talking so much, Radhika. I am not going to eat anything. And you will shut up too, both of you. This is my house and there will be no talk of nice not nice, Labour Department and betelnuts. I have had enough, you hear? And if anyone chooses to eat, just for God's sake eat in silence.' There were tears rolling down his pale eyes. He drank the last bit from his cup and walked away.

Nobody had ever heard Chimanbhai talk so much. They watched him leave in silence. He had not cried ever since...ever since he received Meenakshi's wedding card...

SIX

Chimanbhai looked as tragic as Bharat Bhushan, Radhika's fantasy hero from her teenage years. His eyes were sad and he was staring intently into his morning tea as though it were going to give him all the answers.

His outburst had surprised her and she was wary of asking him anything about it. On the other hand she was dying with curiosity.

'Chiman, you want to eat toast with Milkmaid?'

His eyes brightened for a minute, and Radhika took that as a yes. That was his comfort food. And god knows he needed comforting. She turned to open a can and put the toast on. She did not notice that Chimanbhai had gone into a quiet flashback mode. His eyes were glazed as he remembered the days when he had taken Meenakshi on his new bicycle to Inayat Khan's dhaba where they had eaten toast with Milkmaid. The taste of that perfect toast was still in his mouth. He had longed to go back to India—to that easygoing life and to his Meenakshi. But he had never found enough courage to leave Radhika and do that. Besides, Meenakshi was already married and she must be happy and settled in her life there. Why would she leave everything and come to him now?

Radhika hid her dislike of the sweet toast very well. Bread was such tasteless food anyway. It needed butter and jam. Even the simplest of their bhakris had taste. Some jeera here, some ajwain there...

She watched as Chimanbhai bit noisily into the toast and ate it with his mouth open. The munching sound disgusted Maya and Suraj, but she knew that it was just Chimanbhai's way of showing appreciation. She wanted to find out what had happened the day before. So she pushed a saucer for his tea. Chimanbhai liked to drink tea the way people did back home—from a saucer. It was an art, mind you, to pour just enough tea in the saucer so it would cool quickly to slurp. You had to then hold the saucer between the thumb and the forefinger and bring it close to your lips, then close your eyes and blow softly on the tea, so it would cool off to just the perfect temperature to drink.

She waited until he had finished drinking the second saucerful when she pushed another Milkmaid toast at him. 'Saambhlo ne, tell me what happened at work yesterday...'

Chimanbhai had mellowed like the condensed milk on his toast. 'Why you want to add karela to my toast, jaaneman! But I guess you need to know.' Chimanbhai paused and slurped the last of the tea from the saucer. 'We reached the shop as usual, and they wanted to start immediately, those godless people. So I told them that I had to light a candle to the gods first. Funnily, it was the kaalia Elmore who bowed his head. The white boy just hung around, picking random bottles of achaar and sniffing them like a dog.'

Radhika sniffed in response. Her little sniffs spoke volumes. Chiman knew what they meant too. He would often joke and say that had the English known Radhika when they were making up proverbs and those quotable quotes, they would certainly change one saying to 'one sniff can speak a thousand words'. Anyway, he returned to his story.

'They had never seen a betelnut, Radhika! So they wondered what they were going to do with it. It's a good thing I spent summers at Dadaji's feet learning how to cut betelnuts really fine and make paan for him. I gave them both a cutter each. And showed them how to cut the nuts fine. Gora toh kehta hai...'

'Say Dean, na. You sound racist, ne! Remember how bad you felt when the highway cops called you brownie?'

'You want to lecture me or hear what happened?'

'Arre juo, for me you are perfect, ne. I don't want anyone calling you racist, that's all.'

'Samjhee gayo. So I take them to the back of the store and show them where the betelnut sacks are kept. I know they are not going to be able to do a damn thing. So I leave them there and deal with the store. I watch them once in a way on the CCTV. Stupid bastards! At first they just sat around chatting, not doing anything. Then woh goro che na, sorry, Dean, realized that there is a CCTV camera. He pointed it to Elmore. That must have triggered off a frenzy of work. That's when they cut themselves. I watched it all on CCTV. They are stark and utterly mad. I have told them that the traditional cutter is not sharp as a knife, but when both blades are used together, they can cut through bone. But these foreigners! They only know how to bash things. This stupid kaalia tries my electrical drill on it! In one minute his hand has a hole, because the nut just shatters on his hand! I hear his yell and run to the back of the store. There is blood everywhere. Dean is laughing. I tell him, "Arre moorakh, get the first aid box", and he still laughs, so I run back to the till and get the box myself. When I reach the two morons, I see Dean clutching his head because Elmore has taken the cutter and hit him with it! Bhagwan! And this is only the first day!'

Radhika listened shell-shocked. 'Chiman! You dealt with these two madmen alone?'

'I had no choice ne! I quickly emptied a Soframycin tube on Elmore's hands. Full $4.99 worth. And not counting the bandage for his hand. I told him to sit still...'

'You told him to sit still and he sat still? Chiman! Itna daring!'

'At that time I was not thinking, just doing! Then

I look at Dean. The stupid kaalia had hit him with the open cutter, and his head was bleeding. No more Soframycin! I run back in the store, take the $1.39 packet of turmeric and pour it over his wound.'

'Oh Chiman! That was most brilliant. You get ten out of ten!'

'I told them to stay right there and relax. That Mrs Kulkarni from Hillsborough had just entered with her maid. She comes to China Fong's na, for her ladies' lunch. She usually give me the list and flicks her hair like this and goes off, leaving the maid to collect all the groceries. This time she tells me in that awful screechy voice of hers, "Oh Mr Shah, you give me good discount for not going to other store!" Hah! I know why she comes here. Cannot stand that Supriya. Mrs Kulkarni's wrinkles show na when she stands in front of that Supriya! I want to laugh like Maya, what you say for that laugh?'

'Giggle?'

'Exactly! But I know my age, ne! I don't giggle. I take the list and she goes out. The maid asks me if I can hear someone whimpering like they are hurt. I tell her to stop watching so much TV. She follows me in the aisles pushing the cart.'

Radhika poured more tea for the two of them. It was good that the whole house was quiet.

Between slurps, an excited Chiman continued. 'Madam came more than half an hour after she said she would come. I played a tape of *Kuch Kuch Hota Hai* for that stupid maid.'

'And those two?' Radhika asked.

'Those idiots! Instead of staying quiet, they called Officer Hudson. Soon an unmarked police car pulled up in front of the store.'

'Who called?'

'I think it was Dean.'

'I thought he was the smarter one!'

'Anyway, Officer Hudson came in clutching a bunch of papers. He had a videotape recorder. I didn't know why he had showed up, but he sternly said, "Where are the two injured chaps?" and I promptly took him to the back of the store. He started to sneeze with the smell of the fresh chillis that were stacked there. Funny how none of us even notice the smell. And even those two didn't react.'

'Chiman! What did Officer Hudson do?'

'The moment he saw the two men lying there all bandaged up he started videotaping them, just as they show on *CSI*.'

'Arre *CSI* is about dead people ne, these two were alive!'

'Dean accused Elmore of trying to kill him. Elmore accused Dean of making fun of his injury. I let them all talk. You know how weird they all sound with that accent and all.'

Chimanbhai paused to sip more tea. 'Then he turned to me and asked where I was when these two were hacking each other to death. I told him what happened. Then I showed him the CCTV footage. He took the little tape, and asked me to take them to the hospital. Full $12 nuksaan! But the two didn't want to go. Good thing they said no otherwise we would have to pay so much! Our work insurance does not cover their injuries. Officer Hudson examined their injuries and scolded Elmore for using a drill and for hitting Dean with the cutter. He asked me if I wanted to press charges.'

'You should have! We would not be dealing with them any more!'

'What was the point? The Labour Department would have sent two more men. God knows who else we would need to deal with.'

'Barobar, barobar. You are right Chiman. I had not thought of that at all!'

'What had you not thought of, Mom?' piped in a curious voice. Suraj was awake and was standing at the kitchen door. 'Why are you having tea at the kitchen table?'

Chiman looked at his watch. 'Suraj beta, is Neeraj awake?'

'Puppa! Neeraj and Maya didi are already awake and talking to the killers.'

'Arre, they are not killers! How many time I have to tell you this?' Radhika scolded. 'Get ready for school. And don't you dare talk about any killers to anyone at school, okay?'

'Fine, Mom. Just don't give me theplas, okay? Give me lunch money and I will shut up for ever and ever. Just remember, no matter which killers you use, the Indian one, or the guys staying with us, only I can help you make the bomb that can blow up Supriya the Bombshell's store.'

'Go now!' Radhika yelled. 'And let that Kali out. She's been scratching the door for the last hour.

Suraj grabbed an apple and escaped.

'What now, Chiman?'

***

'What do you call this food?' Elmore asked, making a face as though he'd just tasted hell.

'Now, now Mr Slutty Toe...'

'Sutloe,' Elmore automatically corrected. 'That's what my old man was called. I was always Elmore.'

'El-more?' Maya's expression changed as she emphasized 'more', arched her eyebrows and made the word more suggestive than it was.

Elmore wasn't clever with words, but he knew exactly what Maya was hinting at. He laughed.

Neeraj and Dean watched them open mouthed. Neeraj was surprised to see Maya flirt. Dean didn't care. His head hurt.

Elmore ate a spoonful of the sticky goop again. He was hungry. Maya was laughing again.

'What are you doing up there, Maya?' It was Radhika calling from the bottom of the stairs behind the garage.

'Explaining what "daliya" is, Ma!'

'Enough! Come down now. Puppa wants to talk to Neeraj,' Radhika shouted, then muttered as she walked back to the house, 'I know what you are doing. If this was India I would drag you by your hair, beat you black and blue, and lock you in a room until you are married off.'

Inside the house, Radhika heard Chiman singing loudly upstairs. 'Now why is Chiman singing?' she thought and decided she had had enough of them all. She would fix Chiman's lunch and then lie down watching *Sa Re Ga Ma* tapes. Music would soothe the savage rising within her breast. She had picked up that phrase from Suraj's lesson. At first she was alarmed by the picture of her breasts turning savage, but Suraj had explained.

'Why are you scowling, my sweet Chikkoo?' Chiman asked. He smelled of Keo Karpin hair oil and Colgate tooth powder.

Radhika was surprised. It was years since he had called her Chikkoo. 'What's with you? There Maya is flirting with those two, and here you...'

'Arre, today these two will stay at home and I will be alone at the store! Maya, you handle. I have always said only you can control that girl. Now where is that Neeraj? I will tell him to look after the two. Now I had better go.'

Before Radhika saw her plans for a quiet musical afternoon crumble, Chimanbhai was gone, leaving a trail of Keo Karpin and Colgate behind him.

'Maya! Maya! Where is this girl?' Radhika yelled for the girl, but the hiss of milk boiling over made her retrace her steps. She cursed her luck and mopped up the milk after switching off the burner. So much was happening in their lives, that everyday ordinary things were just falling apart.

'What died here?' Maya was screwing up her pretty little nose.

'Stop leaning like that! You look like some cheap item girl.'

Maya rolled her eyes, then unbuttoned one more button on her shirt. 'Now I look like your Hindi movie item girl! Now, did you have daliya yet? You eat, I will make some tea for you.'

Radhika sat down to eat, grateful that Maya was still her daughter with Indian values, in spite of all the American craziness.

***

'Neeraj beta! What are you doing here?' Chimanbhai woke with a start.

'Chiman uncle? Chiman uncle? What are you thinking?' said Neeraj, who had just come into the store.

Dean was there too, watching Chimanbhai with a bemused expression on his face.

'Arre, why are you smiling? Didn't I tell you to rest?'

Dean's eyes were hard. 'Look Mr Shah. I don't know what you know about Elmore and me. But this is our last chance. You know the law three strikes? We've been in for two already. I haven't killed anyone, yet, but I am damned if you are going to send us back because of some stupid nut you want chippered to slivers.'

Neeraj was quaking in his boots. 'But...but...'

Dean ignored Neeraj. 'It's not like we are getting paid minimum wage even. But right now we need you. And from the looks of it, something tells me that you need us too. Elmore has a short fuse. He and I have been treadin' thin ice for the last four years, from state to state. He won't hesitate to do something thoughtless. So I suggest we get on without jobs. Three months the officer said. Then we can go back to dole and you can fuckin' go back to slivers of beetles and nuts.'

Chimanbhai had sat down on his chair behind the till with his hands on his head.

'Uncle, you don't worry. I will show Dean how katri supari is made.'

Chimanbhai did not want to know. His head was hurting so much, he did not want to think. Nothing was going right. First he was robbed when Menon did not sell him the store, then Supriya ruined his business, and now these two thugs were making things worse. Could anything ever turn out right?

***

Neeraj and Dean decided it was easier to scrape the blood off the floor and the walls instead of washing it off. Neeraj had smoked up on the way to the store and had let Dean drive. He was happily buzzed. He found music in the combination of sandpaper and wall, and saw a parade of gods in the resulting design on the scraped-off wall. Dean took charge of the floor and soon the floor was as good as new. It was Dean who insisted they wash their hands before they started cutting up the betelnuts. Neeraj was happy to wipe his hands on the seat of his pants and had sat down among the wall scrapings.

After a dusting of the back room, they were ready to begin work. Neeraj held out the betelnut cutter to demonstrate the cutting again. 'Look carefully at the betelnut cutter. It's like a pair of scissors, but heavier, isn't it? In India, we call it soodi. This one is plain, but in India we get really fancy ones with designs. My dad had one which had a naked god on one side of the scissors and a nude goddess on the other, and when the nut was placed between them to be cracked, the kids would have a good laugh even though they did not understand its *Kama Sutra* connotations.'

Neeraj showed Dean how to hold the cutter carefully and placed the hard betelnut in between. He pressed hard. Nothing happened. The nut was supposed to break into two. Dean laughed. 'We went through that yesterday. And that's when Elmore had the bright idea of disintegrating the damn thing by drilling it.' Dean and Neeraj decided to try it together.

Neeraj cursed loudly, 'Motherfuckin' nut!' and pressed the ends of the cutter. The nut fell apart in neat halves.

'Aha!' said Neeraj.

'Gotcha!' Dean was delighted. 'This one didn't need force at all. I just sort of squeezed the handles of the cutter.'

They tried several nuts. Cursing each time they pressed. 'Fuck!', 'Fuucccck!', 'Ffffuuuuck!', 'Mother faaaaak!', 'Bhenchod!', 'Maadarchod!', 'Yooo fuuuuckkkk!'

Chimanbhai could not sit still at the till any more. Although there were no customers, the two were painting the back room blue with their curses. Chimanbhai did not want a repeat of yesterday. He didn't want to see any more blood. So he ran to the spice aisle and pulled out a one-kilo pack of turmeric. It was slightly dated and kept right in front of the row. Chimanbhai visualized two men bleeding back there. He remembered that Elmore had chopped off the tip of his finger when cutting the betelnut. Tearing at the turmeric packet with his teeth, he ran to the back room, spilling the yellow turmeric on his favourite shirt, leaving a trail of the yellow powder all the way.

'What happened? Who is hurt?'

He came upon a scene that stopped him in his tracks. Neeraj and Dean were squatting on the floor, looking very pleased with themselves. Around them were neatly cut halves of betelnuts in a huge pile. Between the two of them they had managed to cut up half a sackful of betelnuts.

'Stoppppp!' Chimanbhai screamed. The two froze in their gleeful cutting job.

'I don't need them in halves, I need them in slivers!' he screamed.

'Slivers?' both repeated in unison, looking like naughty boys caught doing something wrong.

Frustrated, Chimanbhai threw down the turmeric pack and fell down on his knees before the two of them. 'Please stop. Please stop now. These broken halves by themselves are no use. For pujas they use whole betelnuts. Halves are no good. We need slivers. If you cannot make slivers, it's no good! And why are you guys cursing?'

'It becomes easier when we curse!' said Dean.

Mr Shah could deal with it no longer. He lapsed into the Hanuman Chalisa to protect himself, 'Sankat kate hate sab peeda, jo sumire Hanumat balbira! Save me from these dangers, Hanuman ji!'

That's when the mobile in his pocket began to ring.

The tableau froze. Dean and Neeraj expected Chimanbhai to answer his phone, and Chimanbhai stunned by the volume of the ring so close to his hands joined together in a plea to a higher authority.

'Chimanbhai! Phone!'

Chimanbhai was startled into clumsily groping for his phone in his pocket. He said 'hello' almost reverentially as though it were God himself answering his prayer.

'Kya Chimanbhai, kitna phone kiya. Why you are not taking my phone? What happening to my visa? Once I take supari, I must complete my job! Supari also has rules, you know.'

It was Osmanbhai. Chimanbhai should have been laughing hysterically, but he handed the phone over to Neeraj. Osmanbhai was now yelling the same sentences again and again, 'It's *my* supari! Where is the visa? It's *my* supari! Get my visa fast! It will be my first supari in Amrika!'

Neeraj cut Osmanbhai off. Chimanbhai was shaking in his Bata no. 8s until lunch. Neeraj and Dean had stopped the cursing (and the cutting). Chimanbhai put his head into the account books and drowned himself in numbers. This he was used to. This was normal.

***

Neeraj and Dean woke up with a start. They were still at the shop, asleep among the betelnut halves. It was quiet in the store. They walked a little dazed by the morning's events, to the restroom right beside the sacks of Canadian potatoes. One after the other, they peed long and hard. Dean laughed at the fish soap hanging from a lone hook by the mirror. By the time he had washed his hands and emerged from the restroom, he saw Neeraj sitting down and looking carefully at the nut in his hand.

'Let's just do this. How difficult could it be?' Dean said.

'This difficult.' Neeraj was showing him a sliver of his thumb and forefinger. And before Dean could react, he had fallen down with a huge thud. The chap had fainted. His bleeding hand was now clearly visible. Dean looked at the bloody floor, and wondered for one fleeting second if he would have to clean up the blood again tomorrow.

He quickly grabbed the ghastly yellow spice

powder that had stopped his bleeding the evening before, and poured the entire packet on Neeraj's bleeding hand, then yelled for Chimanbhai.

Chimanbhai awoke with a start and clutched at his heart. He was riding his brand new Raleigh bicycle with Meenakshi perched on the bar in front of him. The hair on his hands were like a thousand tiny antennae, receiving pleasure signals from the touch of her soft sari and muddling up his brain. What was this unearthly scream?

'SHAAAAAAAAAAAAAAAAAAH! Mr Shaaaaaaaaaaaaah!'

Chimanbhai was forced to look at reality. Racks and racks of Indian goods lined up in front of him, and the two boys working in the back room. Dean! It was that luchha gora who was shouting. Neeraj! What had happened to his nephew?

Dean was holding Neeraj in the classic Pieta pose. Neeraj had fainted. There was turmeric everywhere. Dean had blood on his shirt. Who was hurt?

Chimanbhai fell to his knees, hoping for a miracle in front of this bizarre rendition of the Madonna, and asked, not really wanting to know, 'What happened?'

Neeraj did not move. Dean said, 'Fingers...'

Chimanbhai's imagination was on video mode, and the pictures it painted weren't pretty. Neeraj sitting outside the Tigard church with a begging bowl. Neeraj outside the Palitana temple, at the mercy of strangers, spreading his fingerless hands for coins. Neeraj at the dole queue. He didn't rein in his imagination from projecting other uncomfortable clips like where the entire Shah clan was on one side, pointing fingers at him, and he crying all through. And the one where Supriya was dancing naked on top of a heap of betelnut slivers wearing a necklace of fingers around her neck.

'Mr Shah?' Dean was saying. 'Mr Shah? Oh, shit!'

***

Dean drove Neeraj and Chimanbhai back home that evening. Blood and thoughts were pounding in his head. He would call Officer Hudson the next day. This was not a regular fruit-picking job. This should have been classified as 'working with hazardous materials' job. Two people injured in two days. In his dictionary 'betelnut handler' was not like 'picking hazelnuts'. What on earth was Officer Hudson thinking! He drove silently on. A niggling thought kept popping up in his head. Could it be that the officer was just making sure they were heading straight to jail? Maybe the Labour Department was making the most of cutbacks in their department and were trying to prove that they were still doing their jobs by locking up Elmore and Dean for good? He hit his hand on the steering wheel in frustration. What the hell kind of mess had they gotten into!

He would need to speak with Elmore and maybe both of them would figure out if Elmore's original idea of making the escape and crossing the border for a bit was really a better idea than this mess. Maybe he would think it through before asking Elmore. Elmore anyway was too mad to be of any help.

***

Elmore was blue around his mouth and resting on the Lazyboy when Dean walked into the house escorting not one but two people. Chimanbhai was still shivering, and plonked down heavily on the second Lazyboy. Radhika looked at Chimanbhai's state and opened her mouth to question him. But good sense prevailed and she scurried away into the kitchen. Neeraj was floating in and out of consciousness. The turmeric powder made him look like one of the Indian gods watching over them from the shelves above the dining table. Dean just sat down on the third Lazyboy and hoped he would just pass out. But the glorious smell of spices in milky tea wafted out of the kitchen and all he could do was wait for it.

Elmore saw the tea trolley and just groaned. He wished aloud for beer very feebly and everyone ignored him. There was no sign of Maya or Suraj. Dean accepted a cup of tea quietly, grateful for not having to answer Radhika's questions about the day. Radhika held the saucer for Chimanbhai and made him drink the tea. Neeraj had fallen asleep.

Just then Suraj decided to make an entrance. He came rushing down the stairs, heavily. And then, stupid as he was, went straight to Elmore who had just barely woken up. He held on to Elmore's arm and shook it. He looked very excited about something. 'Elmore, Mr Elmore! I have good news for you. I know how to make the bomb. What say? Should we make it?'

Bomb? Dean was careful to hide his surprise. Why would they need a bomb? Elmore was a little less measured in his response. He caught hold of the kid and despite his injured arm, yanked him around. 'What motherfuckin' bomb are you talking about?'

'To bomb her store. That's what you are her for, isn't it?'

Radhika yelled 'Suraj' so loudly that it reminded Dean of the Kung Fu flick he had seen when they were incarcerated last time. But that didn't take away the power from the yell. Chimanbhai Shah was now fully alert. Elmore had let go of the pesky kid and was staring at Radhika goggle eyed. Dean realized that his head was hurting. They were at the Shahs to bomb some woman's store? Why were they cutting betelnuts? What was going on?

Radhika had pounced upon Suraj and caught hold of his ear, twisting it with a vengeance. Suraj yelped in pain. Dean and Elmore, afraid to intervene, watched Radhika giving Suraj an earful. After she let go of the ear, Suraj just stood there, holding it and crying. Radhika was now circling Suraj, ranting and raving, although her decibel levels had gone down considerably. Chimanbhai kept shaking his head because he would try to interject and Radhika would stop him by an irritated wave of her hand. Even Elmore, who had seen enough abuse, felt sorry for the lad. Dean decided to change the subject.

'Neeraj, how are you doing, my man?'

Neeraj had come to and was looking bleary eyed. He had picked up a cup without thinking. His fingers were bleeding again.

Chimanbhai reacted. 'Oh Bhawani Ma! What is to become of this boy! Will he join the ranks of beggars outside your temple?'

'Oh, shubh shubh bolo, Chiman! Why are you always speaking of bad things! What happened to your hand, Neeraj?'

Neeraj, now fortified with the milky cup, was not about to faint. 'Radhika chachi, Dean and I cut up half a sackful of supari today! Just that when I was trying to cut the halves into slivers I think I cut up the tips of my two fingers. It just bleeds so much...'

Radhika was easily distracted. 'Neeraj! Why were you cutting supari? You know what "supari" means! As it is there have been too many injuries...' Then realizing that everyone was staring at her, she put her hand over her mouth. Everyone knew that she had put her foot into it.

'Yes, Neeraj, tell us what it means. We're tired of injuries to,' said Dean.

'Maybe we should ask Suraj. He even knows how to make a bomb,' Elmore added.

Suraj looked eager. But Radhika would have none

of it. She sat down and poured herself a cup of tea. Between sips she explained. 'We have a problem...for the last six months, the girl at the new store...'

'...which should have been mine,' Chimanbhai finished.

'Well, it isn't yours. She has almost ruined our business so Neeraj suggested we call the supari man...'

'Supari means "betelnut",' said Neeraj.

'A betelnut man?' Dean said, thoroughly confused by the conclusion.

'In India, there's this cool tradition...'

'Shut up, Suraj. What do you know of tradition? So in India when we want to get some work done...'

'Work means murder,' Suraj interrupted his mother again.

'Shut up, Suraj! Neeraj knew someone who would do the job. But the man wanted to move here. That's why we applied for an H1-B.'

'H1-B?'

'Mr Elmore. That's visa. So people come here and work. Legally.'

'Damn! Why bother with visa? Heck, they can give them a Mastercard and just let them come here. It's not like I wanted to work at all...'

'And Officer Hudson thinks you want betelnut pickers?'

'We couldn't explain.' Chimanbhai looked relieved that they were coming clean. 'And we could not say no either. So we agreed. How I wish we hadn't. Two days, just two days and who would know... There has been blood, blood, and more blood here than I have seen in my entire life.'

'Chiman! Have another cup of tea.'

'So what are *we* doing here?' Dean asked.

'Hey, no one said anything about murdering. Dean picks locks. I know how to steal things and have been in a brawl or two. That's what we do.'

'Yeeeeee...Haaaaaa!' Suraj had forgotten the scolding and was now rubbing his hands in glee. 'I told you these guys were crooks! I am sure they could kill too. Like Rambo. Bare hands!'

'Rambo was frikin' white. I am better even on a bad day. But murder? No fuckin' way.'

'She's just a girl!' Suraj said.

Everyone ignored him.

'We don't think murder is right either but we have a business to run. Everything is right in business and war, wise men have said. Sometimes we have to eliminate competition before our competition eliminates us.'

Radhika snatched the cups from Dean's and Elmore's hands and dumped them on the trolley with a clatter. She smiled at Chimanbhai and took his cup away as well. She began pushing the trolley towards the kitchen. But having grown up on TV serials, she knew her moment of drama was now. Stopping for a moment, she said, 'Three men bleeding. One useless. I have dinner to make and a plan to cook up. You two can decide whether to go to jail or help us.'

Suraj looked at his mother with newfound respect.

***

Dinner was lentil soup that was mildly spiced but sweet, and some sort of bizarre bitter greens cooked with potatoes (also sweet), and tortillas with sweetened butter spread on them. Maya was still not back. Radhika served the men. Chimanbhai devoured tortilla after tortilla, and Neeraj and Suraj ate a couple and slurped up the rest of the lentils.

'Eat up, daal is good ne.' Chimanbhai was expertly tearing off the tortilla with his thumb, index, and middle finger, grabbing a bit of the gooey, potatoey mess and then dipping it in the lentils. The drippy lentil–vegetable left a trail from the steel bowl on the melamine plate to the point where Chimanbhai's mouth was leaning over.

Dean had tasted Indian food before at curry houses. This was dessert compared to the spicy fares. It was so sweet it ought to have come with a warning for diabetics. Elmore just hated it. Dean asked for Tabasco and doused it all liberally. Elmore looked at Dean and did the same.

'That's $7.98 from your wages.' Mrs Shah served yet another tortilla to Suraj who protested.

'What for?' Dean and Elmore looked at her, incredulous.

'Tabasco doesn't come as part of the food that you get. That's extra.'

'But the bottle was already here, used!'

'If you don't like the food, tell that to the officer and go.'

'If we go, we shall tell the officer what you really want to do.'

'Mr Dean, who will believe you?'

Dean thought hard. The officer had already seen them bleeding from the effort of cutting the betelnuts on day one. They had chosen to not go to the emergency services. Neeraj had cut off his fingertips on day two. He had left the turmeric powder all over the back room. If the Shahs complained about them, they would be in jail so fast they would not have time to explain why betelnuts were given as a token offering by Indians to murderers as something to seal a contract, and why the Shahs were looking to bring a contract killer all the way to America.

Arms akimbo, Radhika was watching them with a triumphant smirk. 'Another tortilla, Dean?'

SEVEN

Osmanbhai swaggered in his trademark lungi and kurta up to Raasbehari's dhaba-cum-PCO.

'Ek chai de re bhai ko, malai maar ke!' shouted Raasbehari, who was suitably obsequious. He shooed away the customers sitting on the front bench drinking their morning chai, and cleaned it with his own gamchcha. And when Osmanbhai sat down, he yelled again, 'Ek bun maska bhee!'

'You going to maska me? Smart boy. Butter is good. Buttering is good.' Osman had a feeling in his bones. He would dip the buttery bun in the spicy ginger tea and then make his call.

The tea came in two three-inch glasses just as he liked it—one to dip his butter bun, and the other to drink from. He hated finding bits of bun with his last sip of tea at the bottom of the glass. The bun was placed on a broken glass saucer, but he didn't mind. It was going to be a good day.

Raasbehari stood attentively until Osmanbhai finished his chai, then said reluctantly, 'Bhai?'

Osmanbhai was sitting as quietly as a Buddha. He had closed his eyes and was savouring the taste of the sweet, milky, ginger tea. The ginger would help him make his overseas call. That was why he was at Raasbehari's PCO.

'Chal, phone laao.'

'Erm...Bhai...you have to come here. Wire...'

Bhai was in a rare mood. 'Haan, haan! Why not! I understand! Wire is short. I go to the phone if phone not come to me. No problem.'

He dialled an incredibly long number. Raasbehari checked quietly. America! Osmanbhai was calling America! He bit back a curse that crawled up his throat. Osmanbhai would not be paying for this call. Bhenchod!

But Raasbehari was in luck. Osmanbhai's call was just not going through. He had tried six times already. All of a sudden Raasbehari felt an iron grip choking the life breath out of him.

'Phone out of order? Cheating karega?'

Raasbehari tried to say that the phone was fine but no one was answering the phone, but the only thing he could say was 'Ackk! Byawk!'

One of Osmanbhai's henchmen reminded him that Raasbehari couldn't answer if his neck was being wrung and Osmanbhai let go. The sudden rush of air had Raasbehari gasping like a fish. Osmanbhai kicked him. 'Bol saale.'

'Bhai, America mein kya time hua?'

Time? Osmanbhai hadn't thought of that at all! That's why nobody was picking up the phone! Maybe all of them were working. And the womenfolk were not allowed to pick up the phone. Or maybe it was night, and they were all asleep. He kicked Raasbehari again.

'Why you didn't tell before? Saale kutte! You wasting my time!'

Osmanbhai and his henchmen left Raasbehari clutching his stomach.

***

The two men stared at the ceiling in the little room above the garage.

'I wanted to run for the border.' Elmore was nursing his hand.

'But we are here. So lemme think.'

'Fat lot good it did to us.'

'So *you* think.'

'I am not thinking now. You've ruined it. You think.'

'Fine. We just wait.'

'Then we get swallowed by that shark in a saree at breakfast.'

'Elmore, let's just wait and see, okay? Maybe things will change over breakfast.'

Elmore just muttered something about sweet eggs but Dean did not hear it. The bed was narrow but comfortable and the heater was working fine. He had had a tiring day and the Tabasco-laced lentils had filled him up. Sleep was not far.

***

Elmore was used to sleeping light and ready to bolt. He looked out of the little window and knew he had to get out there. Maya had just stepped out of the house, with a cat. She was wearing the shortest shorts and a tee. She was not wearing a bra. Elmore clambered out of bed and took two steps at a time and presented himself in front of the temptress.

'I'm walking the cat,' she said.

'I'm walking with you,' he said, wolfishly.

'Isn't it too early to be flirting?' she said coyly and began to walk ahead. The cat walked beside her as if it were a dog.

'In my book, it is never too early,' he said, and joined in the walk. 'How strange. A cat that goes for walks.'

'Not just any cat. Cali. Short for Caligula.'

'I've seen the movie. The kinky king.'

Maya grinned knowingly. 'Hmm...mm.'

Elmore kicked at a stone as they walked on the rain-washed path. She kicked it ahead. They walked quietly following the cat. The rolling of the stone was the only sound breaking the peace of the neighbourhood. There was a refreshing little nip in the air. Elmore knew he had to stay. Even if the only reason he had was to hold that breast walking next to him. Caligula, his tail raised, had spotted something and was sniffing it. They stopped at a respectable distance. A cat and its interest had to be given space.

Timing wasn't one of Elmore's virtues. He just grabbed at the breast that had distracted him from the start. Maya stepped away, but did not look surprised.

'Crap!' she said. 'Not in front of Mrs Chopra's house. She'll be watching.'

Elmore's brain had sort of woken up with that touch. Did she mean he could when no one was watching?

EIGHT

It was Suraj who climbed up the stepladder to the room above the garage and shook Dean awake.

'Dean! Dean, wake up! Elmore is having breakfast in the dining room already. Mother was asking for you. Everybody is waiting for you.'

Dean had been awake. He had been thinking. Elmore was right. They needed to get out of this and go underground for a few months. By his calculation, Lou would be out of the Cook County jail by now. He would be holed up in Chicago somewhere with that Chinese girl. They would find him and get some papers made. Then they would be free. But first they would need to scare these bloody Indians into keeping their mouths shut. He needed to threaten them with something concrete.

He pounced on the boy and covered his mouth so the little bastard wouldn't scream.

'Give me the plans to make the bomb!'

'MMMfffffmmm!' The boy tried to wiggle his eyebrows in answer. He was struggling so much he managed to get himself entangled in the duvet.

'I swear I will kill you if you scream. Now tell me, where are the plans?'

Dean took his hand off the boy's mouth.

'Wow Dean! You are strong! But why would I scream? I've got many plans. They're on my computer. I can print out all of them. In fact it would be awesome if you let me help you with the planning. I have lots of ideas! We would need to dispose of the body too you know. Mom does not like bombs. She says bombs don't always kill the target and sometimes only end up destroying stuff instead of people.'

'You discuss bombs and killings with your mother?'

'I have been telling Dad since the day he got to know that Mr Menon would not give him the store. We must get rid of her. She's caused us so much loss. I would have got the Nintendo Wii two months ago for my birthday. Now Puppa says I have to wait until he makes up for all the losses. I hate that woman. If you let me help, I promise you will never get caught. We have watched every episode of *CSI* and every episode of *CID*, the Indian show. I have lots of ideas: from poison to murder. And I know you are perfect.'

Dean could not believe what he was hearing. These people were all insane! Elmore was right. They needed to get away. Vanish. Mr Shah could deal with Officer Hudson alone. He shuddered involuntarily.

'But why did you think I would scream? Mother says that you two are like her sons and she will take good care of you.'

In his head Dean was already headed eastward on I-80 racing away to Chicago, with or without Elmore.

The boy was tugging at his sleeve now.

'I'm going, okay? Come down as soon as you wear some pants.'

***

'I'm going to hurt the brat before we go,' Dean promised himself, as he buttoned his jeans.

Elmore was sitting on a low stool just outside the front door and before Dean could ask him why or what was making him sit outside, he spotted the plate in Elmore's hand. There was nothing on it but two teaspoons each of salt and pepper.

Just then Maya came sauntering out with a saucer that had a single boiled egg on it.

'Breakfast!' she announced.

Elmore extended his plate and accepted the egg. He shelled it with haste and scarfed it down. Maya just stood there giggling. Dean watched the two of them with growing disbelief. She handed a plastic bag to Elmore.

'For the shells.'

Elmore tipped the plate into the bag and handed it to Maya.

'Mr Dean, you better have your egg too. I will get it for you. Wait here.'

After Maya had left with the plate, Dean said, 'One egg? One fuckin' egg? And you sit there smiling as though you've just had an all-you-can-eat at Denny's.'

'What's eating you, man! I had more stuff in there. It's weird food, but I am stuffed.'

'Then why eat the egg sitting on the doorstep?'

'They're Hindus. Don't eat meat.'

'They're weird. Let's not get involved.'

'Mr Dean, here is your egg. Have it here and then come inside. We're Hindus, you see...'

'And you don't eat this stuff.'

'Right! Never inside the house.'

'Does that mean you eat it outside?'

'No, Dean. Some people might. But we don't.' Maya shrugged her shoulders and rolled her eyes in a gesture Dean had seen in many women but never understood. 'But Mum's made poha for all of us. So eat this quickly and come in. There's tea too.

'Of course there's tea,' said Dean, not bothering to decipher what other delights awaited him. The egg smelled odd, but he doused it with pepper and gobbled it up. Stifling a peppery sneeze, he entered the house.

Dean froze as he stood by the food. There was a terrible smell of what could best be described as a synthetic fart. And amid that smell sat Mr and Mrs Shah and the rest of their ilk. Sitting like happy Buddhas who could not smell a thing. Their plates looked like they had already eaten whatever was making them all smell so bad.

'Dean! Good morning!' Suraj grinned.

Radhika was grinning, 'Good morning, good morning! Please sit down. You ate non-veg ne? It is such strong smell.'

'Strong smell?' Dean started laughing hysterically. This was some ghastly olfactory nightmare. He pulled a chair which Chimanbhai had patted and looked longingly at the pot of tea lying near Radhika.

Radhika was ladling out some steaming hot yellow mush from a casserole. 'Very happy today, Mr Dean! Good, good. Now eat. Gujarati special it is.'

'Poha, it is called.' Chimanbhai had started slurping on the tea.

The lone egg had disappeared in the vast hollow that was his stomach and he was not going to be able to argue logically with anyone. He needed to have a straight head on his shoulders. Maybe some tea would help.

'May I have some tea? The egg comes up as a burp otherwise.'

Maya had sat down beside Elmore. She giggled. 'Ma, let him have his tea. Egg hitchki...yuck!'

Radhika reacted to the words 'egg hitchki' far better than she had to his idea of a burp.

Bloody weirdass Indians and their foul, fart food! Dean poured himself a cup of the hot, spicy, milky tea. He held on to the cup as he drank it silently as though it were his last connection to sanity. Everyone watched him as though he were some cable access segment, difficult to understand but not at all artistic.

'Eat, Dean,' Chimanbhai said, breaking the spell.

And propelled by reflex action Dean stuck a forkful of the yellow stuff Radhika had served, into his mouth.

At first he didn't taste a thing. His mouth was too full of little plump flakes to allow him any taste sensation. But then he removed the fork from his mouth and the suicidal fatty morsels willingly let themselves be chewed. That's when he felt his mouth explode with taste sensations he never thought he possessed. He knew when he was biting into the hard bits, that these came out of the jar, and had he smelled the forkful before he had eaten it, he would be inside the crapper right now, on his knees. But at that moment Dean was like a boy who had just tasted his first exploding candy. The stuff inside his mouth was not bacon, but it had everything going for it. When chewed, the food sort of became grainy-pasty but there were round bits that were odd, there were leafy bits that were odd, and then there were some bits that were plain potato.

'What do you call this, again?' Dean asked, wanting to hate the stuff, but could not. Not when it had potatoes in it. He was looking at his plate now, which was almost empty. What kind of magic was that?

'Poha.'

'Right. Po-ha. Now that breakfast's done, let's get down to business, shall we?'

'Aww, Chiman, this is a sign from Bhawani Mata! See! In two days, he become pure Gujju. You talking business.' Radhika was beaming. 'Deanbhai, take more tea.'

Dean wasn't sure he liked what Radhika had just called him. Especially because it had Maya, Suraj, and Neeraj sniggering.

'You have been Gujjufied!' Maya declared.

'What's a "bhai"?' Elmore asked.

'She called him "bro"! My mom's talking like the boys in the "hood"!' said Suraj.

'No shit! She called you bro?' Elmore too was sniggering now.

Chimanbhai and Radhika seemed to have been transported to another world altogether as they drank their tea, oblivious to this exchange. Dean beat his hand on the table in frustration.

'Fuck all this. Mr Chiman and you...you, Mrs Shah. Listen very carefully. Elmore and I are leaving. We don't care what you really want to do, and what you have told the government. We will keep quiet about all of this if you pay us $300 each. Wait, let me finish. That will help us get out of your hair, and you can then do whatever the hell you want. Tell the cops we stole the money, or whatever. I've had enough of this beetle shit.'

'Six hundred dollars? To keep quiet?' Radhika started laughing. 'Keep quiet about what story? You have not been thinking have you, Deanbhai?'

Dean stared hard at the people at the table. They were staring right back at Radhika and Dean. Even Elmore did not look like he was on Dean's side.

'Elmore?' Dean was looking for support. 'El...more?'

'Dean. She's right. We oughtta stay.'

Dean kicked himself. Elmore was looking too comfortable to be ready to run.

'Stay? You want to stay? You? Did you forget how you begged me to think ways out last night. You hated it here. You did not want the pain any more. I stayed up most of the night thinking of ways to escape from this place and these people. And now you want to stay?' Dean was ranting. Elmore kept shaking his head as if to deny all charges.

Dean paused for breath. He had noticed how Maya had shifted her chair closer to Elmore. He had noticed how Neeraj and Suraj had shifted their chairs closer to each other, and how Mrs Shah was laughing silently. Dean ignored her and looked squarely at his buddy.

'Why do you want to stay here, Elmore?'

He just muttered something about changing his mind. But it was Radhika who answered.

'Deanbhai, who are you? What you have done in your life? Neeraj found out that you run from one place to another place. Sometimes living on—what they say—dole. You don't want to be big man? You don't want to be Don?'

'Big man? Who Don?'

Suraj piped in to explain. 'Don Corleone. You know, the Godfather.'

'Godfather? The movie? You guys are crazy. I don't want to be the Godfather or anything. Elmore! You want to be a Godfather? A Don?'

'Dean! Listen to Mrs Shah. I don't want to be a Don either. But I am tired of living on minimum wage. Want to make more money, man! Just listen to her.'

'Please, Dean. We have been honest with you. Tell him, Chiman. Tell him how we have been humiliated by that...Menon woman. Tell him!'

'That shop is mine, I tell you, mine. I paid money for it to Menon, but he gave it to his niece. Once upon a time I had twenty-twenty customers coming in daily. After she opened the shop, it is so bad I am getting one-two, one-two customers in two days, three days. If this goes on, I will have to sell at loss and go back to India. There I have nothing. My work of twenty years, all gone! That's why we are asking for you help, understand?'

Radhika said, 'We just want to live the American Dream.'

'American Dream!' Dean snorted. 'So why didn't you report about the other shop?'

'Would you report if you were in our place?'

Dean stopped in his tracks and poured himself another cup of tea.

Radhika continued. 'In India they say you can finish the competition in four ways: saam, daam, dand, bhed. Suraj samjhao, ne!'

The ever obedient Suraj was happy to explain. 'Saam means intelligence. Daam means money. Dand means force. Bhed means divide. You need to use all these to beat your competition in business. You know, you stay top dog.'

'So why have you guys gone straight to force?'

'Deanbhai, my Chiman knows better than anyone else how to do business. There was no other store doing business like him in the Greater Portland area. But they come with more money. So we begin to suffer. You can steal her money when you finish her. That money is yours if you like. We won't say anything. But we want you to finish her for us.'

'Finish her? As in kill her? Do you know what you are talking about? It's not easy killing someone. We haven't killed anyone. Elmore, tell them.'

Elmore was thinking about Maya. 'I am willing to try.'

'You? Killing? Do you even know how to hold a gun?'

'Dean! You always treat me like an idiot.' Elmore flexed his muscles. 'If I put my mind to it, I could kill.'

Suraj said, 'I know all about guns. We can download it.'

Dean could not believe he was listening to this. 'Wait, wait. I need time to think.'

'Think later. Neeraj will tell you what Osmanbhai was going to do. I need to prepare lunch for Chimanbhai,' Radhika said and walked off with her cup of tea towards the kitchen.

'Osmanbhai? Osama bin Laden? What are you guys mixed up in? Who are you people?' Dean looked stunned.

NINE

Osmanbhai's thugs had broken down yet another PCO booth. The owner, a skinny man, stood shivering in his chappals in front of Osmanbhai who was sitting on a chair, watching the mayhem his men were wreaking on the booth. People gathered there to watch, but nobody dared do anything such as call the police.

'Osmanbhai, tell me, meri galti kya huyee?'

'Galti? Mistake bol. I learning Amrikan. Ei Baban, dikha be! Show him.'

Baban, Osmanbhai's spoken-English coach, whipped out a much-thumbed English Learning book. The thin man looked suitably impressed. He joined hands shaking his head.

'Please, Osmanbhai, tell my mistake,' Baban prompted.

'Please Osmanbhai...' the owner could not continue.

Osmanbhai was pleased with the effort. 'Your booth can no connect to Amrika. I go Amrika. I need to connect. Your booth no connect. So we break it. No point it has. Waste. Open chai shop.

More use for people. Now go. Make me chai.'

He would eventually learn to say 'America' but Baban was rather proud of his student.

'Aur kitne PCO baaki hain re?' Osman forgot his obsession with things American as soon as the glass of chai was placed in his hand.

'Cheh bhai.'

Before Baban could say *Sholay*, Osmanbhai was beaming like the Buddha himself.

'I sound like Gabbar Singh from *Sholay*, no?' he asked.

Now Osmanbhai's chaps knew how many times their boss had seen the Bollywood blockbuster. If he was enacting a scene with himself as the big bad villain, Osmanbhai must be very happy. They knew this was the right time to ask for a favour.

'Bhai! Aaj ke liye bas kya?'

'English, foolish men, speak English. How will you come to Amrika otherwise?' Osmanbhai was on a roll.

'America, bhai? How we go America?'

'Arre! I have contacts. Neerajbhai Shah is fixing my visa. I go Amrika first. I fix your visa. You come, then Chandni come. I fix visa for all.'

Chandni. Now that was an idea. Osmanbhai had had enough of breaking booths. He told the men that he was off to Chandni's. They should also go home except Baban. Baban could give him English lessons later.

***

'I cannot believe you guys want to bring a contract killer to the country. Where do you get these ideas?'

'Look, Mr Dean, in India, it is far simpler to have fight with competition. If they fight fair, like give extra discounts, then you too can have a super price war. But if they don't fight fair, you can fight unfair. All you need to use is brains.'

'You must indeed have brains to try and get someone called Osama a visa.'

'Not Osama, his name is Osman. Big difference. Osmanbhai is one of the best. His head has a hundred ideas on how to eliminate competition. He would need to use a gun only when there was nothing else. He is said to have killed two men simultaneously with his bare hands.'

'Well, you haven't got him. And how much were you paying this guy who can kill two birds with his two hands?'

'Two thousand dollars. That is the price he charges for a kill. He is double awesome.'

'People in India have that kind of money?' Elmore piped in, but before he could suggest a move to India, Neeraj said, 'I am sure they would offer the two of you the same terms. Just listen to Radhikaben's plan.'

Dean stared at Elmore. A strange sense of foreboding passed down his spine. But he put it to poor thermostat levels in the Shah home. They were weird people. The house was cold as a coffin during the day, and hot as hell in the evening.

Radhika walked into the room, but ignored the three silent men. She yelled, 'Mayaaaaaaaa!'

The three were shaken out of their personal visions.

Maya, like all children, understood the urgency in that yell. She took two steps at a time and came downstairs to see four pairs of eyes on her.

Radhika recovered first. Maya was too old for a supervised wardrobe, but her shorts had recently got really really short. And where did she find that ganji? It looked like the undershirt Hrithik Roshan wore in the movies, but this was not the movies and Maya was a girl, not some hero.

'Put some tea on and go wear some clothes. And don't argue.'

For an instant, Maya looked defeated. But she went to the kitchen quietly. Radhika turned to the three boys.

'Neeraj, have you told them about Osmanbhai?'

Neeraj nodded.

'Deanbhai, Elmore, you understood what we were really looking for?'

Dean nodded but Elmore was still staring at where Maya would have been.

'Come to the dining table. We talk there.'

The three boys obeyed her without any unnecessary questions. Maya had squished the ginger perfectly, and had gone upstairs to change. Radhika added ginger to the milk and stirred the tea leaves once more. Maya came down wearing track pants and a proper T-shirt. Radhika did not notice how well the track pants fitted around Maya's curves. She waved Maya to the kitchen and went around to where the boys were sitting.

'Neeraj beta, Osmanbhai ka phone aaya?'

'No, Radhika aunty. Osmanbhai has not called me. He did call Chimanbhai though. He sounded completely upset that his visa was delayed.'

'Hmm. Call Chiman. I want to talk to him.'

Dean and Elmore sat quietly. Dean's mind was racing like a freight train and he was feeling happier by the minute at the turns the train was taking. Elmore was happy simply because he had seen Maya look like some Indian love goddess.

'Chiman? Hello, Chiman?' Radhika was on the phone, but she was so loud, using the instrument seemed pointless. Everyone in the neighbourhood could surely hear her, and by that logic, Chiman would have heard her as well.

'Mommmm! Volume!'

Radhika nodded her head and lowered her voice so much that Dean sitting across the table could not hear. When the conversation was over, Maya had brought in the tea and was watching her mom.

'Well...?' Maya asked.

'Osmanbhai has not called Chiman, and I told him to not worry if he does call. We ask Osmanbhai to wait. We now have Deanbhai to help us. If these two can do the job, it's all well and good. If not, there's always Osmanbhai.'

Elmore said, 'I will do this kill. I am ready to do this kill.'

Dean rolled his eyes. 'Fine, Elmore. We will do the kill. But Mrs Shah, you will need to pay us. And I am not talking minimum wage here. I am talking rates you would have paid had your Indian killer showed up here.'

Radhika was a thoroughbred Gujarati. She loved dealing with money and she liked a good bargain. Dean did not have half an inkling that she held all the cards. He was being set up to a bargain and he had no experience at all. If people had tails to express what they were really feeling, Radhika's bushy tail would be swaying slowly like a little tigress's, in anticipation of an easy kill. But this talk of money from this callow boy was too funny to resist. An involuntary giggle escaped Radhika's mouth, which she soon muffled into a cough.

'Neeraj beta, did you tell Dean that Osmanbhai was doing this for us free?'

'Free?' Dean said. 'It is costing you $2,000, Mrs Shah.'

Radhika poured tea for them all. Pushing one cup towards Dean she said, 'Less actually. Once we figured out we don't need the lawyer, the costs came down drastically. But we let Osman believe that the visa process costs a lot. With you, I don't have to play games.'

'I am not playing games either, Mrs Shah. It is going to cost you $2,000 to convert us into murderers.'

'I not forcing you, Deanbhai. I ask, if you cannot do the job you say no. You have said yourself, you are not killing anyone. So if we let you do the job, you should be paying us, for helping you begin new career. Osmanbhai is professional. He can kill two people at one time with two hands.'

'Yes, we know. And Osmanbhai may be professional, but don't underestimate us. We are also willing to do the job for free. You will be paying us to keep quiet. And since there are two of us, $2,000 apiece sounds like a neat round figure. And I am not counting the costs at all. We would need to buy a gun, and the bullets and...'

'Sixty-five dollars. That's what you get.'

'Sixty-five dollars? Are you kiddin' me?'

'Sixty-five dollars. I will get you a gun. And the bullets. And you will keep quiet about the killing otherwise you will go to jail so fast...so fast... Before you say Chimanbhai Jayantibhai Shah you will be in jail.'

'We've been nothing but nice ever since we've come here. Eaten the sweet Indian food you made us although we hated it. We even ate egg outside the house like we were some homeless people. The two of us sleep in a room above your garage and you pay us minimum wage for a job that is concocted. It is not a real job. You knew that cutting up those nuts was not exactly easy. But we tried our best and we even have injuries to prove that it is a hazardous job. Now you come up with this ridiculously low number and you think we will kill this person you have in mind for a few measly dollars?'

'Here, have another cup of tea. And sit down. Good thing Maya put ginger in the tea, or you would burst a couple of blood vessels.'

'What? Are you completely nuts? You have the nerve to offer me peanuts and then tell me to calm down!'

'Look the $65 is free. Can you do math? In one week, with minimum wage you would earn $8.4 an hour working ten hours a day. In the store you won't work ten hours, but maybe maximum five. So you earn $42 a day. Understand so far?'

'If we work for a week, we earn $300 at least, right?'

'Neeraj beta, show calculator. You boys! We learnt to do math in our head. See, you earn $294 dollars. Assuming you work seven days a week, which you won't. You will work five days. So that's only $210. You stay with us and eat with us, that's fifteen dollars a day for stay which makes it $105, $20 a day for two meals which is $140. So I cut $145 from your wages. That leaves you exactly $65. Thank your god that I think of you and Elmore as my sons and am not charging you for breakfast. That would be extra.'

'You will charge me $15 to share that small pokey room above the garage?'

'Find something cheaper and stay there. But think about it, you will have to spend your own money to get to the store. This way you save gas money because you travel to work with Chimanbhai.'

'The food you eat is crap. I am not paying nine ninety-nine to eat the Indian shit.'

'Eat where you want. But you get to and from diners on your own. The nearest diner is in Tigard. Four miles away. I won't pay for petrol. But tea, see, as much tea as we drink. No problem. You are like my sons only.'

Dean realized he was well and truly stuck.

Elmore was watching this exchange with his mouth slightly open. It was going a trifle fast for him. But by Dean's expression he knew that Radhika had won. Radhika sat there like a Cheshire cat, sipping tea from her red mug, satisfied with the outcome.

'Sixty-five dollars! But then that would be what we have earned, isn't it? That's not enough to keep our mouths shut. You have to buy our silence, Mrs Shah.'

'Look. You have no experience. We are taking too much risk already by putting you on the job. I cannot give you any money. Like I said, you can leave.'

'Chachi,' Neeraj interrupted, 'what if we let them take any money that is in her shop? Then the cops will think that she was killed when she was robbed.'

'That is not our business, isn't it Neeraj? I cannot guarantee that she will have lots of money in the shop. Even if she is robbing us, she might not have too much money. If these guys want to steal from that shop, it is not my business.'

'What you are saying, Chachi, is that they are free to take whatever cash is there in her till.'

'I am not saying anything. Do you think I will sit under the gods like this, drink the milk from the holy cow in my tea and tell these—two godless people to steal? You know Gandhiji said stealing is a sin, and my mother comes from the same town as Gandhiji's mother, so I am not about to encourage people to steal.'

'Momm!' Maya interjected. 'Don't be so holier than thou! Just the other day you were hoping someone would ransack the shop!'

'Shut up, Maya! My wishing is one thing and then telling people to steal is another thing. When will you understand the difference?'

'Where is this shop?' Dean asked. 'We would need to begin planning soon. And when we are planning, we get paid separately. Do we have a deal?'

'Fine, but I want to know what you are doing when you are planning. You cannot tell me you are thinking with your eyes closed and catch naps like you've sold horses.'

Neeraj and Maya laughed. Dean looked confused. These Indians had an odd turn of phrase. This bunch was madder than anyone he had come across. The faster they finished the job and got out, the better it would be. He would take the $65 and steal anything and everything of value in that store. The problem with him was that he didn't hate anyone enough to want to kill them. But the way these Indians spoke about killing their competition, they made it seem trivial almost, to take someone's life.

'Where will we get the gun?'

'Leave that to me. You just fill the bullets and shoot to kill. We won't get too many chances—one chance, six bullets. That should be enough to kill that kutri.'

'That's "bitch", in Gujarati,' said Maya.

'Sounded like that,' Dean said.

'I need to sleep,' Radhika announced. 'You discuss more. Suraj will be back home in an hour or so, and I want you to take his help with all the killing ideas he has. My Suraj has lots of knowledge about the Internet. I have told him to show all.'

Radhika walked upstairs leaving Elmore and Dean sitting at the table with Neeraj and Maya.

***

Suraj was over the moon, sharing his ideas with them. Dean was disgusted. He could not stop himself from saying, 'Calm down boy! Your spit is flying all over the place.'

That didn't dampen Suraj's enthusiasm at all. He wiped away all the spit on his sleeve and the rest with the back of his hand. Dean stifled the rising bile that tasted like the gingery tea, and listened to the child.

'We can poison her. Rat poison. It will give her huge stomach cramps and then kill her. We'll follow her to her house and poison the food she makes for herself.'

'What if she calls 911 when she's suffering?'

'Ha! We cut the phone lines.'

Elmore couldn't believe his ears. This child was demented. 'Won't she know?'

'Indian food has so much spice, she won't taste a thing!'

Then the boy sat looking glazed at the two 'killers'.

'We can stab her to death. You gag her then stab her. That will be fun.'

Dean could not help joining in for a bit of fun. He added, 'Wouldn't it be messy? Blood on our clothes? Maybe we take chainsaws. It will be faster.'

'Chainsaws are noisy!' Elmore said.

Dean wished he could roll his eyes like Radhika and Maya. 'How about burying her alive?'

'Yeah, Dean! Super idea. Pedro Almodovar showed it in his movie. Maya didi, don't tell Mom I watched an adult film. We can knock her down and then put her in the freezer and bury the freezer somewhere.'

'How about we feed her to the chickens?'

'Elmore! We cannot feed people to chickens.'

'Why not? It'll be fun!'

'Maybe we can throw a grenade into her shop when she is doing her tally for the day. Woohoo! She'll be all over the neighbourhood.'

'How about we dunk her in a vat of acid?'

'Maya! That is gruesome. Where will we get a vat of acid?'

'If we have to kill someone, why don't we do the job like super villains. Why just kill her with a gun?

Guns are too easy. Bang! She'll be dead. Revenge for what she has done to Dad and Mum must be a little more satisfying. No?'

Everyone stared at Maya and the vehemence in her eyes. Elmore felt a huge stirring in his loins. This was a goddess.

'Maya is right. Revenge is what we want. We can find acid.'

Suraj said, 'If acid is the way to go, we have acid at home. If the two of you tie her up, Maya can make her drink battery fluid. That should kill anyone.'

Neeraj was watching with his eyes glazed. 'What was that episode where he feeds her two tubes of toothpaste to kill her?'

'Toothpaste?' Elmore asked. 'How do you die by eating toothpaste?'

'Fluoride poisoning.'

'Is there such a thing?'

'If *CSI* says, there is, then there is.'

'I've had enough. We cannot do this. I don't even know this woman.'

Maya said, 'That's easily rectified. We will go on a recon trip, and we will figure her out.'

Suraj was delighted. 'I'll bring my super spy binoculars.'

'No doofus. They are toy binoculars. We will use our eyes, thank you very much. And you have school.' Maya's sisterly reminder brought a wail from the boy, who gathered up his laptop and all the bizarre printed pages which had everything from poisoning to blowing up her brains listed out, and left muttering curses on everyone. 'Wait and see, Maya didi. Wait and see. Today you won't let me help you, but in the end you will all come running to me for help. Just remember I have the brains. And Gandhiji said brains were always more important than brawn.'

Dean looked at Maya. 'Your Gandhi said that?'

Maya answered with a shrug, 'I doubt it. But we have grown up on so much that Gandhiji said that we don't really know whether he said it or not. All I know is that he was an old chap who was like a peacenik or something. But right now we have to think how we are going to follow Supriya and figure out how to kill her.'

TEN

Chimanbhai came downstairs, his hair slightly damp from the shower, to smells of parathas made in ghee. Radhika must be very happy to have made parathas. He wiped the cutlery with the paper napkins from the first drawer. They would all collect unused napkins from restaurants they visited for use later. The kids had laughed at first, but they changed when they realized all Indian families did that. Teabags, dairy creamers, napkins, sugar sachets, ketchup packets, toothpicks—it was all there. He remembered how Radhika had poked herself with a plastic fork when she was looking for something in her purse, and from that day he did not allow anyone to bring home plastic cutlery from restaurants. He used to be tempted by spoons, but the pain in Radhika's eyes reminded him of Meenakshi's expression—from the last time they met—when she told him that she was getting engaged to be married to a boy her family had 'found' for her, how their horoscopes matched, and how she could not marry him because he was just not rich enough for her family. And Chimanbhai did not want to be reminded of the day his heart was broken.

He wiped the forks that Elmore and Dean would use and then he placed them on the plates, not knowing which side of the plate the forks should go. He didn't care for spoons and forks, preferring to eat with his fingers. Even the kids were brought up to eat like Indians did. The food tasted better somehow. Only ice cream or basundi (Radhika made basundi better than his mother ever could) was eaten with spoons, and even basundi could be eaten with fingers if there were puris.

'Su karechho? What's on your mind, Chiman?'

'Smells like parathas, Radhika. What else could I be thinking about?'

'One of these days our health insurance is going to go through the roof if your arteries get clogged with parathas, I'm telling you.'

'Let me remind you that my grandmother lived to be ninety-nine, and she loved eating parathas made in ghee.'

'Fine, fine. Eat. Everyone will be coming soon. I serve you hot-hot from the stove.'

'Hey Puppa, how was your day?' Maya breezed in smelling of some heavy perfume.

'Maya! Did you break the perfume bottle?'

'Hey Pops, how much money did you make!' Suraj came rushing in.

'Go call those two first. When you work with me then ask about money,' said Chimanbhai. And when Suraj reluctantly left, he asked Maya, 'Any progress with those two?'

'Mom was just awesome. She bargained with them! They asked for $2,000...'

'Two thousand dollars! Hey Ambe Ma! We cannot afford so much money!' Chimanbhai wailed.

'Puppa! You don't listen ne! I said Mom bargained! She offered them $65!'

'Sixty-five dollars! Maan gaye! Unbelievable! Your mom has not lost her touch. No wonder she made parathas.'

'Parathas! I will become so fat! Momm!' Maya ran into the kitchen to look for an alternative. Chimanbhai sat down for a rare moment of peace.

When the boys came in, they found Chimanbhai dozing.

'Puppa! Please tell Maya didi to take me along for the recon trip. I thought up of so many different ways to kill Supriya. And now that it is time to try it out, they won't take me.' Suraj made his case before his parent.

Chimanbhai was shocked at such talk. He couldn't believe his young son was talking about killing so easily. 'Hey Ambe Ma! We don't talk of such things openly. Where did we go wrong?'

Radhika waltzed in with a mound of parathas on a plate. She saw Chimanbhai sitting with his head in his hands and sighed. 'Now Chiman, don't be so dramatic. Suraj just wants to be a part of the family project.'

'Family project?' Chimanbhai looked horrified. But his objection was drowned by Neeraj's smacking appreciation of his wife's cooking.

'Eat, Chiman. Don't worry about all this. We have planned out everything. Eat, Dean. Eat, Elmore. Suraj, you want more ghee on the paratha?'

Radhika served parathas to everyone. Maya emerged with a plate of watermelon and a bowl of yogurt. Dean looked at the watermelon with interest, but it looked like Maya was not about to share. He turned his attention to the parathas. Elmore had started tucking in with a fervour of a starved man. Dean tentatively put one piece into his mouth. There were spicy potatoes in the bread. Dean saw red. The spice went straight to his head and he felt each cell of his sinuses open up with joy! He watched the others eat. Everyone had the same glazed look. He watched Chimanbhai make a neat cone of the bread and dip it into the yogurt before eating. He did the same. The cool yogurt was a brilliant contrast to the hot, spicy bread. Elmore was licking his fingers just as Neeraj and Suraj were doing. Dean realized that he had eaten four of the round breads. He paused because Radhika was now bringing a platter with a napkin covering the food.

'What is it, Ma?' Suraj asked.

'Don't touch it.' Radhika ate two of the breads so rapidly that Dean was stunned.

No one dared ask what it was until all the dishes were cleared away and Suraj and Neeraj were sent away to wash them. Maya put away the leftovers in the fridge and the mango pickles. She had eaten only watermelon and fruit yogurt.

Everyone was back at the dining table.

Radhika pulled the tray towards her and removed the cover, and there was a collective exclamation of surprise. It was a gun. A very old gun. Radhika picked it up gingerly and then very dramatically announced, 'For the kill.'

Elmore started laughing. Dean looked at everyone and began laughing too. These guys had no clue at all! This was a not a gun, it was a museum piece! No one could shoot to kill with this thing. Dirty Harry maybe, but not Elmore, not Dean.

'Where did you find it, Mrs Shah? You robbed a museum?'

'What? Museum?'

'Is that what you did today, Mom?' Suraj asked.

'I have bullets too,' announced Radhika.

'Oh, no. No. No.' Elmore now looked serious. 'Dean wouldn't be able to shoot with that thing.'

Suraj was rubbing his hands with glee. 'Yes, he will. I will help fix the gun. I have read on the Net, you know, how to clean a gun. This one probably needs oiling of the parts. Lemme go get my computer.'

'Dean, are you going to use this gun? It looks so old it might explode if you used it.' Elmore looked scared now. 'I think we should let these guys do it themselves. I am happy to get out of this while we are alive.'

Maya was posing with the gun now. Neeraj and Elmore were staring at her. Chimanbhai was sitting there looking stunned, staring at the gun as though it would jump up and bite him.

'Hey Jagdambe! Now we have a gun inside the house!'

'Chiman! Don't start that all over again. You said yes and that's why I have gone through all the trouble. If we had the money, we could have afforded to bring Osmanbhai on full payment. We didn't have the money, so we agreed to his condition, yes or no?'

Chimanbhai nodded a meek yes. But Radhika was now going full force. She wanted to make a point.

'If Osmanbhai had not put us in this position to beg, we would not have had to bring any gun home. Or these two either. He would have come anonymously, strangled the kutri with his bare hands and left the country! If only we could pay him. Pan ye Neeraj bhi! Because you did not want to pay money, Neeraj suggested to Osmanbhai this work visa idea, and that horrible man! Oh god! We still need to deal with him! That man now wants to move to this country! And we are now going deeper into this! But I am sure with this gun we will be able to finish off the girl and then we tell Osmanbhai his visa application was rejected. Simple it will be. Here, Dean, make it work.'

Dean took the gun from Radhika and examined it. The gun looked like it was jammed. It probably weighed a couple of pounds. He tried moving the safety lock, even using the trigger. Nothing worked.

'I don't think it can be of any use,' Dean said. 'Look, everything is rusted.'

'Rust? No problem!' Radhika said, and started to walk to the kitchen. And before Dean could say 'Colt 45' Radhika was back, had practically snatched the gun from his hand, and doused it with the household kitchen rust cleaner. Dean watched Radhika horrified. He did not think you cleaned a gun with an ordinary rust cleaner. She had drowned the gun in the cleaning fluid.

'The entire gun is going to melt away, Mum!' Maya voiced her concern.

Elmore and Neeraj nodded.

'When was the last time you used a cleaning fluid, Maya?' her mother asked, then sweetly instructed her to go get a sponge and cleaning cloth from the kitchen, 'Do you at least know where they are kept?'

Maya made a face at her mother and sashayed kitchenwards.

Chimanbhai watched Radhika working on the gun with the cloth and sponge and more anti-rust liquid, the hypnotic rhythm making him really really sleepy. Suraj was yawning nineteen to the dozen. Elmore was finding it hard to stay awake too. Only Dean was watchful. Hoping that he would not have to use the gun.

As the table began to empty of people, only Maya, Dean, and Radhika remained looking at the slow transformation of the gun. The first thing that started to work was the slide. Dean was amazed. The bullet chamber in the new guns popped out and one loaded the bullets in the chamber. In this gun, each bullet had to be loaded and the slide pushed the empty casing out. This much Dean knew. But the safety was jammed. If the safety didn't work, they might end up shooting themselves if they dropped the gun by mistake. Elmore could be ham-handed. Dean knew that it was not just a possibility but a certainty that they would end up shooting themselves in the foot.

Radhika's hands were feeling the corrosive effects of the fluid. She knew she had to stop.

'I will wipe the thing off. Maybe tomorrow you can put that WD-40 or something to make the parts working again. Suraj will help you separate the gun into parts. He would have the video on the computer. That boy! Don't underestimate him, haan! He has many ideas. How he has taken birth in my straight family I don't know. But he thinks like some master criminal. You will ask him, ne?'

'We will, Mrs Shah. The boy has some good ideas. Maybe the gun will be workable soon. We have much work before that. We need to find out all about this girl. What she does, how and where she works and all that. Then we make a plan. A proper plan.'

'You don't look intelligent, but maybe I am not used to white people na, so I cannot correctly say. Sorry. You do sleep now. You helping us, thank you.'

Dean should've been angry, but the mere mention of sleep made him yawn. Maya yawned and stretched sexily. Does this girl ever stop? Dean thought, but refrained from saying anything.

'Good idea, Mrs Shah.'

Radhika nodded and waved him away. After wiping the gun, she put it away in the first drawer where all the restaurant extras were kept. Then she locked up the front door, bowed her head in front of the many photographs of the gods and goddesses, switched off the lights and went up to bed.

***

'Suraaaajjjj! Eat breakfast at school, beta!' Radhika's yell shattered the morning's peace. Dean could not eat the boiled egg any more. It just tasted ugh. Elmore was happy to eat Dean's share. Leaving Elmore outside with pepper and salt and eggs, Dean ventured inside. There were no smells of Indian food. There was no sign of either Chimanbhai or Maya. At the dining table, there was Radhika sitting with the gun, her face covered with a scarf like bandits from an old Western.

Dean's first instinct was to flee. But he spotted a bag of discount store sugar flakes and a jar of milk on the table. Radhika waved her hand to the flakes. Dean felt like a little boy who was being waved to a feast. The milk and the frosted flakes tasted like heaven. He watched Radhika spray WD-40 with the nozzle into every crevice of the gun. The wood grip of the gun was corroded by the rust fluid. But it had cleaned up the metal parts. The WD-40 was loosening up more stuff that was jammed.

Soon Radhika was cocking and uncocking the gun with the safety lock working. This was a miracle.

'Mrs Shah, wait. Let me see the gun.'

'I told you this gun would work. You thought I was a Gujju housewife, won't be able to buy a gun ne? See!'

Although it felt like sandpaper, the gun seemed to be working. Now they would need bullets.

'We will need bullets, Mrs Shah. Did you think you could find us bullets that will go with this hundred-year-old relic?'

Radhika smiled and said, 'We have three.'

'Three?'

'Yes, how many do you need to kill one girl? Osmanbhai would not need a gun...'

'Yes, we know. He would have killed her with his bare hands. But, Mrs Shah, only three?'

'But I got them for free. I bargained for three. Don't think you will find any more bullets for the gun. Very difficult now is what Jerome of the pawnshop said. So you have to use only three. Use your brain before you use the gun, Gandhiji said.'

'Gandhi used guns?' Dean just could not understand this Gandhi chap at all. Sometimes they said he said do-gooder things. Sometimes he spoke of guns. And Mrs Shah's mum came from the same town, so she couldn't be wrong.

'Gandhi fought the British. He knew everything about everything,' Radhika clarified. 'Also now you and Elmore go with Maya and find out where she lives. I will get lunch ready.'

Dean realized that he was dismissed. He looked longingly at the frosted flakes and the milk. Elmore came in and grinned to see milk and cereal for breakfast.

'This is kiddie stuff, man! Where is the Indian hot stuff?' Elmore asked.

'Did someone mention me?' Maya had perfect timing. She looked like a frosted flake herself. Dressed in pink jeans and a tight white tee she was the stuff of Elmore's dreams. But Dean knew better.

'So you are ready to take us to where she lives?' asked Dean. 'It's cooler out there. You will need a jacket.'

Maya leaned forward very provocatively on the chair and asked, 'Now Mr Elmore, do you think it's cold out there and I should be covering up? I thought I was hot enough, no?'

Elmore choked on a mouthful of milk and flakes.

'All right, I'll get a jacket until you finish.' Maya rolled her eyes and walked away, swaying her hips again.

By the time Elmore and Dean had finished a second bowl of cereal each, and stepped out into what was another cloud-covered morning in Portland, Maya had managed to change into a short olive green skirt, an army-style camouflage tee, an olive green jacket and funky camouflage tights and boots. Elmore whistled. Dean pushed him to the back seat and walked around to sit in front next to Maya.

'Let's go find out everything about the enemy,' said Maya, as she turned on the ignition of her Toyota Tercel.

***

'You've driven us to your father's store, Maya!' exclaimed Dean.

'Yeah, Supriya's store is right here. But let's go meet Dad first. He was going to tell you about Supriya.'

The three trooped into Mr Shah's India World Store. Chimanbhai was on the phone. He had the oddest expression on his face. It made him look younger, wistful somehow. Not something Dean would associate with someone who had plotted elaborately to literally eliminate their competition.

'I wish I were in Navsari too,' Chimanbhai was saying.

'Dad?' Maya was puzzled. 'Dad! Dad? What are you saying?'

For a fleeting second Chimanbhai gave in to his emotions. 'Had I been in Navsari...with Meena...' Then he suddenly realized that Maya was standing there. 'Oh Ambe! Maya? When did you come?'

Maya was never short of words. 'What Navsari? Where would you rather be? Dad? Who are you speaking with?'

Chimanbhai recovered so fast that Maya had trouble repeating her question. 'So are you ready to start working the plan?'

'Plan?' asked Dean. 'I have barely been told her name. Maya said that you will tell us something about her.'

'Menon is the guy. He promised me that he will sell me this shop space. So I showed him all the drawings, told him how to set up the store, where the grains should go, where the dry foods should go, where to put the perishables and the best place to put the deep freeze. I wanted to put the deep freeze there. Then I made the biggest mistake. I told him of my plans of setting up a larger video section. So many desis moving into the area, what other entertainment do they have?'

Chimanbhai looked at his audience. Dean was all ears, nodding appropriately. He did not see Maya leaning provocatively on the grain sacks and Elmore paying attention only to the cleavage his daughter was displaying. His hate for Menon and Supriya blinded him to everything else. 'You know she came to me for a summer job...'

'You mean she used to work here?'

'Work? She only wanted the numbers of all the young chaps who came in here. That's all she did! Who knew she was luring them away to her store! Yes! That bitch! Menon was just her pawn. He told me sorry and earned interest on my token money! He returned the money! But took away my respect!

My plans were known to everyone in the community. Now they are laughing at me. My business is hurting every day. You must understand that our enemy is very nasty. Her store is in the same mall, on the side of the big Circuit City. Go see. Be careful.'

'Okay. I think I shall do this alone. I will follow her and will come back tonight.'

'Good idea, Mr Dean. Ambe Ma's blessings are with you.'

'Erm...I need some money to follow her...'

'Oh yes. Here's a ten. Will do?' Chimanbhai looked at Dean's face. 'No? Okay here are two dollars more. She won't take a cab. She travels by bus everywhere. Her car is not working for the last two days.'

'Thanks, Mr Shah. I will take the bus back to your home. I shall tell you everything tonight.'

'Okay. We will keep dinner for you.'

***

Dean walked over to Circuit City, and spotted the store. It was new, so it had the flash and the dash of a new store, but looked different from Mr Shah's smelly overcrowded one. This store was called Indian Exotica. He walked past the store, peering into the display window. It looked cool, expensive somehow. There were DVDs displayed there, and weird lamps that Dean had seen in the dining area where the hundred gods were kept, and touristy posters of India. And there were people, shopping! That meant he could slip inside and take a look.

But maybe he should just watch the store from afar.

So he did. He walked up to the bench near the nail store that was shut, and stood watching. It was a good place to watch the front door of the store. He was not too far that he would need binoculars to spy on the store, nor was he so close that people would notice. Making a mental note that he would go around the store and check it out, he settled down to spy. Sheesh! He was beginning to sound like the brat Suraj, in his head. He put his hands inside the pocket of his hoodie and leaned back on the bench. The frosted flakes had worked their magic. He was still full when he realized that people who worked at nearby stores were stepping out for lunch. But no one appeared at the door of Indian Exotica to hang the 'Closed for lunch' sign. In fact, more customers showed up at lunchtime. Indian ladies in funny shapeless pants stuck in the bum and oversized floral shirts were driven to the store by Indian men who must be their husbands (the men and women wore matching sports shoes, and the men walked meekly behind the women!). Then there was car after car after car that unloaded young Indian men who dashed in and came out with DVDs in their hands. It was odd that all those lads would want to comb their hair before going into the store. Maybe it was an Indian thing. But he hadn't noticed either Neeraj or Chimanbhai combing their hair ever. Yes, he had seen the boys at the pub run their hands through their hair when the broads gave them an extra look. But he knew that the chicks didn't care much for that sort of stuff from him. He had perfected the art of leaning. When he had the cash, he would lean back on the bar, elbows resting lightly. When he had no cash, he would lean against a wall, his thumbs hooked in the loops of his favourite pairs, cocking his head at just that perfect angle to look at the ladies. And he would not smile at them, like the other wolves. He would squint his eyes into the dance area, light up a smoke, and watch them calmly as though he had all the time in the world. He had read that in a book somewhere...or was it in a movies, he wondered, that the ladies really put out for the strong, silent types?

Suddenly he saw someone pulling the shutters down on the store, and locking up. Who locked their store in the afternoon? Especially when they had worked through the lunch hour? Strange. He sat up. Alert now. The person who was locking up must be the girl that had put the Shah family in a tizz. He watched her walk around the corner. He followed her. She was sitting on the hood of a blue Ford Fiesta, eating an apple. The first thing Dean noticed about her were her legs. She was Indian, but she was not wearing the sports shoes he had seen everyone wear. She was no ordinary Indian. She was wearing boots. He pulled the hood over his sandy hair and went past her, then bent down to remove his shoe and shook an invisible pebble from it, so he could take a look at the long-legged enemy of the Shahs. He was a tits man. And the white shirt she wore made him want to tear it right off and…fuckkk!

Some arsehole had bumped into him just as he tried to put his shoe on and picture her naked body on the hood of her car. When he accepted the man's helping hand, and dusted off the seat of his pants, she had gone back into the store. Her car was there, and his fingers began to itch. He walked to the hot dog stand and stuffed his face quickly. Dean made his way back to her car and with the help of his practised fingers opened the boot of her car. It had some old Indian magazines and a whole bunch of empty DVD covers. He pushed them around and made enough space to fit in. Then, without thinking of the consequences of being discovered, he got inside and shut himself in. He would follow her home, or wherever she went.

ELEVEN

Maya flipped through a two-month-old issue of *Filmfare* and drooled over the muscles of Shah Rukh Khan. They always had Shah Rukh Khan. Chimanbhai had put Elmore to work. Elmore was hauling rice and lentils when he saw Maya's orgasmic expression. After dumping the last of the bags into the storeroom he walked up to Maya and stood behind her looking at the magazine. Maya turned back to the photo spread and said, 'That's the hottest star ever. His name is Shah Rukh Khan. Look at his body!'

Elmore grunted. 'Not that hot. See mine.'

'Okay! Let's go,' said Maya. 'Puppa! I am going home. If you are done with Elmore, I will drive him home. Otherwise you bring him back with you, okay?'

Chimanbhai wanted more work done, but the prospect of driving back home with that scary, big kaalia was more daunting than the temporary rest he was getting with someone else doing the lifting and the storing for a change.

'No, no, deekra, take him home. I have been doing all this work myself for so many years, I will manage. If Deanbhai comes back in time I will bring him back home.'

Maya flashed a triumphant smile at Elmore. Although Elmore did not understand what had just happened, he was happy to drive back with Maya. He had not had a woman for so long, and Maya looked more than willing.

The two walked out to her car. 'Seatbelt, Elmore!' is all she said when they got into the car. She played *KINK* FM radio loudly and drove as fast as she could, slowing down at the speed traps by instinct. Elmore wanted to tell her to slow down a couple of times, but held on to his fear that saying anything might spoil any chance he might have with her.

He knew he was going to be violently ill when she took the curves that brought them to Winderly Heights. Maya looked at his green face and began laughing. She made an elaborate attempt to open the front door while he threw up in the hydrangeas by the driveway. Radhika would just have to replant the damned bush.

Radhika had gone off for the monthly 'bhisi'. She had debated in her head about the prudence of staying at home as she knew she could not stop chattering once she got started. And the women would inevitably mention that bitch Supriya, just to get a reaction out of her, especially Mehtaben who loved to needle Radhika. But not going to the kitty party would mean sending the money over and not tasting the hara-bhara kebabs Darshana would make today. Besides, she had the green Satya Paul saree which she had especially kept for the occasion. Her Motiben had had the saree especially embellished by Kantibhai. Darshana had a wonderful little black leather-stuffed chair. If she could snag that chair before anyone else, her green saree would look really nice. Jagruti had called and she had said yes to the car pool for the kitty.

Maya saw the note and an involuntary whoop escaped her lips. She handed Elmore a glass of water and when he had drained that, he had a sip of her Red Bull. She stared at him as he downed a fourth gulp. With every gulp she stepped back and stopped when she felt the dining table touch the band of her military-style olive green skirt.

Elmore watched her retreat wide eyed. She was unbuttoning her shirt. Her smile was an invitation he could not refuse. He did not even think of Radhika.

The hundred-odd gods with their large eyes and a thousand hands, and the lone velvet Elvis watched the two disapprovingly as they sprawled over the dining table.

***

The car must be doing at least eighty, if not more. Dean could feel every pebble of every mile, lying there in the trunk of Supriya's car. She was driving like the devil himself, and took corners as though the car were a motorbike. Dean was thankful that his bones were intact when the car finally stopped.

He counted twenty before he heard her step out and lock the car. Thank goodness for the chewing gum he had jammed in the lock or he would have been locked in. He stepped out of the trunk gingerly, and shook his head. He steadied his feet and looked around to see where he was. He was in the parking lot of the Powell's Bookstore. After running a hasty hand through his hair, he walked around the cars and on to the street to the entrance of the bookstore. The bookstore assistants were used to all kinds of people coming to the bookstore either for books or for the delicious tea and cakes at the coffee shop, so Dean's scruffy appearance did not warrant more than a passing glare. The bookstore was huge, and finding one slip of a girl, no matter how long legged and exotic she was, was not exactly an easy task. But Dean decided to take a chance. The rough ride to the bookstore had wiped the girl's name from his brain completely. But he remembered what Mrs Shah called her again and again. He looked at the nerdy assistant at the information counter and walked as casually as he could towards him.

'Excuse me,' said Dean. 'Did you see Kootri come in?' He wanted to swallow the words as soon as they came out, but he hoped the library assistant did not understand Indian.

The nerd looked at him owlishly from above his glasses. 'Excuse me?'

'Sorry. Did you see an Indian girl come through? She was wearing boots and blue jeans and...'

'Aaah. Yes. I saw her. She went through thataway.' He pointed in the general direction inside.

'Thanks.' Dean made a face. He would have to search the whole damned store. He went straight ahead checking out the people who were looking at new books. Not there. He went down to the Rose Room. There were too many people there, the cookery section seemed to be crowded. Someone was signing a book. He scanned the queue. But his gut instinct told him she would not be a part of that queue.

He moved quickly through the other sections and stopped short when he saw her engrossed in a graphic novel. She was leaning against the tall bookshelf and reading. He panicked. He grabbed the nearest book, opened it, and pretended to read. The words were all blurry though and he could hear his heart pounding in his head. He suddenly felt a craving for Mrs Shah's milky tea. He closed his eyes and fleetingly wondered if it was four o'clock. That's when she made that spicy milky tea. When he opened his eyes she was standing six inches from him, staring at him.

'You like Jay Wiseman?' she was asking.

He did not answer.

'Then you must be following me. Are you?' she asked, eyebrows arched, her large Indian eyes lined with soot.

She was really something. Dean couldn't say a damned thing.

'It's all right to follow me, you know. So if you

are, come, hold my books, and talk to me.' She thrust her basket at him.

Dean followed meekly. He watched her giggle as she read a comicbook. Then he glanced at the heavy basket. His eyes widened upon seeing the cover of the book on top. It had a funny Japanese man in a dress (or was that a woman?) standing behind a tied-up Japanese woman. The book was written by someone called Midori and it was about Japanese Bondage. He looked up again, and found her watching him.

'Erm...interesting read,' said Dean, looking away.

'Yes, isn't it? You turned on by bondage, Mr...'

'Dean.'

'Last name or first?' she asked.

Gosh! Looking down was useless. Her legs were amazing. He needed to look away.

'Huh?'

'Dean is your first name or last?'

'Dean. Just Dean.'

'Okay, Just Dean, come with me. I shall buy you coffee. For holding my books for me.'

She began walking towards the sunlit coffee shop inside the store. Dean did not know what to do but follow. He stood behind her as she ordered a coffee for herself and then looked at him.

'And for you, Dean...' she asked.

Dean had scanned the blackboard and said, 'Chai latte.'

She raised her eyebrow again, but didn't say

anything. She just paid for the beverages and pointed Dean to the empty table in the far corner of the room. He put the basket of books on the floor and sat down. Instead of sitting across the table from him, she pulled a chair next to him and sat down. Her legs were brushing his. He felt trapped for some reason. But first he had to stop being dazzled by her smile.

Dean steadied himself by proceeding to turn the ear of the teacup to his right. It was not enough. So he reached for the sugar jar and held his spoon under the spout. She was sipping her coffee and watching him. He poured three spoonfuls into his tea, and then stirred the sugar when she started laughing softly.

'You drink tea like an Indian!'

'You're wearing cowboy boots, so I must be Indian, no?'

Tea had given him Dutch courage. But she must've thought it was cute because she laughed.

'Now tell me, why are you stalking me?' she asked him, looking at him with no expression at all on her face.

'Stalking you? Yeah, sure. I wanted a free cuppa tea. So I stalked you.'

'Cuppa tea? Cuppa tea?' She started laughing loudly now. A few people turned to look at her.

Dean looked totally puzzled.

'Had you said that to an Indian person, they would have cursed you right back, saying, tu kaptee, tera baap kaptee, tera khandaan kaptee!'

Then she laughed more. She just waved his question away. 'Ask someone,' she said. 'So why are you stalking me?'

'Why would you think that? I don't even know your name?'

'Supriya,' she said, pouting her red lips on the first syllable and sighing with the last.

Dean had never heard a sexier name. But by now Dean had caught on. She was just being cute.

'Actually, Supriya, it was the cowboy boots that caught my eye. I am going to chop you into bits and take your girly boots.' He wiggled his eyebrows like a roué and dared to hold her hand.

'You like Midori, you read Jay Wiseman, you notice shoes. Are you gay?'

'Would you like me better if I were?' Dean said. The tea really worked miracles. He knew it wasn't like him to say such things. He didn't think he was half as intelligent. But Supriya looked satisfied with the answers.

'I gotta go. Need to pay for the books and go.'

'But we've just met!' Dean protested. 'Why do you have to leave?'

'All right then, walk with me,' she ordered.

He drained the last of the tea and followed her. She was sashaying ahead with the basket of books. The nerd at the information counter was helping out with sales. He looked curiously at Dean. Supriya was sorting out the books. Dean made a zip-your-mouth gesture with his thumb and forefinger, warning the nerd not to say anything. He didn't. He quietly checked out the books that Supriya handed to him. Supriya watched the clerk silently as well. Usually the clerks made intelligent conversation about books, this one probably had had a tough day. Supriya took the paper bag with the books with a smile, and turned to Dean.

'So what are we going to do with you?' Supriya looked at him with amusement.

'Where do you live?'

'Aaah. So now we know. You might as well take my boots now.'

'No, no, please don't get me wrong. I was hoping you were going my way, so I could hitch a ride with you.'

She sighed and said, 'Hillsborough.'

'I'll get off, I promise.' Dean looked at the reluctance in her whole demeanour then added, 'It's all right. Thank you for the tea.'

Then without looking back, he pushed the door open and walked out onto the windy Burnside Street, leaving her with the bag of books. He wanted so badly to turn around and see her reaction, but then he had seen the reaction many, many times in westerns he had watched when incarcerated in Montana. She would be surprised, then as she would walk back to her car, she would begin to regret her reluctance. He hoped the damned bus would come and rescue him. He pulled up the hood of his jacket and walked away into the night.

***

Maya's eyes opened wide at the long peel of the bell.

'Oh fuck! Fuck fuck fuck fuck fuck fuck fuck fuck!' Maya said. 'That's Suraj!'

She pulled Elmore's head from between her thighs and got off the table. Elmore looked even more dizzy than she felt. But Maya knew the little snitch would spoil everything for her. She stuffed her panties into the band of the skirt, pulled down her tee, and made her way to the door. Elmore got off his knees and made his way to the bathroom.

'What Didi! Why did it take so long? I need to pee!' Suraj ran upstairs.

Whew! That would give her enough time to set up a scene. Something that would explain time spent at home alone with Elmore. She spotted the TV. She walked up to the Lazyboy and sank into it. One flick of the remote and she found herself face to face with the Amitabh Bachchan fest on the Indian channel. One movie had ended and the other, a bulletfest, was just about to begin.

'So that's why you couldn't hear me ring the bell!' Suraj had poured himself some cola and was sipping it through a super bendy straw he had saved from Atul mama's fiftieth anniversary party.

'Coolio! *Shahenshah* is next!'

Maya smiled, knowing exactly what was keeping Elmore from joining them. But when he finally did join them, Maya was ready to let Suraj do all the talking.

'Hey Mr Elmore! Come sit down. They are going

to play the best Indian movie ever!' Suraj raised his arm and pretended he was dodging bullets exactly as Amitabh does in *Shahenshah*.

Elmore sat down on the Lazyboy and for the next three hours he was educated like never before. He was an eager student and Suraj was an enthusiastic teacher.

'How the hell does he kick so hard with his skinny legs?'

'He's taller than you, dude!'

'Why is he pretending to be such a sleazebag? Clark Kent doesn't have to be a sleazebag, and he's Superman!'

'Arre! Vijay has to be like that only! How else will he sneak into JK's gang?'

'What on earth! His mouth is bleeding!'

Suraj laughed so much he snorted out the cola from his nose. Elmore thumped him on his back.

'Go to the bathroom right now, Suraj!' Maya yelled, but she too was laughing with Suraj.

Elmore did not understand why the two were laughing.

Maya explained. 'See what he's eating? It's called paan. I love the taste, but the stuff turns your mouth red. It's in the *Kama Sutra*. An entire chapter on how to seduce with paan.'

'I thought the *Kama Sutra* was only pictures.'

'What have I missed? What have I missed?' asked Suraj, returning from the bathroom.

'Nothing, Suraj! Nothing he's not going to say at least a hundred times through the film.'

'Rishte mein toh hum tumhare baap lagte hain,

naam hai Shahenshah.' Suraj was posing in front of the TV, facing Elmore and Maya.

'What does it mean?'

'In relative...related to you...Maya! Will you translate?'

Maya thought for a minute. 'This cannot be translated. But I will explain.' She waited for another minute. Then she explained, with an eye on the commercials. 'Anyone who is better than you is called "baap" that's "daddy" for you.'

'Yeah, Maya didi! That's it! He's saying, "I'm your daddy. Call me Shahenshah".'

'He belongs to your community? Like Chiman Shah, Maya Shah, Shahen Shah?'

Maya and Suraj started laughing. They both laughed so hard that they missed the look on Elmore's face when he saw Vijay romancing Meenakshi Sheshadri.

'Hey Maya! Suraj, dude! Stop laughing so much. What is he singing?'

'When you romance an Indian girl, you gotta be able to sing songs...' Maya teased Elmore.

'Bleacccchhh! And she will make you chase her around thousands of trees!' Suraj added, completely missing the chemistry between the two.

Elmore looked shell-shocked, but at the same time he could not take his eyes off the screen. 'Man! Is she stacked!'

Maya threw a cushion at him, but Elmore caught it and continued to be mesmerized. 'I could do her man! I could do anything for such a woman.'

'Anything, Elmore? Even kill?'

Elmore looked at Maya. She had said it so softly that he almost hadn't heard. But he had.

He nodded. And answered just as softly as she had asked, 'Yes.'

Shahenshah kept them all involved. Elmore loved Shahenshah's sneer, his steel armour that was bulletproof, and the noose... What was with that noose? A trifle morbid, he thought, but he was now slowly beginning to understand the Indian need for revenge. That woman who had indeed taken the store that should have rightfully been Chimanbhai's was like JK. Elmore wasn't exactly Vijay, but he fancied himself as Shahenshah. He could imagine Maya as Shalu, prancing about in tight conical bras, midriff exposed, singing, 'You could be my jailor!'

Radhika unlocked the door to hear Amitabh Bachchan's voice booming through the living room. It must be Suraj. He would not stop playing that Kaalia again and again. She added milk to the water and set the pan on the stove, and as she spooned the tea leaves in, she yelled, 'DVD ghis jaise, Suraj! How many times I need to tell you, deekra!'

She bustled towards the TV to see Elmore, Maya and Suraj glued to the TV watching Kallu in jail, mouthing his famous dialogue and then kicking the heck out of the baddies in jail.

'DVDs are digital, Mom, they won't get wiped out,' Suraj protested. But Radhika would have none of it. She picked up the remote and pressed random buttons on it and then blurted out to Maya, 'I had a bad afternoon... Why won't you all stop?'

In an instant Suraj had picked up the right remote, turned the DVD player off, and Maya had offered, 'I will make you tea, Ma. Come with me.'

Elmore got up. Radhika was looking at him exactly like JK looked at Vijay's dad before hanging him. He got off the Lazyboy with super haste, and doffed an invisible hat to her, and made his escape out to his room above the garage and decided he would wait the storm out.

Maya found the tea boiling, so she stirred in the spices, and added some extra cardamom. Her mom would like that. She would hear over tea what had transpired at the kitty party. Radhika had shooed Elmore away. Maya sighed into the tea. He was talented, that Elmore, she thought and smiled.

'Why you taking so long to make tea, Maya?' Radhika was now sitting at the table, swallowing Saridon.

'It's ready, Ma! I have poured it in your favourite cup.'

'Saambhal! Take care, Maya! You will break the cup. We have only one, Chiman bought it for me on our honeymoon at Niagara Falls.'

'Yes, Ma! I know. Here, drink your tea.'

Radhika watched her mum drink tea from the mug her dad must've bought from a cheesy souvenir shop when they had gone for their honeymoon. On the one hand Maya despised the whole middle-class existence of her parents, romance between the two was best not imagined and their way of living was not exactly aspirational. In fact, Maya and most of her Indian friends hated the way their parents lived somewhere between their imagined Indian lives and their suburban American reality. On the other hand, Maya could not but help love the two people. They had been strict but had given up once they realized that their little girl was beyond their attempts at 'grounding'. They had taught her everything they knew about India, but had not tried to stop her from 'becoming American', something most other families tried to do to their girls and boys. If Maya accompanied her parents to the Oregon Gujarati Samaj festivals it was not because they were forcing her to, but because she loved getting dressed up in the shiny ghagras and cholis. It showed off her perfect figure and of course she scandalized the bitches of the samaj. A couple of them had spoilt her mum's afternoon, and Maya was ready to hear her mum out.

'That Jigna!'

Maya narrowed her eyes. Jigna was older than Radhika but looked younger because she was always at the gym. She looked like the super tanned South Beach old ladies and was such a super bitch, not even food wanted to stick to her body. Reed thin, she made it her business to know about everyone's business. So it was Jigna's long nose that had burst Radhika's bubble this afternoon.

'It started when Darshana started talking about recession. Instead of making ten dishes like each time, she had made only eight. Jigna asked her and quite nastily too, if they were all going to now pay her less because of recession. I like Darshana ne, so I said, leave it ne Jigna. Darshana's homemade dhoklas are far better than those bran theplas you served us. Everybody started laughing because they remembered how the next day we were all constipated. Jigna remembered that and laughed too, but she kept giving me dirty looks.' Radhika stopped to drain her cup. 'You don't want some chai too?' she asked Maya.

'Yes, Ma.' Maya pushed her chair back and felt something fall. Fuckkkk! It was her panties she had hastily tucked into her skirt band. Radhika would kill her.

'What happened?' Radhika asked.

She hadn't seen it fall! Maya kicked the panties under her chair and moved to the kitchen to pour herself some tea. She brought the cup and the flask to the table and refilled Radhika's mug.

Radhika started narrating the events of the afternoon, while Maya tried in vain to step into the panties and drink tea at the same time.

'Jigna was wearing green-yellow nimbu-coloured pants! And pink and yellow dot-dot shirt! Oof! So bright! Oomar ka koi khyal karna chahiye ne? But she is ready to tell other people what to wear and what not to.'

'Oh, what did she say?'

'She told Maniben she should not wear brown colour sarees as it made her complexion look sallow, kootri! Maniben just bought that saree; it has very nice pink flowers embroidered and very expensive Swarkovski diamonds on it.'

'Swarovski, Mom! Not Swarkovski!

'Same thing re. You should have seen Maniben's poor face. Maya! Why are you fidgeting so much? What are you doing?'

Maya had managed to get her panties up to her thighs, but they were rolled up, and the skirt was so tight, there was no way she could hitch them up without Radhika noticing. She made up a story fast.

'I keep telling you I need to buy some new underthings. This panty keeps sliding down. It's bad enough when I am wearing jeans, but with a skirt... ugh! Good thing I am at home now. See!' Maya got up and pointed to the panties on her thigh.

'Hey Ram! What are you doing? Pull them up now! How can they become so loose? Better throw it now and go upstairs and wear another one.'

Maya yanked her skirt up and wiggled her panties into place, then heaved a sigh of relief.

Radhika was now totally puzzled. 'I don't understand you at all sometimes, Maya. The skirt is so tight but your chaddis...'

'Leave it na, Ma! I am going to change my clothes soon. But you have not told me about Jigna.'

'Haan, so Jigna then took it out on me. The kootri

said, "You don't advice anyone about clothes. You are still sending old sarees to India so your Kantiben can add sequins to them. Then you wear them and pretend they are new."'

Radhika imitated Jigna so perfectly that Maya had to laugh. 'Ma, you are great!'

'I was so angry I got up and flung my whole glass of lassi on her face.'

'Mom!' Maya said, horrified at first but then giggly at the thought of her mother doing anything so...

'If Jigna knew what I have planned for Supriya, she would not be talking to me like she did. She would be very afraid.'

'Mom! You didn't say that to them!'

'Of course not! Darshana was laughing. Maniben was laughing. Swati, who came with her mother-in law for the first time, was also laughing. Jigna had said bad things about her small-town roots ne, it was everyone's revenge in that glass of lassi that accidentally fell on Jigna. And that brainless Poorvi was screaming as though it was the end of the world. Maniben was laughing so hard, she slapped Poorvi's back, and Poorvi was eating dahivada.'

'Mom! Stop! So why did you say you had a bad time?'

'Jigna said something about Chiman. And now that I have had tea at home, and my brain is working, I think she was lying, but in my heart I know your Puppa would have preferred to have been married to...never mind. Remind me to never, never

160

send another saree to India for the sequins. Jigna figured it out with her oatmeal- and bran-fed brain. I don't want anyone to ever say anything about me that makes us look like we are giving up on our life here, you know, recession. I did not send the saree to India because of recession, and we are not going to follow the clothes back to India like Jigna says. We are going to...how did Neeraj put it? Yes. Finish off the competition.'

Maya stared at her mother and her new-found vehemence. 'I think I should go upstairs and get changed.' She pondered on the discovery and allowed her discomfort to carry her upstairs.

Radhika stared at the honeymoon mug she was washing from habit. 'So that's who you are thinking of when you have that look in your eyes. I won't think like this. I won't think like this...' Radhika repeated the thought again and again, then made a decision. She threw the honeymoon Niagara Falls mug in the garbage bin kept under the sink.

TWELVE

Chimanbhai was reading the latest issue of *India Abroad* when his cellphone rang. His heart skipped not one but several beats when he recognized the India number. Osmanbhai! Should he even look at the phone? What could he say to Osmanbhai? He peered at the number carefully, not wanting to touch the phone. If it were a +9179 he would have to throw his phone away. But it wasn't. His fear now clouded his vision. Blinking hard at the number flashing incessantly on the phone, he pressed the green key and said, 'Hello, who is speaking please?'

He could always say 'wrong number' if it was someone he did not know and put the phone down. He could say nothing and still put the phone down. He could... 'Chiman?' a woman's voice asked.

No one else called him 'Chiman' like that.

Chimanbhai answered a tentative 'yes' and no sooner had he said it, a recently familiar voice poured honey into his ear. Chimanbhai shivered pleasurably. It could only be Meenakshi! She began to sing a song that used to play on the radio at the dhaba where they would eat fafda in Ahmdavad. Chimanbhai watched the lone customer prowl the aisle, pushing the cart slowly, reading the list, consulting the coupons, and then looking at the price again but the phone was glued to his ear.

'Tu mera chand, mai teri chandni,' she sang.

'Yes, I am your moon and you are my moonlight!' said Chimanbhai. For that one moment he forgot the many years that separated them. Why was she calling him now after so many years? he wondered. How much he had missed her! He felt that he could tell her everything about his horrid complicated life. Tell her about how he had taken to daydreaming about a life that could have been, a life without that bitch Supriya who had managed to turn his ordinary suburban household into a place for murder-plotting meanies. Hey Ambe Ma! He too had started cursing. And he had missed the song Meenakshi was singing for him. She was saying his name over and over again. 'Chiman... Chiman...Chiman?'

'You ready to ring this in?' Chimanbhai's reverie was broken by the lone customer. Chimanbhai's eyes widened upon spotting the cart. It was loaded.

Commerce beat Cupid and he simply switched the phone off and rang up item after item on the register and he was thrilled to see the total. He could not stop beaming. Nine hundred and twenty-three dollars and thirty-two cents! He asked the customer to wait. He bought the bottle of lemon pickle, scratched off the sticker that marked the sell-by date and grabbed the nearest wipe cloth. Wiping the bottle, he presented it to the customer.

'The bottle costs $8 only, should I add it to the cart? It's very good pickle. Tastes just like home pickle.'

The customer simply nodded his head. Chimanbhai could not believe his luck. It was changing around for the better. First Meenakshi called and now this. He helped the customer fill the bags, and also double-bagged the last package because it had spice bottles.

He even carried the bags to the door and was about to offer to carry them to the car when he spotted two women walking towards the store. Radhika! And with her was the Northwest's biggest gossip, Mrs Desai. What did they want from the store?

Radhika saw Chiman at the store entrance helping some customer with bags. She hated to see him carrying bags like he was some help, but these days many bags meant that the cash register was not empty. She smiled. Desaiben was still going on and on about Dr Patel.

'He has told everybody that Swamiji would stay at his home because they had specially heated floorboards. Hanh, hanh! All of us have heating in our homes, but Dr Patel has to claim that his is best. And he is grabbing all the good luck by having Swamiji stay in his house. Why are you smiling, Radhika?'

'I was just thinking of Roopaben. How she is going to have Swamiji in her house? I will go for satsang, but I can never sit in front row.'

'Why?' Mrs Desai asked, and then suddenly realized what Radhika was hinting at. She roared with laughter just as they neared Radhika's husband's store.

Poor Chimanbhai stared at the two women stuffing their pallus in their mouth, slapping each other's backs and cackling like a pair of hyenas on feast day.

'Radhikaben! You are very funny! Swamiji is naked! That's why you won't sit in front row! Hahahahaha!'

'Mrs Desai! I am God-fearing. Chiman is God-fearing. My whole family is God-fearing, and I liked the satsang with Swamiji as much as anyone of the thousand people. But the first time I saw that he was naked...oh gawd! I am being honest with you, the first thing that I thought was how does he travel by plane naked?'

Both women laughed again. Then Mrs Desai became serious. 'Tell me, Radhika, we all respect Dr Patel because he is rich and famous doctor. But is it fair that he is going to Indian people's homes and campaigning so he can become head of Hindu samaj and have Swamiji stay in his house? So cheap na? Famous doctor driving door to door and begging for votes. Hello Chimanbhai, kem cho?'

Chimanbhai raised his hand and smiled hesitantly. 'Hello, hello!'

But the two women did not pay any more attention. Mrs Desai began to look at *India Abroad* while Radhika went inside to pick up something she needed for the house. Chimanbhai stood quietly by the door, hoping the two women would leave quickly, and that Mrs Desai would not stop reading the newspaper and begin chatting with him. But his gods were asleep.

'Ei Chimanbhai! You heard ne? Dr Patel wants to be president of Hindu Samaj. Don't vote for him. We Gujaratis have decided that we will not vote for him. I just wanted to tell you that you must support community, ne?'

'But Dr Patel is also Gujarati!'

Radhika had come to them and had heard this exchange. 'Chiman is very simple, Mrs Desai! He doesn't understand politics.' Then turning to Chiman she said, 'Tsk Chiman, don't get into something you don't understand. I have taken one mango pickle jar. Come, we should go now. Bye!'

Chimanbhai watched the two women walk away. He suddenly realized that he had left his phone by the pickle row when he sold the customer that old bottle. He made his way to where the pickles were kept. The phone wasn't there. It was sitting on the counter. Radhika must've seen Meenakshi's call! He was a dead man! Or at the best, a marked one. He was indeed afraid of Radhika, really really afraid.

***

'You like Maya, no?' Suraj asked Elmore, who was sitting on the floor, going through the VHS collection.

And before Elmore could answer, he continued, 'Puppa will have a heart attack if he guessed.'

'Guessed what?'

'That Maya didi's perfume rubbed off on you.'

'You are a vile kid. If you keep sticking your nose where it should not be, I swear I will kill you before I leave here.'

'Why don't you take the supari for Supriya instead. Killing me will get you nothing.'

'What's a supari?'

'Lemme show you.' Suraj disappeared up the stairs so fast that Elmore had no time to react. He stared at the stack of films. Each had a sneering hero against a backdrop of flames, or pop art. The large-eyed girls were stacked, and wore sequins mostly. There were odd villains. He was amazed at how much happened in those three hours in Indian films. Most of it was improbable, but he was hooked.

Suraj was bounding back down the stairs, his laptop stuck under his armpit. He switched on the computer, and then put the movies away carefully. Then Suraj clicked furiously at the keys, babbling away. 'See I am going to search for how killings got to be called supari...see...Elmore I am doing this so look carefully...yeah, so we were talking about the word "supari", see let's click here...long time ago the people who agreed to kill for money were said to have accepted a beeda...you remember Amitabh Bachchan eating the paan? ... No no, Amitabh was not killing anyone in the film. Never mind...there must be an easier explanation...wait, here it is...Marwaris gave supari as a token of accepting a deal. The practice was later adopted by gangsters to signify a deal. Now everyone knows it as supari...got it?'

'I get it. It's a sign. Like a contract, not signed.' Elmore paused. 'Then why did your dad make us cut those nuts?'

'We didn't want you two.'

'Those cutters should be made illegal!'

'See, Puppa wanted to get Osmanbhai. He's a professional. But the government guys asked Puppa to go downtown and Neerajbhai and Puppa had to prove that no American can do Osmanbhai's job. Obviously, they had to listen to the government guys. That's why you are here. But I know you can do this job even better than Osmanbhai.'

Elmore was stumped. This was insane. These people were insane. He understood this much, if they screwed up on this job, the coppers would have them behind bars faster than he could eat a grilled chicken. And if they listened to the Shahs, they were fucked anyway. Betelnuts were fucking lethal. Killing that bitch was probably the only way to stay out of jail.

Suraj heard a car stopping outside and ran up to the window to look. It was Radhika. 'It's Mum,' he announced.

Elmore's stomach protested and an acidic burp that was more fear than burp rose from deep within his stomach. He craved for some crumb-encrusted chicken.

Radhika said, 'Jai Shree Krishna' to Mrs Desai and walked up to the front door. Her mind was like the muddy well in her village. Full of dark and depressing thoughts, and she felt dragged down by them all. Suraj opened the door even before she put her key to the lock. He snatched the bottle from her hand. He hoped it was Indian jam. Ugh! Achaar!

'Mom! You bought achaar? Disgusting!'

Suraj dumped the bottle back into her hand. Radhika didn't notice it. As if on auto pilot she went up to the kitchen and put the electric kettle on. She put a pan of milk on the gas and added tea leaves and a sprig of lemon grass. She stirred the milk and watched the swirling patterns. Who was calling Chiman from Chicago? She was sure Chiman did not know anyone there. Maybe it was a wrong number. But why would he chat with a wrong number for an hour and a half? Who did Chiman know who could afford to talk long distance for so long? The tea kettle was whistling now. She added water to the milk and spooned in sugar. Was he talking to a woman? Who would want her Chiman? He had been handsome once, even Radhika had to acknowledge that. But now? Who would be waidi enough to want him now? But if they did? Chiman with another woman?

The milky tea was boiling over. She switched off the burner and strained the tea into the flask. She poured herself a cup and sat down. She did not realize there were tears running down her cheeks. But the tea was good. And she knew she had to stop crying and take care of her home. She put her cup down forcefully on the table, the teaspoon which she had used to add some extra sugar to her tea (her mum always did that for her whenever Radhika cried. 'Extra love,' she used to say to Radhika) fell to the floor with a clatter. As soon as she bent down to pick it up, a thought flashed in her head. Since Osmanbhai was going to come to America to settle down and begin practising his dhando here, she could get him to do a favour and get rid of the Chicago caller, especially if it turned out to be a lady caller. And maybe threaten Chimanbhai a bit as well.

Happy at the simple solution that she had figured out for her troubles, Radhika hoped she would not take a violent dislike to Osmanbhai. She had hated Gabbar Singh. She hoped Osmanbhai would turn out to be a nicer killer.

THIRTEEN

'Kya Chandni! How can I stitch in this light? I asked for only one ordinary tube light. Pink light se mera sar dukh raha hai! Big headache I am getting! Do something!' The tailor was sitting on the floor among partially stitched blouses and ghagras and sequins and zari gota of all fluorescent colours. His assistant Abdul was sitting on his haunches, staring unblinking at Chandni. He had never seen such a beautiful creature ever in his life. Basheer, his boss, would go into raptures describing her when they would be carefully stitching the gota on the edges of the ghagras, in swirly patterns, imagining how Chandni would dance and twirl round and round for her rich customers, especially the dreaded Osmanbhai, a man who could kill two men at the same time with his bare hands. Abdul was an assistant, so he sewed the buttons and the bows, made eyeholes, loops for the hooks, and finished the hems of the garments neatly.

Today he felt as though it was Id. He was sitting at the foot of Chandni's bed watching her preen and pout, try on one dress after another, flounce and stamp her foot if the fit was not perfect, and titter when the dress fit her like a glove. She changed behind the wooden partition, and Abdul would get to see a flash of her skin in the little mirror hung by the partition. Her skin was smooth, just like malai kulfi. He wanted to imagine her on that bed, spread on the colourful bedspread wearing nothing, and he, Abdul, helping her put clothes on—a blue sharara with sequins in a starburst pattern. She would then say thenkoo to him. And that word coming out of her red lips would be his payment. English words they were, and she would put her little pink tongue to her upper teeth to mouth the 'th' and she would dimple to complete the rest of the word. Did she have dimples? He realized that his eyes were closed. He opened them only to realize the two were looking at him: Chandni and his boss, Basheer.

'Aaaei shaitan ke shagird! So raha hai kya?'

Chandni tittered at that. Abdul shook his head. He held up the blouse he had been working on. He had finished taking it in and making it tighter. The first time he had done that, he had wondered if Basheer mian knew magic. No way could that...that bit of Chandni fit into what he had stitched. But she did! And she inevitably asked for the blouses to be taken in. Magic! It was Abdul's job as an assistant to unravel any stitching, and make a temporary running stitch along the new tighter mark Basheer made by putting two fingers inside the seam of her blouse. He even put in a hurried but beautiful backstitch if she wanted to wear the blouse and ghagra that very evening. One day he would be the one checking how much he needed to take the blouse in by putting his fingers into her blouse. His fingers, her butter-soft skin! Basheer mian was hopeless. Did he not feel anything?

Abdul felt a chappal sail over his head, barely missing it. 'Saale!' Basheer was cursing him, 'Do some work! Otherwise I will send you back to your Chuchajaan in Jaunpur where he will beat you black and blue for no reason, then you will learn! Bhadwe! Kaamchor!'

'Sorry!' Abdul yelped.

Basheer mian was hitting him with the chappal now. Chandni was amused. She had been giggling before, now she had gone hysterical.

A growl from somewhere near Chandni's door interrupted the duet between Basheer's hand-held chappal that was coming down upon whatever body part it found attached to the lazy bum called Abdul. Chandni's laughter had frozen mid-air as well.

Osmanbhai!

He had walked in unannounced, and did not like what he saw. 'What is this? Mad you have become!'

Chandni knew this was Osmanbhai practising his English for America. She was not afraid of Osmanbhai. She looked at Basheer and Abdul frozen in fear. She was not about to lose her tailor to someone who had been talking big for the past few weeks. Big money, big travel plans, and of course big breasts. And she knew that the Americans were not even answering Osmanbhai's phone calls. Chandni was not used to waiting. And it had been more than three weeks. The other girls had learnt that Osmanbhai was going to take her to America. But three weeks later he was still coming home, learning English from the book instead of pushing her down on the bed and making the whole building shake with his power. Now the girls sniggered behind her back. That bitch from Nepal even asked her if Osmanbhai now needed Viagra, and if she had turned into Mother Teresa and was running a school for her clients. She did not know who or what Mother Teresa was, but she certainly wasn't about to turn her room into a school. Not even for the sexy beast called Osman.

'What is going on here?'

'New dresses, Osman! You learning Angrezi so you can kill the Angrez, I am going to dress Indian and kill Angrez!' said Chandni.

'New dresses? Why? In Amrika, every woman wears a bikini,' Osmanbhai said. 'I studying English, understand? Neerajbhai said there are many Indians in Amrika, so my bijness will be full on. But I want to be better than Godfather. That's why English.'

Chandni glared at him, 'Bikini? Ai-hai! You think I am stupid?' She threw a pillow at Osmanbhai. He fielded the pillow, sat down on the bed and pushed the pile of new clothes aside. The two tailors were still standing there, shivering. He hated seeing men shiver in front of him. Everyone who saw him reacted like that. He wanted to kill them simply because he hadn't killed in three weeks, but he wanted to stay under the police radar. And these two insects weren't worth the trouble. He turned away from the three and opened the chapter he was struggling with. It was correctly called 'tense'. Saala, he didn't understand it. Past, present, perfect and future...the chapter was correctly named.

Chandni told Basheer to gather up the clothes and sit in the little veranda outside. Abdul looked crestfallen. She watched them leave her room with the clothes, her hands on her hips. Abdul would store that image in his head for ever and ever.

Chandni should have been mad at Osmanbhai for making her the laughing stock of the kotha, but she could not resist him. He was a bastard, but such a stud. She should have changed but had to ask, 'How you like the bow, jaan?'

The colossus on her bed turned to her. A sharp thrill went down her spine and the little bells sewn on her skirt jingled and jangled. He stared at the bow strategically placed on her blouse. He stared some more. So she jingled and jangled some more as she walked towards him, toying with a seasoned coyness with the bow on her blouse.

The Nepali chick in the dingy rooms downstairs would not take cheap potshots about Viagra any more.

But curse the Angrezi book! It crunched between them and he was distracted. But alas! The distraction was not temporary. One of the pages was torn. Osmanbhai pushed her away and stared in horror at the book. Torn! Torn! Torn! Was it a sign that he was never going to America?

'Kuttee! Saali! You did not like me to study Angrezi! You are the reason why my trip has been delayed!' He was mad now, wanted to slap her across her face. But before he could hit her in his anger, Chandni was screaming loudly as though he already had. And boy, could she scream!

That scream was like a police siren. Osmanbhai stood there shocked, with his hands on his ears. Soon there were frantic bangs and shouts from outside. 'Chandni!', 'What's going on!', 'Open this door!', 'Osmanbhai!', 'What are you doing to our Chandni!', 'Open this door now!'

Chandni was still screaming. It was Osmanbhai who opened the door. Girls from the kotha, their curious customers, the pehelwaan with his big stick—everyone came trooping in. They looked at Osmanbhai, who raised his hands in surrender, 'I did nothing!'

The whole group was staring at Chandni who was sitting on the floor, with her fingers in her ears and was screaming like a woman possessed. Osmanbhai was a big man, and he welcomed all the attention directed at Chandni's screaming. He picked up the torn book and quietly made his way down the stairs.

He stepped out into the road clutching the English

book, heaving a sigh of relief. Then he made the mistake of looking up at her room. Chandni had opened the window and was looking out for him. The moment she spotted him, she yelled out, 'Loser!' And before he could grin at her, she had disappeared. A moment later Osmanbhai felt a bucketful of water coming down on him. It happened so fast that he had no time to duck. All the morons in the alley started laughing. A wet Osmanbhai called her all sorts of names, kicked a couple of chaps who came within kicking distance and made his way to the public phone booth.

***

Osman had dialled the number so often that he could now punch in the number blindfolded. It was hot in Mumbai, and his clothes were almost dry. The call had connected and it was ringing. One ring. Two. Three. Four. Five. Six. Bastards. Seven. Eight. Nine. Ten. Osman was determined. He would sit there and let the phone ring until they picked up. He clicked his fingers at the owner of the shop quivering outside. His assistant was quaking too. The chai was spilling on to the tray while the phone kept on ringing. Saale.

The owner opened the door tentatively. He asked, 'What I can do for you, bhai?'

'Angrez ki aulad! Bring chair for me!' Osmanbhai barked.

The owner kicked himself for speaking in English.

He had seen Osmanbhai with the English textbook and was hoping to earn a few brownie points with the giant who was occupying his phone booth. He knew he was not going to get paid for the phone call, but he thought speaking English with Bhai would at least ensure that his bones would not be broken. It wasn't working. He pushed the chair gingerly at Osmanbhai who was counting.

'Twenty-five, twenty-six, twenty-seven. Haan, thank you for chair. Now give tea. Twenty-eight, twenty-nine, thirty. Bastards!'

The public call booth owner regretted the stars under which he was born. He cursed the day he had agreed to the weedy banker who had advised him to start his phone booth business. He cursed the telephone company manager who had made the application process so easy. And before he could curse the man who was currently occupying the phone booth, a tea glass came whizzing from behind him and crashed on the floor. He turned and froze.

Osman tried the number again and started counting. One, two, three, four, five, six, seven, eight, nine, ten, eleven, twelve, thirteen, fourteen, fifteen...

'Hello!'

Osmanbhai bit his tongue saying sixteen. 'Kaun hai be?' he growled on the phone.

'Suraj Shah here, who is this? Kaun?'

Osmanbhai filled air in his lungs and exhaled, 'Osman.'

There was silence. Osmanbhai laughed like he was Gabbar Singh. His name could now strike fear even in Amrika.

The person on the other side of the phone suddenly sounded like he had woken up. 'Osman? You mean Osmanbhai the killing machine? Have you really killed two men with bare hands at the same time?'

Osmanbhai was amused at having his biodata read out to him through the phone. He threw back his head and laughed. 'Yes, yes. Osmanbhai. Where Chimanbhai? Neerajbhai? Phone kyon naheen uthate tum log? Saala kitne dino se phone kar raha hai apun! Chootiya samjha hai kya?'

Suraj laughed at all the curse words. He knew saying 'saala' and 'chootiya' was bad. But he was excited at speaking with such a dangerous man.

'Dad and Neerajbhai, Dean and Elmore ke saath hain.'

'Hain? Deanandelmore kaun hai?'

'Deanandelmore naheen, Deanbhai, aur Elmorebhai, do log hain. Aap naheen chahiye. Yeh do hain na ab. Isi waaste Dad aur Neerajbhai are not answering your phone.'

'What you saying? Kya keh rahe ho! Koi aur mera kaam kar raha hai? Kaikoo? Neerajbhai apun ko promise kiyela hai...'

'Promise? Yeh pata naheen. You ask so I am telling you. Maybe you are not needed here.'

'Saale! Wait I coming to Amrika. I will kill you

and I will kill Chimanbhai and that Neeraj. I will make Neeraj into fifty pieces, fry them, and eat them. Wait I coming.'

Osmanbhai did not slam the phone down. He pulled the phone off the wall and smashed it to bits, then stormed off into the night.

***

Radhika Shah was sitting at the dining table with a grim and determined look on her face. She had not cooked. She had sent Suraj and Maya to Anjali Krishnan's Woodlands to bring back south Indian food. The kids would eat dosas there, so that would give them an extra half-hour to discuss things. She was so not in a mood to discuss things. She was tired of having these foreigners in the house. The faster they did their job and got out of her house the better she would feel. Chiman was no use at all. Neither was Neeraj. He had come back from his girlfriend's house looking as if a tornado had hit him and fried his brains. Chiman said something about drugs when the boy could not be woken up despite several attempts by both Chiman and Radhika. In sheer frustration, Radhika had even kicked Neeraj, but he had keeled over and was asleep again. Chiman hated seeing Radhika kick Neeraj. He had always hated seeing anything even mildly aggressive and over the last couple of weeks everyone in the family had gone crazy.

Dean and Elmore looked puzzled at the empty

dining table. Chimanbhai sat in his usual chair, cowering while Radhika looked like she had much to say. She came straight to the point.

'Do it now.'

Elmore understood Radhika's need to finish the job. Watching the Indian movie had taught him one thing about them. About Maya. She might be hot for him, but she would need a hero like Amitabh Bachchan like all Indian girls. And the only way he could be like the biggest hero would be to destroy the enemy of her family. He imagined Radhika offering the red mark before he went to battle and Maya on a platter afterwards. He gave Radhika his most reassuring, 'Yes, Ma!' just as the big guy had in the movie *Path of Fire*.

Radhika looked at the big black guy who had just called her 'Ma', and narrowed her eyes. She did not want to be related to the ugly man. She just ignored him and turned to Dean. 'Deanbhai, you saw girl today, no? Tell us why you cannot kill her today. Finish this, ne. It is taking too long.'

Dean was lost. Strangely, he had taken to the girl. He knew that Chimanbhai's business was suffering hugely because of the shop that had opened in the same mall, but he was hoping something else could be done. Elmore and he were not really killers, and to shoot down such a magnificent pair of legs and breasts and eyes, and... It was not such a nice idea. He cleared his throat and said, 'Mrs Shah, I am sure something else can be worked out, killing...'

Chimanbhai gathered the courage to interrupt. 'I think we need to think this through...'

'Bas!' Radhika was suddenly furious. 'Kill her tonight!'

Dean was stirring now. 'Mrs Shah, we need to think this through. Killing her would be easy and we have agreed to it. But maybe we could do something else and get the same result.'

Elmore was hungry and there was no sign of food. And now Dean was sounding as though he was having second thoughts. He growled, 'Do what else? Finishing her would be the fastest. You are the one who's asking me to keep focus. Wait a minute. You saw her this morning, yeah? You come with me.' Then looking at Radhika he muttered, 'I gotta talk to him. Alone.'

Dean's chair scraped the floor as he reluctantly followed Elmore to the TV area.

Elmore's stomach was growling, and Dean needed to know how important completing this task had become. Maya would be like the heroines waiting for him if he vanquished the enemies of the family.

'Dean, if you won't do this now, I shall do it alone.'

'At the Cameron place you didn't have the courage to taser the night guard and we were caught. And you're talking about killing someone? Think about it. I followed this girl. She's not the devil like these people told us she was. They're trying to fuck with us. She's...'

'Fuckin' with us? You're crazy. If you are turning chicken, I will kill that devil woman myself.'

'And what do we get? If we get caught, we go straight to the chair. Remember three strikes? I'm not about to travel across the country dodging the coppers. I just wanted enough money to grow my own grass and smoke it. What ants got into your pants?'

'Maya said...'

'Aah. Maya. So that's what it is! Man, that blow job has blown your brains!'

'Fuck you, Dean!'

'Don't you see, man, what this has done to you? She's Indian, man! Not about to go away with you into the sunset. They'll probably have us arrested after we kill. We cannot...'

'Hey you two, the food is here!' Maya held up takeaway bags.

Elmore and Dean stared at her. Dean saw the look in Elmore's eyes and cursed under his breath. Maya did not miss anything. 'Elly, Deanbhai being mean to you?' She cocked her head to one side and spoke in a flirty baby voice.

'No,' said Elmore. 'I'm starving.'

Elmore was now confused. Dean could tell. He followed the two back to the dining area where Radhika was busy organizing plates and glasses. Chimanbhai had placed two restaurant plastic forks and placed them in front of Dean and Elmore.

'You do it, Elmore, Dean does not have to. He

can stay at home and give Chimanbhai company. Neeraj can go with you to help.' Radhika was serving some sticky rice on the plates. It smelled strongly of spices.

'I can go with Elmore. Don't know when Neeraj will come out of his self-induced coma...'

'Actually I was thinking, we should wait until Osmanbhai comes...'

'Chiman! How many times I have told you that Osmanbhai is not going to come.'

'Dad! Not going to happen.'

Both Maya and Radhika practically jumped on Chimanbhai. Suraj was playing on his PSP when he heard Osmanbhai's name being mentioned.

'Mom! Dad! I forgot to tell you.'

'Not now, Suraj!' Maya reprimanded.

Suraj had just remembered the phone conversation with Osmanbhai, and he knew it was important.

'Mom! Dad! I forgot to tell you that there was a call.'

'Suraj! Stop being such an ass! Shut up!'

'Call from India, Dad!'

'Don't make up stories, Suraj. Grown-ups are talking here. Maybe you can go find something to do. Like a Mithun Chakraborty movie? We could dance to Gunmaster G-9, eh?'

'I'm telling you there was a call...'

'Suraj! Get out of here. Do as Maya said. No more imaginary friends, no imaginary calls. I am tired. Now don't get me angry.' Radhika was having no more nonsense from Suraj. Already he had blurted out things to Elmore.

'Dad?' Suraj was looking for help now from the last quarter.

But Chimanbhai had done what he was best at doing. He had shut up and was now lost in the narrow alleyways of Ahmedabad on a bicycle, with the girl with the most beautiful eyes.

Suraj just shook his head and left the room. 'It was important, I tell you. It was important.'

***

Osmanbhai had wrecked another PCO. He was sitting on a chair and was calmly drinking chai. Yet another owner was on his knees, holding on to a cheek bleeding from the whack he had received at Osmanbhai's hand, from the silver bracelet he was wearing.

'Bhai, very sorry, bhai. You right breaking booth. No problem, bhai. But why you call America?'

'I call for visa. Saale they not telling. Ek ek ka bhurta banake saala parathe ke saath kha jaaneko mangta hai. Visa nikalne ke itne din lagte kya?'

'Arre bhai! You tell this first, na. Booth todne ka zaroorat hee naheen padtaa tha.'

'Wot you saying, kutte? You can get Amrika ka visa? Uth! Get up! Saale you think I am some chootiya or what?'

'Bo bhai! Chootiya toh I am. Bleddy chootiya! I should have told you about Dhunbhai.'

'Dhunbhai?'

'Arre woh apun ka sagewala lagta hai. He my relative on my aunty's side. He is visa expert. People go Muscat, Dubai, even South Africa. America is what kind of chicken? He will fix it. Here bhai, I send you his business card.' The owner was no longer shivering in his boots. This he knew.

Osmanbhai's kick came at him before he could say 'Dhun'.

'Bijness card bhejega! Kutte! Dial number now.'

'Yes, bhai. Yes, bhai. I should not business card his number. I call him now.'

Dialling a number with Osmanbhai over your head was not an easy task. After fumbling twice and after narrowly avoiding the chai glass Osmanbhai threw at him, he finally managed to get through to Dhun.

'Salaam Dhunbhai, main Ashfaaq, Shelina bibi ki Gauhar chachi ka beta...'

'Haan, salaam...haan, bhai...'

Osmanbhai grunted his disapproval at the extended salaams. Ashfaaq hurried. 'Bhai, important kaam tha, bhai. Aap Osmanbhai ka naam sune na? Yes, yes, same Osmanbhai...two men...one hand. He need visa help. Haan, bhai, baat karo.'

He handed his battered cellphone to Osmanbhai. 'Bhai, speak with Dhunbhai.'

'Osman speaking,' he announced, and then without waiting for salaams he asked, 'I need US visa urgent. H1-B too much waiting. I think saala Shah goli diya.'

Osman began to smile as he heard whatever Dhunbhai was telling him. Ashfaaq was relieved. He knew if Osmanbhai left for the US with Dhunbhai's help, he, Ashfaaq, would be hailed as a hero by the twenty-odd public phone booth owners. Not to mention the number of people who would be happy to see the menace leave. Osmanbhai would not be calling him a kutta now. But if he had a tail, Ashfaaq would be wagging it real hard.

'Haan aata hoon main.'

Ashfaaq caught the phone Osmanbhai flung back and heaved a sigh of relief. Thank god he had not given in to the temptation of buying a new phone and had bought Ammi's medicines instead. Had it been a new phone it would have certainly shattered. Osmanbhai saw the worm grab the old phone held together with rubber bands and laughed unkindly. Kutta saala, he thought in his head.

'If Dhun turns out chootiya, I will come back to kill you.'

FOURTEEN

Maya was lighting a small lamp by the dining able gods when Elmore and Dean entered the house for breakfast. Chimanbhai was looking even more morose, like he had had a bad night. There was no sign of Radhika.

Dean had tried to reason with Elmore but it was pointless. He had suddenly become a huge dick. No brains, only this need to please Maya. Dean had a bad feeling about everything they were about to do.

'This is called an aarti. Women prayed for warriors and put a red mark on them to come back victorious.' Maya was pointing to a plate where there were flowers, three small bowls—one with sugar, another with rice, and the third one with red paste—and the little lamp she had just lit.

Radhikaben had just made an appearance. She looked tousled and not in an attractive way. She had overslept. She saw them all staring at her and said, 'I was so worried I couldn't sleep a wink. I fell asleep at five in the morning.' Then seeing the aarti, she beamed at Maya. 'I am glad some things went into your head. Grandma can now cross over and join all the other ancestors. She was always worried about you.'

Maya rolled her eyes. 'Ma, have some tea. I don't care if Grandma's still hovering over our house. I did this to give Elmore, and yes, also Dean, some moral support.'

'What are you going to do?' Elmore asked.

'Watch me!' Maya said.

Dean groaned. Radhika was otherwise a sharp woman. Why had she not noticed Maya flirting with Elmore? Even now she was pouring chai from the flask as though nothing else mattered.

Radhika and Chimanbhai sat at the dining table drinking chai, watching Maya perform the aarti. Radhika was too zoned to notice the expression in Maya's eyes as she put the vermilion paste on Elmore's forehead and then marked Dean's forehead similarly. Dean saw the wink and cursed Maya in his head. If she were his daughter, he would be spanking her flirty butt until she forgot to wink.

Aarti over, Radhika ordered Maya to boil extra eggs for the two warriors. Maya complied. A bowl of sugary pops was thrust at Chimanbhai who picked up the milk jug and poured it over them. He watched them until they had lost all the crackle. He picked up the spoon and looked up at the rest of the lot at the dining table. 'If things seem to go wrong, or if you should change your mind about the killing, tell me.'

***

Dadar was too respectable. Osman did not like the pious smell of the middle class. This was it—the building that was going to change his future. The building was dilapidated, but it had a dignity that Osman hated. He preferred the grime of the slums. It was honest. Even when people did bad things, there was some honesty about it. This middle-class area with its middle-class people made his skin crawl. They had too many rules and they lived like ants. Orderly, but saala, why live like that? And then they chose to live in these buildings that outlasted people. These kinds of buildings looked down on people like him and made him feel like a cockroach. He was climbing up the wooden stairs that were old but swept clean. Yes, there were corners decorated with paan stains, but there was no garbage strewn, no bandicoots. Osman was used to the big rats. As a child he had hated them, but now he could kick them away without a twinge of fear.

He climbed the stairs. Why would this moronic Dhunbhai have an office in a building where there were old ladies staring curiously at him? He stared back at one of them. Just so he could get his khunnas out. He was ready to kick the old cow when he realized that she had that chootiya motiabind! He spat in disgust. In his profession he would never last long enough to have his vision clouded by some old-age shit. He knew there would be some smartass somewhere whose fist would be stronger than his, someone whose gun would be faster than his ability to dodge the bullet.

There it was. Saala kutta kaheen ka. Dhuni ka office. Chootiya! Third-floor office. Kutta saala. Osmanbhai pushed three fellows who were sitting on the bench outside the office and sat down. He yanked the handkerchief tucked between the neck and collar of his pathan suit and fanned himself by spinning it. He looked at the three quivering idiots he had dislodged from the bench and said, 'What you looking at? Dhuni ko bulao saale!'

One idiot who dared to come close to Osmanbhai and tell him confidentially 'Dhunbhai making deal, wait!' got kicked so hard he knew there was little or no chance left of having children. He howled. The other scampered down the stairs and the third one nodded a hasty 'yes' and ran inside to get Dhunbhai.

God had not been kind when he made Dhunbhai. He resembled an unhappy hippo for starters—beady eyes, pink mouth and all. But to make up for his unkindness, he had allowed the goddess of wealth to reside in the big iron safe behind him. Dhunbhai was speaking simultaneously on three phones. His fat fingers were separated from his palm by fat, shiny gold rings. The gold rings had precious stones of all colours and shine. He was wearing the whitest kurta pyjama except for the long green stain on the button flap where he had dribbled chutney when he had the vada pau in the morning.

'Dhunbhai, Osmanbhai!' the man said, bursting into his room, and then promptly fainted.

This was going to be a tough morning. There were three kabootars panicking. If they backed off now, he would need to pay for his wife's diamond earrings some other way. She had already bought the baubles, and would wreak havoc if the earrings did not arrive in time for her next kitty party which was three days away. And now there was that Osmanbhai. Dhun had heard much about him. But if Osmanbhai needed to go to America so badly, there must be some catch.

Dhun grunted into the phones which looked like toys in his fat hands. He heaved himself off the sofa and propelled by that effort waddled to the door.

'Osmanbhai! Good morning!'

'Teri ma ki morning! Seedhi kaise chadtaa tu?'

'Maaf karna, Osmanbhai. Building ka doosri taraf Saadi ki dukan hai na, unka lift leneka. Next time.'

'Next time? Finish this today. I have no time for next time.' Osmanbhai cracked his knuckles. He had thought of kicking the man, but he was too fat. All that charbi, he wouldn't get hurt. Maybe he would be better off pushing the fatty down the stairs.

'Osmanbhai...' Dhun started off. He was afraid of this guy. Although Osmanbhai had a reputation, he needed Dhun's help to get that visa to America. But you could not play games with the man and make him come back again and again with extra money. Dhun would need to finish his work quickly.

'First to first, you give me chai. My brain not working. Then get me visa to Amrika.'

'No problem, bhai!' Dhun said, more relieved than anything else. Then he leaned over dangerously from the corridor balcony and yelled for chai.

'Come to my office, Osmanbhai, please come.' Dhun opened the door wide and made a sweeping hand gesture asking Osmanbhai to go in first.

Osmanbhai did not like people who behaved all 'please, please; come, come'. Dukaandaar saale. These type of people had something to sell. He went in nonetheless. He saw the man who had gone in to inform Dhun about his arrival sitting on the floor nursing a bump on his head. Osmanbhai smiled and said as the man stood up shaking, 'Darpok saala!' He kicked the man hard. The man first collided into Dhunbhai and then bolted out of the door.

Dhun saw twenty 25,000 bolt out of his room and mentally added that amount to Osmanbhai's amount. He opened his mouth to get started, but realized that Osmanbhai had wanted chai. He switched the air conditioner on and adjusted the fan speed. The chaiwalla showed up at the door, saw Osmanbhai, and his kettle and teacups began to clatter.

Dhun rolled his eyes and reached for the delicate English china cups a grateful customer had given him. The boy poured chai into the two cups and left the kettle on the table on the side and ran for his life. Osmanbhai was grinning. He liked people being afraid of him. But this did not affect Dhun.

'Happy customer gifted. His case was very difficult. Beautiful, na?' Dhun offered a teacup to Osmanbhai.

The teacup seemed to vanish in Osmanbhai's large paw. He closed his eyes when draining the cup. Dhun stared at Osmanbhai. When the cup left Osmanbhai's lips, Dhun took in a breath sharply. Osmanbhai's eyes did not miss that. So the fat hippo was attached to the cup. Osmanbhai looked at Dhun looking at the cup.

'So foreign ka cup hai?'

'Haan, Osmanbhai, bahut pyaara hai na? Ek dum jhakaas!'

'Ekdum bakwaas. Saala unglee atkeli.'

Osmanbhai held up the dainty cup, its ear stuck in Osmanbhai's little finger. The way it was dangling, Dhun knew why Hindi movie heroes felt the need to be violent towards the villains. Swallowing a big lump of emotion he never knew he had for the floral cup, Dhun distracted Osmanbhai. 'No problem, bhai. When you want to go America?'

Osmanbhai grabbed the cup tighter. It disappeared in his fist. 'Jaldi. Now. I want to go tomorrow.'

Why did Dhun not expect that answer! He said, 'Osmanbhai, ek aur chai maaro, I make one phone call, okay?'

Dhun was surprised to see the little cup intact in the man's hand. He poured chai in the cup, and pushed a plate of Jim Jam biscuits towards Osmanbhai. Then he dialled Pathakji. Of course you heard the 'Om Jai Jagdish Hare' each time you rang him. He had almost memorized the bhajan. His grandmother had freaked out when she found Dhun humming along during one of the hundred Hindu festivals celebrated in the city, but Dhun knew Allah was far too great and his own faith was so firm, just humming a bhajan was not being untrue to his religion. After all great singers like Mohammed Rafi sang bhajans in movies! Oh, he had finally picked up.

'Pathakji! Dhun bolta hai.'

Pathakji grunted. Dhun knew he had interrupted one of those many quick visa fee barter sessions that Pathakji so loved. 'Kya Pathakji, morning-morning you found girl! But this is very important customer. Full VIP. Anything happening in Caneda? New Jersey? Los Angeles ho toh very good.'

Pathakji grunted. Dhun held the cellphone away from his ear. Osmanbhai was watching, so he explained, 'Pathakji ladki ke saath lagaa hai,' and made a crude gesture with his hand.

Osmanbhai dangled the teacup again. 'I don't care what Pathak is doing. You fix visa for me. Now.'

Dhun put the phone to his ear. He could hear Pathak saying goodbye to someone and assuring her that her visa was as good as done. Pathak said a hello into the phone. Dhun was sitting on the edge of his chair (not that anyone could have guessed) with an eye on the little cup still held hostage in Osmanbhai's hand.

'Kabootar udana hai, Pathakji, bhaari kabootar...'

'Ek Los Angeles mein dandiya group jaaneka hai. Shaadi ka waaste. They want—how they say—cute men. You think your kabootar will fit?'

'Cute?' Dhun asked, then looked at Osmanbhai getting jam out of his teeth with the nail of his little finger. 'Haan, cute hai.'

'Photo batao. I will fix it. If passport is okay, interview in one day and then they fly in four days.'

'Thank you, Pathakji. Thank you.'

Dhun smiled in relief. Osmanbhai would be out of his hair soon. But now he needed to tell the monster that he needed to pay Pathakji's and his fees. And the visa fees over that.

Osmanbhai had heard enough. 'Saala you called me cute and kabootar! I am looking like pigeon or what?'

Dhun was alarmed. He thought everyone knew what kabootar meant. He pacified the big man. 'No, no, Osmanbhai. Kabootar is simple code word. Means we take passenger to America, UK, Australia, Europe, wherever. We take thirty-forty in dance troupe. But then we don't bring them all back. Out of thirty-forty, three-four don't come back. They run away and hide! Phurrrr! They fly away, just like pigeons! Then become...'

Osmanbhai cursed. Run and hide? Him? He was like a full-on stud. Why would he hide?

'Bhai, hide bole toh, you just have to relax in a

safe place. If they catch you without papers, problem is big!'

'Why not make papers from here?'

'I cannot make papers from here. My contact there makes papers. You need to be there to make social security and other cards. Bhai, not to worry. I am doing this business for last ten years.'

'Then I can be Amitabh Bachchan.'

Dhun groaned. 'See, bhai, it's the same reason why you cannot be Gandhiji. And with Amitabh Bachchan everyone knows he's dancing in Europe somewhere.'

Osmanbhai did not look happy at all. 'You tell me what I should go as?'

'Erm...bhai, there is big cultural programme. You will fit in perfect.'

'What programme?'

'Bhai, you not worry. Tell me one thing, can you dance?'

He should have seen it coming. He shut his eyes as soon as he said it, he cringed. He imagined Osman's manly slaps raining down on his face, right to left. They didn't come. And when he opened his eyes, the delicate floral cup was sitting in front of him, without the ear. Osman cracked his knuckles and asked, 'Why saala?'

'Bhai, bhai, don't hit me. Listen, please. We getting you into America for cultural programme...with a dance troupe. The American Consulate might ask you to show dance moves. Dandiya steps. Thoda dance mangta!'

Osmanbhai narrowed his eyes. Humiliation was not on his list of life experiences. He just didn't understand what this guy meant.

'Dance kaikoo? Why Amriki want to see me dance? Dancers get easy visa? Saala country of Godfather, they should give Osmanbhai free visa. Why they want Osmanbhai to dance?'

Dhun thanked the star he was born under. He was smarter than Osmanbhai. He needed to spin a tale quick. 'Osmanbhai, listen. We Indians already ruling their country. Computers bolo, movies bolo, cricket bolo...ab Godfather is very Amriki, isn't it? Their own property. If you go there, you will be better than Godfather, na? They want to remain champion for bhaigiri. Godfathergiri. If you go as Osmanbhai, they will not give you visa easy. So we take you into America as dancer. In disguise. Just like Don changes costume...'

Osmanbhai knew Dhun was praising him. He didn't mind the idea of a disguise, but as a dancer... He would push a bit more and see if this Dhun guy was able to do something else.

'Dizguys I understand. Why dancer? I can go as James Bond, na!'

'Bhai, bhai!' Dhun moaned. 'They know James Bond. You will be caught in a minute!'

Osmanbhai took a deep breath. This man was right. He ran through a list of people he could pretend to be.

'Osmanbhai, dekho. Pathakji's cultural troupe

is our last and only resort.' Then looking at the complete confusion on Osman's face, he explained, 'Bhai, this is fastest way to reach America. In three days after you have that interview, you will be flying to America. Bas, aap thoda say "yes", and then I do the rest.'

Osmanbhai said nothing. Emboldened by his silence, Dhun ventured a little further.

'Bhai, aap passport laaye kya?'

'That also I bring kya? Saala! Then what you are doing?'

And before he knew it Dhun had said, 'It will cost more.'

For a big man Osmanbhai was very quick on his feet. He was out of his chair and around the table so fast, Dhun did not see it. He only felt Osmanbhai's hands tightening around his jowls.

'Cost? Meaning money? You charging money for this rubbish?'

'Bhai, not me, bhai!' Dhun yelped. 'I not charge you money. All the people I work with, they need money na...for passport, for immigration, for social security car, everything costs na, bhai! If you let go I will show you many passports. You choose.'

Dhun thanked his stars again. His neck hurt. But he was happy to show a bunch of passports to Osmanbhai. But trust Osmanbhai to pick the wrong one. 'Osmanbhai, yeh naheen. Iran ka hai. America aur Iran...thoda problem hai...'

Osmanbhai had had enough. This was too much

drama, he thought. 'You choose the passport saala, aur meri photu chep de.'

'Chep?' Dhun asked, then realized that Osmanbhai knew that these were not new passports but stolen ones with original photographs still in there. Osmanbhai knew Dhun would replace the photographs.

'Photo. Yes, yes, bhai, we go get photograph for passport and for Pathakji's interview.'

He grabbed a not-so-used passport from the pile, locked the others in the drawer and then stood up.

'Let's get your passport fixed. Come Osmanbhai, I take you.'

***

'Elmore,' Dean pleaded. 'I've seen the girl. She's too nice. What the Shahs say and what I have seen doesn't seem to add up. Why don't you listen to me?'

Dean and Elmore had driven for over forty-five minutes from the shop to where she lived, and they had waited and waited near her home but there was no sign of her. Dean was hoping she had taken the day off and driven somewhere. They had driven up to a truck stop and gorged on bacon and eggs, and now Dean was driving Maya's car back to Supriya's home with Elmore. But Elmore was stuck on proving something.

'That Maya is mine now. At first she was just another hot fuck. But I want more of her. Maybe you should find someone after we've fixed this Supriya bitch for Maya's parents,' Elmore said.

Dean slapped his hands on the steering wheel in anger. 'You're not listening, Elmore.'

'You just back off, Dean, I have told her that I will kill her. You're becoming soft, Dean. Fuck some chick, get that mojo back.'

'What makes you think I have not found someone? You've been too busy slipping your head under Maya's skirts.' Dean was angry.

They drove in silence for the next mile. It was when Dean began to park the car opposite Supriya's house that this piece of information began to sink into his brain. 'Wait a minute. You were shadowing Supriya. Who else could you have met? You now say she is a very nice girl. Aaaaaaaaarrr rrggggghhhhhhh! You fucker! You like this Supriya girl! That's why you don't want her killed! You baaaaasssssstaa-aarrrrrrrdddddd!'

***

Osmanbhai was clearly soaked. It had taken an entire bottle of foreign whiskey and two whole tandoori chickens to make him amenable. It had taken three men to undress him (one swore he needed extra money when he discovered Osmanbhai wore no underwear) and get him into the dance costume. The costume was elaborate, and rented from Mumbai's famous Maganlal Dresswala. Dhunbhai propped the big man while the two boys put the kediyu on Osmanbhai. The big man looked very silly in a kurta that looked like a baby-frock and nothing else. The photographer suggested he take a couple of naked pictures of Osmanbhai but Dhun knew if Osmanbhai ever saw the pictures, it would be the end of the photo studio. Besides, once Osmanbhai was sent away to the other side of the world, who would really care to see his naked pictures?

The dhoti in place, Osmanbhai looked less ridiculous. Soon they had dressed him with the bracelets and a hat that looked like an upside-down pan. The bright red-and-yellow combination of the outfit that had a thousand mirrors drained all colour from Osmanbhai's face. The photographer suggested they add a bit of makeup.

'Are you mad? Makeup on this tiger? What if he wakes up and finds lipstick on his mouth?' Dhun practically fainted at the very idea of putting makeup on the baddest man he had ever come across.

'Red lipstick saale! Chandni's red lipstick!' This was a very drunk Osmanbhai, muttering about some Chandni.

One of the boys turned out to be brave. He put foundation on the man saying he was just wiping the sweat from his face. And he quickly added rouge.

It wasn't a professional job, but would do for the photo. The cultural troupe was not meant to know perfect makeup. It was a herculean task, but the photographer managed to make a very drunk and yet primped up Osmanbhai look like a professional dandiya star. It was tougher getting Osmanbhai out of the dandiya kediyu and putting a decent

T-shirt on the man for the passport pictures. It was almost five by the time the pictures were taken. And Osmanbhai came to when the photographer was haggling with Dhun.

'Dhunbhai! You cannot be serious! I need some money. What do I care if the man is a notorious criminal or not? If he is a criminal, you just let me call the police. They will pay me.'

Dhun saw Osmanbhai's eyes come alive and alert at the mention of 'police'. He prayed to all the gods at once. The photographer saw alarm on Dhunbhai's face and knew Osmanbhai was awake and right behind him. He continued. 'Akkha Mumbai you can search, but Osmanbhai will make the best Inspector Vijay, better than Amitabh Bachchan.'

'What are you saying about police, kutte?'

The photographer whirled around. 'Bhai! What I say! You will make the best Inspector Vijay.'

In a few seconds, the photographer was out cold on the floor.

'You saala think like this also?' Osmanbhai asked Dhun.

'I don't think, bhai, I don't think,' Dhun conceded.

One of the boys was smart. He brought a steaming hot towel for Osmanbhai who was pacified by the gesture. Fortunately all the makeup also came off with the hot towel.

Dhun knew he would have to pay the photographer double tomorrow.

***

'You moron! You were supposed to follow the girl. Not fall in love with her!'

'I didn't want to. I am telling you she is a nice girl.'

'Nice girl? She's been out until now, and there's a car in her driveway. Is that her car?'

Dean looked. The car was not hers. Whose could it be? Who had brought her home so late? He secretly hoped it to be family or something.

Elmore was holding the gun. Dean hissed at Elmore, 'What the fuck are you doing?'

'My job, unlike you.' Elmore was vicious.

They waited for the next twenty minutes. Dean knew he was going to stop Elmore from taking a shot at Supriya. Elmore on the other hand knew Dean would try to stop him. If he missed killing Supriya, he would make sure he killed Dean. He had promised Maya he would do the job. He was the warrior her family chose. He felt the place where she had put the red mark that morning and knew he would do the job, and to hell with Dean.

Then suddenly Supriya's front door opened and a man silhouetted by the light in her hallway stepped out. Behind him was Supriya, wearing what looked like a short robe.

Elmore looked at Dean. He looked so disappointed that Elmore thought Dean was going to start crying. He saw her wave the man goodbye. And before Elmore could aim his gun the man had reversed his car and she had closed the front door. Shit!

FIFTEEN

'Don't think I am going to let you go that easy! You cheating pig!'

'But Radhika...'

'But? You saying "but" now! Where was that "but" when you are with her? You don't say "but" to her ne? I am taking care of this shit and you dare to say me "but"?'

'Radhika! Listen to me...'

'I am listening to you have phone calls after phone calls with her. You hiding this from me because I making khandvi like your mother, ne? Or because I give Maya and Suraj to you. You tell me what she can do? If she make better khandvi, I will leave this house and then you can say "But Radhika" for ever and ever and I won't come back.'

'She called. I didn't. Why you don't understand?'

'I knew many handsome boys in my time. How come they don't call? You must've told her my wife is stupid woman, straight from village That's why she called, ne? You did not put down phone saying no I am married. You gave her story and she call in sympathy. You can think I am stupid, just let me tell you I am not.'

'No Radhika!'

'Panditji was right, Maha Rahukaal is going on, and I should have listened to him. Rahukaal all day! Hai Ambe Ma, come take me away from this horrible man.'

Chimanbhai sat down on the chair in the middle of the room, his hands covering his face, while Radhika strode around him, her hands gesturing wildly to an invisible audience, like an angry satellite.

Just then Suraj popped his head into the room. He had heard his mom rant and rave at his dad, which was nothing new lately, but the word Rahukaal was.

'What is Rahukaal, Mum?'

'Time of total destruction, my child!' Radhika answered without thinking. On any other day she would've shooed the kid out if she was scolding Chiman. After all he was their Puppa ne. Boys needed to respect theirs Puppas.

'Destruction? Really? Cool! Actually I have downloaded the CIA assassination manual from the Net. We could make a nitro bomb and blast Supriya's shop into space!'

Chimanbhai looked horrified at the boy. Who was this monster who spoke about bombs and blasting shops into space? Could this be his son?

Radhika was staring at her son too. He watched too much TV! And this computer she did not understand. Why was CIA telling him how to build bombs? She wanted Supriya dead, but she did not want to soil her own hands, or the hands of anyone else in the family for that matter. Here was this boy whom she had raised in the womb on a diet of Raj Kapoor films talking of bombs. What was he growing into?

She yelled at him almost at the same time Chimanbhai found his voice. 'Suraj! What...what bomb...what are you saying?'

Suraj mistook the horror in his parents' voices for enthusiasm. He began, 'The CIA manual states...'

His mother's hands that had been gesticulating wildly before now found an outlet for the aggression she was feeling. Not only did the hands come down smartly on his back, but they propelled him out of the room. Radhika was yelling at him. 'How many times I told you all this work should not be done by us, we have those...those two for help. You want to go to jail? No? Then, shut up. No more bomb talk.'

Suraj was used to being ignored. But this was really insulting. Nobody in the family respected his genius. Elmore had looked at his maps and plans to plant mines and plastic explosives at Supriya's store with more interest than his so-called family. He would get even for all the insults. He would show them!

***

'You ring the doorbell, and I will do the killing when she opens the door.' Elmore was enjoying his moment of superiority. Dean had been the brains of their two-man operation for too long. Maya had instilled lots of confidence in him, and he did not waste any of it.

'Elmore, you are not a murderer. If we get caught, you'll get the chair!'

'Then I might as well kill you too. They cannot kill me twice.'

'Then what about Maya?'

Elmore had no answer. Maybe he hadn't thought of that. But a car drew up into her driveway and a man stepped out.

'Another man! Your bitch is a fuckin' 'ho!'

The man rang the doorbell and stood waiting for Supriya to open the door. Elmore stepped out of the car and made his way to her house. He would kill both of them. Dean got out of the car too, hoping he could stop Elmore from shooting her. Dean hissed, 'Elmore, what are you doing?'

Elmore whispered back, 'I'm going to kill her that's what I am doing. I don't trust this old gun. The closer I get to her the better.'

'What about the man?'

'Heck, I'll kill him too!'

'Elmore!'

They were now crouching in the bushes near her home. It looked like the man who was at the doorstep had changed his mind because he was walking back towards his car.

Elmore extended his arm to shoot. Thinking he

had missed seeing her open the door, Dean simply gave in to instinct and tackled him. The man was startled by the sudden noise and assuming that it was a racoon, he made shooing sounds.

Elmore began to curse and kick, hampered by the fact that he was holding a gun in one hand. Dean did not care if they were found and sent to jail. He could not bear to have Supriya shot. Elmore kicked Dean hard. Dean wished the old gun would backfire and kill Elmore instead. He scratched Elmore's face hard with one hand and held him down with the other. Elmore was wriggling so hard that Dean had to use all his strength to prevent him from crawling forward. Dean wished he were as strong as Elmore, but it was as though he was being pushed by a supernatural force.

Then all of a sudden the gun went off.

The shot was so loud that for a moment Dean thought he had become deaf. Elmore looked shocked as well but more so from the recoil and the gunpowder soot all over his hand than anything else.

The next instant they heard a thud. The man had fallen on the hood of the car, face first. The light on the porch came on but Dean and Elmore had reacted like jackrabbits and had bolted for the car. The moment Dean put the keys in the ignition, Supriya screamed as she saw the dead man in her driveway. Her scream brought out the neighbours, and Dean put his foot on the accelerator and zoomed off. The street was dark enough and he hoped Supriya had not noticed the licence plate.

Before he rolled up the window, Dean heard Supriya scream again.

***

Chimanbhai was sitting morosely before the TV set in the living room flicking through channels. He sighed. He did not understand American comedy, neither did he understand why Suraj would sit for hours watching the science fiction channel. Maya watched the songs, but thankfully she watched them upstairs in her room. American pop songs, too, were beyond him. Radhika watched Hindi soaps, and Chimanbhai enjoyed the funny ones. He usually fell asleep when watching the ones where people ranted and raved at each other. But watching TV with Radhika had become such a habit that he was sitting in front of the TV in spite of the fact that Radhika had yelled and yelled at him not too long ago. He watched TV news simply because the Hindi programme that Radhika watched was twenty minutes away.

Radhika was also a creature of habit. Animatedly, she made tea, placed Marie biscuits and Ritz crackers on a plate in concentric circles, and carried the teacups and the glass kettle on a tray to the living room. She had forgotten that she had been upset with Chimanbhai. She was humming aimlessly as she carried the tea tray to the TV room.

Then she saw Chimanbhai sitting in front of the TV, frozen with shock at the news.

A sombre-faced newsreader was announcing, 'A gruesome drive-by has shattered the peace in the Hillsborough area. The victim is a well-known surgeon of Indian origin. He was shot by two or more assailants at point-blank range. The victim was shot in the driveway of a young woman who does not personally know the dead surgeon, and claims that she had not heard the bell ring as she had fallen asleep in front of the TV, and woke up only with the sound of the gunshot.'

The TV was now showing a hysterical Supriya saying, 'I've never seen anything like this in my life! They just shot at the doctor and drove off.'

Supriya? Both Chimanbhai and Radhika looked at each other. Radhika dropped the tea tray from her hand and it fell on the floor with a loud crash.

Maya came running down to figure out what the loud noise was and saw her parents staring at the TV news. The floor was littered with broken teacups, tea, biscuits, and the tray. Had Elmore killed the woman already?

Suraj wandered in holding his laptop and spotted the tableau staring at the TV. 'Aah, Supriya is news already? And here I had news of my own. We can make a nitro bomb from things found at home. This home.'

Suraj hated his family. Like always, they did not pay him attention at all. They never paid any attention to him ever.

***

Elmore and Dean sat at the dining table with Chimanbhai who was wolfing down puri and bhaji.

'I love this bhaji. The puris are a bit of air and oil, isn't it?' Elmore was all enthusiasm. And Maya had made serving food a theatrical production.

Dean ate quietly. Radhika would be the only logical person. Maybe Dean would talk to her later.

Radhika joined them at the table after calling for Suraj. When Suraj did not materialize, she sent Maya off with a plate of food to Suraj's room.

'I think Elmore has caused enough damage already,' said Radhika, her mouth full of food. 'How many bullets did he waste?'

Elmore looked irritated. He had not expected this reaction from Maya's mother. Maya had fawned all over him when they reached home. She had called him a man for having killed.

Radhika continued to speak. 'So you have two bullets left. Useless...useless.'

Dean watched Elmore and Radhika.

'You two must not do anything hasty now, at least for one week. Do you understand? Nothing. The police will be watching.' Then she looked at Chimanbhai who had stuffed himself with puris and said, 'Chiman, how you eat! Now I will have to go to the doctor's funeral with Bhagwatiben, or someone else. You will be half asleep with all the food you have eaten.'

Dean was relieved. He had one week to persuade Elmore to get out of this house and this mess.

SIXTEEN

Los Angeles airport was the noisiest airport ever. And the light was different here. But it didn't matter because he was here! Osmanbhai was finally in America! He did not care if the dandiya costume was itchy, or that the hundred thousand mirrors on the costume were compelling everyone to look at him and snigger.

On the flight he had beaten only one guy who was annoying the pretty girl in a short skirt. That pretty girl was so good she gave him food without his even paying for it. She had brought him food not once but each time she crossed him. Five trays of food he had eaten before he felt full. After that he had shooed off two men who sat next to him and stretched out on the seat to sleep.

Now the same girl was beckoning him. She told him to follow her. He did. He needed to get to the Shahs. She led him to another aircraft and showed him another seat. She told him in very nice Hindi that he would be in Portland in an hour and fifty minutes. He was so happy with the girl that he told her he would buy her and keep her in the big house he was planning to buy for Chandni. He was a big guy. He could handle two women.

The girl smiled and waved goodbye. Osmanbhai would be in Portland soon.

**

Portland airport was less noisy, and everyone was wearing jackets. It was 9 pm but there was sunlight. Osmanbhai was confused now. Saala, yeh kaisi jagah thee? He was propelled by a friendly airplane chap towards his luggage. His one brand-new red suitcase appeared from a hole in the wall. He yelled for a coolie, but then saw everyone pushing their own luggage. Osmanbhai was exhausted and a strong urge to sleep was taking over him. He knew he had to make that phone call to the Shahs to announce that he had arrived.

He fished out the paper with everyone's numbers and walked to the telephone booth. There were letters and numbers on the phone. How did these things work? He stood staring at the booth when someone tapped him on the shoulder.

'Bhai, help chahiye?'

Hindi? He must have been so tired he was hearing things. Osmanbhai whirled around.

It was a little man with funny check pants, a coat that covered him from neck to toe and there was a dead rabbit on his head. No, it was a topi! Because he took it off and straightened his thinning hair.

He asked again, 'Dandiya master, phone karna hai?'

Osmanbhai said 'Hain? Dandiya master?'

'Haan, haan, you! Help chahiye? You look new here.'

'Help? Haan. Phone.' Osmanbhai handed the paper to the silly man and pointed to the first number.

'No, no. I not calling for you. I show you.'

The man took out change from his pocket, and asked Osmanbhai to do the same. Osmanbhai had smashed Dhun's safe and taken out a stash of American money, but he had no coins. He shrugged and fiddled with the big roll in his pocket and took out a hundred. The weird man saw the note and showed him a quarter. 'This is a q-u-a-r-t-e-r, pachchees paise.' He spelled it out for Osmanbhai.

'Chaar phone karne hain, cha-a-r,' said Osmanbhai. 'Where is booth boy?'

The man shrugged and showed him how to make that one phone call. He dialled Neeraj's number for Osmanbhai. Neeraj did not take the call, so the man took the rejected coin and put it in the slot once again. Osmanbhai understood. Saala India and Amrika, phone saala same to same.

The weird helpful man handed the phone to Osmanbhai and asked him an odd question. 'You got jacket?' Then he wore his rabbit hat and stepped out into one of the taxis standing in a queue right outside the glass walls of the airport.

Osmanbhai called the Shah home, and after six rings, the same young boy picked up the phone.

'Hello! Chimanbhai ko bolo Osmanbhai bolta hoon.'

'Osmaaaaaaanbhai?' someone screamed.

Osmanbhai liked that reaction. It reassured him about his status in this world. Nobody dares to say 'who?' to Osmanbhai. His chest swelled up and he took a second to admire himself in the glass wall. Not once did he think that his dandiya costume looked stupid in the midst of people dressed in mostly dark coats and jeans.

'Haan, main...Osman. I come Amrika already. Ab tell me address. I come. I kill.'

Suraj had grown up on a diet of Bollywood. He was so excited at this development that he decided to play his part. 'Haan address deta hai. Likho. Teen sau chaar, Frangipani Drive...Fra-n-ji-pani Dri-vuh...haan raste ka naam hai. Aur likho. Winderly Heights...haan, Win-dur-lee Hai-ts. Tigard. Tie-gard. Samjhe. Lekin tell me. I told you we have already got someone.'

'Matlab?'

'Matlab clear hai. Main tumko bola, we have two American killers. Tum kyon America aaye ho? Kaise aaye? Visa kaise mila?'

'Neerajbhai, Chimanbhai apun ko supari diya. Apun liya. Now I in Amrika. Tell Chimanbhai, I do it. Saala my first supari in Amrika. I give free!'

Before Suraj could say anything about Neerajbhai and Chimanbhai, the operator asked Osmanbhai to 'put in additional 35 cents'. Osmanbhai was confused. Who was this ladki and what was she saying? He could not hear the voice at the other end. Irritated, he slammed the phone and a whole bunch of coins came tumbling out of the return slot. Osmanbhai took it as a sign! He quickly collected whatever he could and put them in the pockets of his kurta and his jacket. He also put some coins in the front pocket of his shiny new red suitcase, then jingled out of the doors.

A curious policeman looked at this jingly, jangly, sparkly tourist stepping out of the airport but said nothing. He had seen enough kooks at the Oregon Country Fair in Eugene to bother with an obviously Indian person dressed in a wild costume. He watched the man react to the cold breeze blowing that evening and chuckled to himself.

Osmanbhai had spent all his life in Mumbai. He knew that a five-star air conditioner could be cold (he had killed one Tamil film producer at the Sea Rock Hotel), but this was more than that! The cold went through his thin dhoti and froze his essentials. The cotton jacket was no protection against the wind either! He could feel the hair on his chest shrivel. He wished he could knock someone senseless and steal their jacket. There was nothing in his suitcase that could protect him against the cold either. Maybe Chimanbhai could give him one for a little while. This thought propelled him towards the yellow taxi queue. He got one immediately.

Fortunately the cabbie turned out to be Indian. Waah!

'Bhai, take me here.' Osmanbhai showed him the Shahs' home address.

The cabbie did not look happy at all. He was a

small man, irritated by his job, unhappy at having to work that cold night. And now he had to deal with an obviously fresh-off-the-boat chap dressed up in a dandiya costume and with a new suitcase. He probably didn't have any money. But there was a policeman standing there watching the two. Getting him involved would not be a good idea. So the cabbie asked, 'Money? You have American money?'

Osmanbhai was slowly getting angry. 'Yes! You think I bhikhari? Standing on road and asking for money? I have money, lots of money.'

'Dikhao! Show me money!'

The police officer wondered what was going on now. He walked up to the two and asked, 'Is everything okay?'

The cabbie could not help himself. 'I wanted to know if he had money to pay the taxi fare. Look at him. He's dressed weird.'

The policeman coughed and said, 'Sir? Is there a problem with money?'

Osmanbhai hated policemen, especially the ones that asked for money. He took out another hundred and gave it to the policeman. The policeman was taken aback. If the Internal Revenue weren't so fucking active, he would have kept the fresh hundred dollar bill. But he had to return the money and help the tourist into the cab and wave it away. He noted the number of the cab and memorized the features of its Indian cabbie and his passenger. Just in case.

***

A big burly man followed Neeraj with a baseball bat. Neeraj was not drunk, he was just coming back home from work. He had been on the bench now for almost four months, and that morning he had almost blown away his boss who had called up to say that they were looking to let go of some of the consultants and that he had to report for work. Neeraj knew he was on that list. He had sweet-talked Guha sir's secretary Barbara into showing him the list. There was a question mark against Neeraj's name because there was no real complaint against him from Intel. It just said that he was tardy.

Several weeks' worth of junk mail strewn on the floor made it tough for Neeraj to push the door open. He chucked the keys into the bowl on the shoe rack. When he turned to shut the door, he saw the man with the baseball bat.

'Mmm...mm...Mr Rigg!' stammered Neeraj.

'You clear out right now!' Riggs demanded, thwacking the baseball bat on his palm for full effect.

'Clear out? But I've paid the rent for this month already,' said Neeraj.

'That's why I haven't opened the place and thrown you out yet. But you gotta clear out now, man. Now!'

'Why are you doing this to me?'

'Take a deep breath, Mr Shah, take a deep breath. Then tell me what died in there.'

Neeraj stepped inside his apartment. It was

stinking. He saw several empty beer bottles in the living room. But it couldn't be just the beer bottles or the pizza boxes. He stepped into the bathroom and quickly stepped out. Juanita! She had upchucked everywhere. Or was it him? He did not remember. The bedroom was no more than a closet, but it stank too. He quickly grabbed a suitcase and threw in the pictures of Bhawani Ma and Hanumanji, his passport and other papers that were kept in the box under the pictures and whatever clothes he could find in the fridge. There wasn't much left here as he was staying with Radhikaben in any case. But he dumped two pullovers, a baseball jacket, one pair of work shoes and stashed the computer CDs in the mess. He hoped Hanumanji didn't mind too much travelling crammed up in a suitcase like that, but this was an emergency. He looked at the duvet that his mother had sent for him, but a box of Chinese takeaway had coagulated on it and a bottle of Coke had left a huge stain.

'What's taking you so long?' Riggs had come in. 'Oh my God! What died in here?'

Neeraj managed to look disgusted himself. 'That bitch, Juanita! She trashed the place!'

'Juanita? That Latina with the big hoo-haas?' Riggs asked. Riggs noticed everything about everybody.

Neeraj nodded his head. Riggs felt bile well up from inside him and looked like he was going to be sick any minute as well.

'I think we need to get outta here.'

When Riggs and Neeraj reached downstairs, Riggs was back to being his nasty self. He had Neeraj's file opened up in front of him.

'Please sign here and get out. Juanita or no, the apartment is in a mess. I should have beaten you into cleaning it, but the cleaning lady could do with some money. So I'm going to take it out from your security deposit, which means that I owe you nothing.'

'But...but your wife is the cleaning lady!'

'So?'

Neeraj eyed the baseball bat and thought rapidly. Radhikaben and Chimanbhai would not even notice that he had been living with them until they were concerned with Elmore and Dean. He had practically no money in the bank except for the almost-half salary that would be his because he was benched. Guha sir's chamcha, that brown-noser Subbu, had asked for Neeraj to be sent to Honeywell to work on a project. That was his only hope. But Subbu would make his life miserable, he knew that. He had no choice but to sign on the paper.

Neeraj tried one last time to coax Riggs into giving him some of his deposit back. 'Please, Mr Riggs, don't take all of it. I've just been benched, so I'm going to get half the salary. Please! Why would you take $1,200 to clean? Can you not take half?'

'No. The trouble my missus is going to go through cleaning that shit, is more than this. Maybe you should clean it up, really.'

'I will. But you must give me the deposit back.'

'We'll see.'

Those two words were like a flashback slap on Neeraj's face. His dad used to say that and after young Neeraj had done whatever was needed, his dad would shrug and deny him the treat. Maybe Riggs was not like his dad.

Neeraj spent the next four hours cleaning his apartment, and he upchucked only three times. Mrs Riggs was very kind. She gave him the vacuum cleaner, an apron, gloves, garbage bags, and liquid soap. The apartment looked clean, but somehow the smells had transferred themselves on Neeraj. And not just on his clothes, the smell seemed to have made a permanent impact on his brain. Neeraj was sure he would not be able to smell anything for the next few days. His bones were aching from so much physical work. He had taken at least ten trips to the dumper. The gloves were no good because the soap had seeped through and his hands had become red and wrinkled.

Mrs Riggs was beaming at him. He returned the cleaning equipment (she made him rinse the apron under the garden tap and hang it out to dry, so now his clothes were wet) to the closet next to Mr Riggs's office, and walked up to him.

'Aha! So you cleaned up the apartment!'
'Yes, Mr Riggs.'
'Sign here please. And here and here.'

Neeraj was so exhausted, he signed on the papers. Then he remembered about the money.

'What about my deposit?'

'After deducting the money for the use of the cleaning equipment from the apartment complex, there is nothing left to give you, Mr Shah. Thank you and goodbye.'

'What?'

'You had better leave now. Or I shall call the police.'

The weight of the sky suddenly made itself felt on Neeraj's shoulders. Too tired to argue with a man who had a baseball bat for company, he simply picked up his suitcase and walked away from the apartment. He should have known Riggs would not give his money back. He should've returned to Radhikaben's home. He pulled his car out of the driveway, and wondered what had happened at the house while he was gone.

***

Osmanbhai was so exhausted that he couldn't keep his eyes open no matter how hard he tried. The lights on the highway looked eerie, diffused in the cold air haze. But the taxi guy was a certified chor in his eyes. After what he did at the airport, Osmanbhai knew he had to stay awake, otherwise the taxi guy would dump him somewhere, take his money and run. So he decided to engage the taxi guy in conversation.

'So taxi bhai, where you are from?'

'What do you mean where? I am from Portland.'

'No, no. Where from in India?'

'Jaunpur. You know Jaunpur? But why you want to know?'

'To talk Hindi, why else?'

'If there's anything else, I have a gun to handle you. So don't step out of line?'

Osmanbhai's laughter filled the taxi and shook it. The mirrors on his clothes sparkled in the light reflected from the highway.

The taxi guy yelled, 'Oye! Stop laughing. See what you doing to the taxi!'

'I can do more to your taxi and you if you take me to dark place and try to dump me after stealing my money. I will make small-small pieces of you and throw you to dogs.'

'Why would I do something like that?'

'You think I am stupid or what? I see English movies.'

'That's why you ask where I live in India?'

'Not really. But if you try something like stealing from me, I shall go back to India and kill every person related to you and their relatives and their children.'

'You seeing too many movies, man! I like this job too much to do something like this. And how much money will you have anyway? Five? Ten thousand? If the police find out they will have me in jail so fast I would not be able to spend a dime. I am simply going to drop you to Winderly and that's that. I keep a gun for protection. So you don't try anything funny.'

'Okay.' The fight had gone out of Osmanbhai. He put his leg on the suitcase and promptly fell asleep.

It was twenty minutes before the taxi turned into Winderly. The taxi guy stopped by the gates and woke up his passenger. Osmanbhai was snoring. The taxi guy shook the man tentatively at first and then used a bit of force. His hand was caught in a grip so strong he thought he would never be able to use it again. He screamed. Osmanbhai had pulled him towards the back seat. Between Osmanbhai and the seatbelt, Osmanbhai won the battle and the skinny taxi guy was now lying on top of Osmanbhai with Osmanbhai's large hand around his neck, choking the life out him.

'Ack...Ack...Gag...Ack!'

Osmanbhai was pissed off at having been shaken awake. He realized that the cab had stopped.

'Kya kar raha tha be?' Then looking at the gagging cabbie, he asked in English, 'What you were doing? Shaking me like that?'

The taxi guy was near faint with pain and lack of air. But still he pointed to his neck. Osmanbhai understood. He let go. The man scrambled first for air. He gasped and gagged some more. Then he asked Osmanbhai, 'What you doing? I only wanted to know house number! Why you trying to kill me? We reached already.'

Osmanbhai looked as contrite as a big brute could. He extended his paw to backslap the skinny taxi guy to show him how sorry he was. The taxi guy winced in anticipation even before the paw touched him.

'311 oye. The number is 311. Sorry yaar. Galti se mistake ho gaya. Sote wakt bhi sab Osman se bach ke rehte hain.'

The taxi guy got out of the taxi and went around to the front again. '311 it is! You can be Osmanbhai or anyone. Boss, I am just going to drop you off and go home. God knows what side of bed I got out today. He shook his head and drove Osmanbhai in.

Osmanbhai stuffed an extra hundred into the taxi guy's pocket. Curious as to who was going to host the man mountain, the taxi guy remained at the door, soothing his neck.

It was Suraj who opened the door to Osmanbhai. Before Osmanbhai could say anything Suraj had come out of the house and was shushing him.

'Osmanbhai! I could never have imagined you in my entire life! But why are you dressed like this?'

It was windy and cold. Osmanbhai had begun to feel shivery. 'Kaun hai tu? How you know my name? Thand hai saali! Cold, cold, cold it is!'

Suraj looked at the taxi guy and said, 'Come in, both of you. But no noise!'

Whether it was the cold or just the surprise of finding a young boy who told him to be quiet, Osmanbhai meekly followed the boy in. The taxi guy looked at his watch. He ought to call it a day, but this was like a scene straight out of some masala Hindi movie. He couldn't resist accompanying the two.

He lugged the suitcase inside just in case someone asked him why he had come along too.

Osmanbhai turned around and looked at him but did not say anything. The boy gestured with his hand and asked the two to follow him up the stairs.

In the boy's room the taxi guy deposited the suitcase and sat down on the floor with the effort. Osmanbhai saw the duvet and wrapped himself in it. He was shivering uncontrollably now. Suraj looked at the two men. The one under the duvet was Osmanbhai. Who was the other guy?

'Who are you? His assistant?' Suraj asked.

The taxi guy's neck was aching a lot. He did not realize that stretching his neck back and then flopping it in front would be construed by the boy as an answer in the affirmative.

Suraj said, 'I'm going to get you tea and something to eat.' Turning to Osmanbhai he said, 'Chai,' and left the room.

Tea was not a bad idea, the taxi guy thought. What's another ten minutes. He could leave any time he wanted to. The warmth of the room was comforting. He was sitting on the floor, pleasantly drowsy. Osmanbhai was still shivering inside the comforter.

The boy was back. He had a thermos in one hand, and two cups in the other. He placed the thermos and cups carefully on the table and unzipped his jacket. He had managed to stuff three large packets of chips in the jacket. The taxi guy started to laugh but the boy stopped him. He hissed.

'Hushhhhh! I told you to keep quiet. Want some tea?'

The taxi guy nodded. Osmanbhai shook the whole bed when he nodded his affirmative as well. Suraj poured tea in two cups and handed one first to Osmanbhai. His hands were cold, so Suraj held on to the cup until Osmanbhai's large hands had held the cup properly. The taxi guy had torn the chips packet apart. Suraj gave him a cupful of masala tea and he accepted it gratefully. His mother used to make this masala tea. The taxi guy put his nose to the tea and took a deep breath. This was the true Indian tea with cloves and cardamoms and cinnamon and ginger, and that elusive...lemon grass.

'You made this?' The taxi guy took one deep sip and asked, full of admiration.

Osmanbhai had finished his cup and had extended it for more. Suraj complied, then offered Osman some chips. Osmanbhai grunted. The tea was warming him from inside. Suraj opened his closet and pulled out a big jacket. He kept it by Osmanbhai's side. He was still whispering, 'For you, Osmanbhai.'

Osmanbhai was cold and tired, but his brain was functioning. Especially because he knew nobody was kind without wanting something in return.

'Kya be? Kya chahiye?'

Suraj hushed Osmanbhai again.

Osmanbhai gritted his teeth and asked again, 'Now tell me who you? Where is Chimanbhai? Why do we need to keep silence?'

'I am Suraj. Chimanbhai is my father. We keep

quiet because everyone is sleeping. I told you, you cannot do the job. We have two Americans doing the job now. Why did you leave India and come here?'

The taxi guy understood this. The Americans were notorious for this. His dad had come to America when someone had promised him a job. When he came here, he was asked to do menial jobs in the house and then on the owner's California fruit farm. His brother and sister had died and his parents had escaped without their passports. After many hardships, the sisters of that big church had taken them in, and set their papers right. But he had ended up working his way up and now he was driving a taxi. Life had been tough, and even though Osmanbhai looked like he could take care of himself, someone ought to take his side.

'Oh, hello! This man does not know you gave his job to someone else. Why will he come all the way here?'

'Oye! You Angrez ki aulad. Why you speak so much English? Shut up. Suraj, you tell.'

'I told three days before, no? Don't come Osmanbhai I say to you, no?'

'Yes, but I must come to Amrika, I also tell you. So I come with dandiya troupe.'

'I understand, that's why I tell you to come in quietly. You stay here, no one can know. You can do the job. I don't think the Americans can do this. I want to show Maya didi and my mother that I am also something. I have good ideas, but they shoo me like a dog. Now Osmanbhai, you do the job. Then I show them who did it. Deal?'

'Deal.'

The taxi guy felt pleased. He did not know what this exchange meant. But something was turning out to be right for Osmanbhai even though he had almost killed him.

'I come pick you up tomorrow, okay? For the job?' the taxi guy asked.

'Yes, yes,' said Suraj. 'I will give Osmanbhai the address. You drive fast, no?'

'Yeah, I can drive fast, if it is required.'

'Oh good, now I will take you downstairs. Quiet, okay?'

Suraj led the taxi guy downstairs. Osmanbhai did not want to get out of the warmth of the comforter, but he had to. He wore the jacket and discovered that it fit him. Barely. He opened the door which he guessed was the bathroom, and used it. By the time Suraj came back up, Osmanbhai was eating from the bag of chips. They tasted weird. But the taste grew on him. It reminded him of burnt chicken.

Osmanbhai asked Suraj to pour a cup of tea for him.

'Why you didn't pour it yourself?'

'Arre. I am Osmanbhai. People do things for me. I kill for them. Chai you pour. I kill.'

'You'll kill for me?'

'Why not? I am here. You father has Angrez godfathers to do the job...'

'Godfathers?' Suraj started laughing, and then

stifled his laughter. 'You should see them! Those two people have been forced by the government, that's why Puppa is stuck with them. But they are idiots. They will not be able to kill anything.'

'Government forced your puppa to hire godfathers? I don't understand.'

'It's too complicated. Not to worry. You just do the killing. I will help you. See I have many many ideas.'

Over the next hour Suraj had shown him all kinds of murder plans—from the most bizarre (skinning victim slowly or hacking off limbs and holding victim in a box with air holes) to the simple (blowing them up by sticking a stick of dynamite to the victim or a single gunshot to the temple). Osmanbhai was amazed at the computer. He had wrecked many, but did not know they contained such interesting information. He was amazed at the boy. He could not but pat the boy every five minutes to tell him how brilliant he was. Suraj was glad to have such an avid student who thought he was the best. Osmanbhai's exhaustion had vanished the moment he saw bombs and dynamite and various ways of killing people. All these days he had just used his strength, and thought it was the cleanest way to kill. But blowing up people? That he thought was a great idea!

'Suraj bhai! You toh have opened my eyes! Amrika is truly great country! I am now convinced I am in the right place!'

Suraj yawned, nodding his head in agreement.

Osmanbhai yawned too when he saw Suraj yawn.

'Osmanbhai, I think we should sleep. I don't have school tomorrow, but we cannot let anyone know you are here. Can you stay quietly in the room without anyone knowing?'

'No problem! I hide from police many times. But you will bring me something proper to eat? Chips is not food,' said Osmanbhai.

'Haan, of course! Nobody will suspect anything since I always bring food upstairs and eat. So not to worry. Let's sleep now. We plan the murder tomorrow morning,' replied Suraj.

And before Suraj could say camp bed, Osmanbhai had fallen across Suraj's bed and was out like a light. Suraj stared at the man and knew he would have to sleep on the lounger. He pulled the comforter and a pillow from the bed and stretched out on the lounger. Then he remembered that he would need to lock his bedroom door. He got up, locked the door and lay back down on the lounger, watching Osmanbhai. For the first time in his life, someone had looked up to him, listened to him, and patted his back. Content, Suraj fell asleep.

***

Suraj's body clock worked for once. He was downstairs with the flask before Maya came knocking at his door. He locked the sleeping giant inside. Radhika had woken up with a headache. She had more than one thing to worry about today. Her heart was broken. By her husband. So many years together and he made her feel like second best. What all she had done for him! Brought up the children almost single handedly, run the house, even helped with the business sometimes...

But some things were even more important. She needed to check the newspaper to see if anyone had seen Maya's car or the two idiots at the scene. Then there was Dr Patel's funeral. She really did not have the strength today to face anyone. In fact, she dreaded going to the funeral because she knew how he had died. She had never liked Bimla Patel either, who was always showing off the expensive dragon's egg amethyst crystal. But that was besides the point. She felt she was indirectly responsible for the man's death. Radhika made chai with a heavy heart. When she saw Neeraj coming down, looking even worse than she felt, she felt sad. She did not like Neeraj much, but he had helped them so much over the last few weeks. And see, now he had lost not only his job but his apartment too. All because he was helping her.

'Neeraj beta, how are you? Today I make the khandvi for you. Your favourite, ne?'

Neeraj was dying for a smoke. He didn't care about khandvi. He wanted bacon and a smoke. He wanted coffee and a smoke. He wanted those titties and a smoke. Titties? Did he just say titties aloud? He opened his eyes. Radhikaben had not heard him say that. It was Maya. She was making a hole in his brain. He should have offered to kill Supriya himself. Then maybe he would be the one in Maya's room. He wanted to tell Radhika that Maya and Elmore...

'Good morning!' Suraj chirped. 'Neerajbhai, how've you been? What an awesome day! Mummy! I am so hungry. What have you made?'

'Awesome day?' Radhikaben was irritated. 'Go away, Suraj. Don't eat my head. Take khandvi and go up to your room.'

'I'm taking some Cheerios and one apple also, Ma.'

Maya had come down to see Suraj collecting all the food. 'You going to hole up in your room and plan to blow up the whole world, eh?'

'Yes, so?' her brother replied, filling the thermos with tea.

'I'm going to come in and tear up all your plans.'

'If you come up I will smear skunk gunk on you. Remember the last time?'

'Mommm! Suraj has got skunk gunk in his room. Last time he sprayed it I got such a bad rash! You must ground him!'

'Look, Maya, my head is aching like hell. He's already going up to his room. We are not going to see him. Just make me some fresh tea and then boil some eggs for those two...' Radhikaben sat down in her favourite place by the gods.

Chimanbhai came downstairs when Radhika was drinking her second cup. He looked fresh and bathed and was dressed in all white. Radhika saw this and wailed, 'Chimannn! Why you are dressed in white?'

'We have to go to Dr Patel's funeral, ne?'

'No, no! You cannot go. What if you started crying there and told them everything? We cannot risk that.'

'Why should I tell them that Elmore shot the gun that you bought from the gun store in Tigard?'

'See! This is what I am afraid of. You will tell and then say how did I say anything. No, no! I am going with the ladies and that is final.'

'If they ask for me?'

'Chiman, trust me, nobody will ask where you are. It will not be a party, ne, that people will ask your khabar. If they do I shall tell them you are not well.'

'I am sick of being called sick all the time. You say I am sick then people ask me how I am and then when I say I am fine, then you tell people I am sick. How can one man be sick all the time?'

'Please, Chiman, please listen to me. You can be man of the house in charge of the two Americans. With Neeraj and the two men you can look after the store so if the cops come looking for Maya's car, they see you working as usual.'

Chiman said nothing but his lips were quivering. Nothing was going right. The woman was still alive, and their plans were failing. He sat down and poured tea into the saucer and began to drink. But the tears decided to spill at the same time the saucer reached his lips. The saucer shook and he dropped tea on his pristine white kurta.

Radhika and Maya both leaped towards him, saw the tears, and reacted at the same time.

'Puppa! Don't cry, I can get the stains off your kurta. Just change it quickly and give it to me.'

'Ei Chiman! Why you cry like baby? Kurta can be washed, ne? I made khandvi. Change, change... Maya will fix it.'

Chimanbhai said nothing. Through his tears the khandvi looked like a wet roll of paper. Probably tasted like it too. He pulled off his kurta and threw it at Maya. Maya caught it and held it under the sink. Chimanbhai pulled the plate of cut fruit that Maya ate and sprinkled chaat masala on it. Maya looked as if she was about to say something but she stopped. Chimanbhai continued to eat in silence. Neeraj escaped for a smoke outside but Radhika had noticed.

'Neeraj!'

'I'm trying hard to quit!' Neeraj sighed.

SEVENTEEN

Osmanbhai woke up to a familiar smell. When he was on a job, he was used to hiding out in all kinds of places. Sometimes the stakeouts would be cramped, other times not. Strange, unfamiliar places did not bother him. He wasn't disoriented for a minute. Only when he saw Suraj did the enormity of where he was sink in.

'I in Amrika!' he said.

'Say Ame-rika,' Suraj corrected. 'Osmanbhai, quiet rehna, please?'

Osmanbhai said, 'Yus, yus! Very quiet. You can get chai?'

'Chai is here and mom made khandvi. Chalega?'

'Waah! Ab thodi tatti ho jaaye. After that I am set to eat.'

Suraj made a face at the mention of the word tatti. Why did people from India always talk about crapping just when food was mentioned? Suraj remembered how Jignesh mama and Sailesbhai had come from Surat to buy costume jewellery and had stayed with them. They would fart at the dining table and laugh, joke about constipation after eating so much bread. Suraj had hated them. And now Osmanbhai too was casually mentioning tatti.

Thankfully Osmanbhai did not add anything more but shut the door behind him when he went to the restroom. Suraj munched on the apple and Cheerios. He hated milk in his cereal. Mumma and Puppa always heated the milk and it smelled funny when heated. He had received so many emails about his query on homemade explosives and bomb making that Suraj forgot to think about the strange sounds coming from the restroom.

Osmanbhai came out sans clothes, freshly showered, shivering again, with only a hand towel covering his vulnerables. Suraj started laughing.

'Why you laughing? How you wash, chootiye! Shower karna pada, na! Soap also you not have.'

Suraj stopped short. 'Soap? Hai na! But it is in the bottle.'

'Water very cold, saale.'

'There's hot water also. Come I'll show you.'

Smothering a giggle, Suraj showed Osmanbhai the hot and cold shower, the liquid soap, and the sponge. Then he handed Osmanbhai a big beach towel to use. Suraj then put the khandvi near his CPU to keep it warm.

Minutes later, Osmanbhai emerged complaining about the smell of Pinesol. 'Good soap, good soap!'

Suraj started to object but stopped short. Osmanbhai's armpits needed nothing less than Pinesol. He handed Osmanbhai the plate of khandvi, poured him a cup of tea, and watched him eat. He put more Cheerios on a sheet of paper and began to eat them one by one. Osmanbhai polished off all the khandvi, and drank two cups of tea. He looked beseechingly at Suraj.

'I am hungry,' Osmanbhai said.

Suraj looked at the watch. Puppa would be leaving home soon. Elmore and Dean would go with him. His mother and Maya would go to the funeral. Neeraj should be gone too. That would leave Osmanbhai and Suraj alone.

'Osmanbhai, everyone would be gone soon. Can you wait please? I will make not one but two cup noodles for you.'

'Noodles? Apun ko pizza, burger mangta. Amrika is famous for burger, pizza, no?'

'For that you need money. I'm all out. In fact I maxed Mom's credit card to get materials to make bombs at home.'

'Money? Not to worry. I have lots of money. Full in suitcase. Two dandiya clothes but full money. Amriki dollars that my friends gave me. How much you want?'

Suraj was stunned. He was wondering why the man had not worn any clothes when he had lugged a suitcase. The suitcase had money! He could not believe his eyes when he saw so many hundred-dollar bills neatly packed in.

'What you thinking, boy?' Osmanbhai asked. 'How much for one pizza?'

'You can buy the whole shop for this kind of money.' Suraj stopped himself from whooping. 'You have so much money, then why did you need Puppa to bring you to America?'

'Money is easy to get. But I want to become famous. Like Godfather. This money was given to me by people who love me. I just called them, and said, give, so they gave. So money is easy. It's ijjat, fame. That is important. I have come to become baap of all godfathers. Baap!'

Suraj stared at this vision of baap of all godfathers wrapped in an Ariel the Mermaid towel.

'You order pizza first. I can't think on empty stomach,' said Osmanbhai.

Suraj whipped out menus from the pizza chains and spread them out in front of Osmanbhai.

'Which pizza is fastest?'

'Fast pizza means everyone at home will know. Let me check if everyone will be gone in twenty minutes. You can have some cookies until then.'

Suraj decided to take the breakfast plate, but if Maya saw him she would wonder why he was cleaning his room, so he let the plate be. If Mummy caught him downstairs, he would make himself a sandwich, or go to the fridge and get some theplas. Maybe he could take some money from Osmanbhai and order some things that would help him assemble a real bomb.

Everything was quiet at home. Neeraj's car was gone. So was Chimanbhai's. Which meant Elmore and

Dean would be gone too. Just then he saw Maya and Mummy watching TV with the sound off.

He tried to sound casual. 'Ma, I'm making a sandwich, okay?'

When the two did not say anything, he asked, 'Ma, what are you watching?'

He saw that the two of them were watching news reports of Dr Patel's death. It was still top news on Portland's four local stations. Before Radhika opened her mouth to scold Suraj, there was a honk in the driveway.

Maya switched the TV off and put her finger to her mouth glaring at Suraj. The doorbell rang and Radhika let Mrs Mehta in.

'Radhika, sorry hain. I wanted to use the restroom before we reached the funeral. Doesn't look nice, ne, going first to restroom before we even sit down and express how sad we are.' Mrs Mehta dropped her handbag on the Lazyboy and hurried towards the restroom. She had visited the Shah house so many times that she knew she did not have to be formal with Radhikaben.

'Okay, okay!' and 'Yes, yes' is all Radhika could say.

Maya rolled her eyes as soon as Mrs Mehta went in.

'Suraj!' Radhika exclaimed. He was getting to be quite a little sneak, she thought. She had not noticed him at all. 'We are going to Dr Patel's funeral. It will take long. But I will be back for dinner. Just make some noodles for yourself. Or eat some theplas for lunch. Okay?'

Suraj just nodded. He did not want to spoil anything by smiling although he wanted to, badly.

***

Even though the house was quiet and devoid of people, Suraj did not let Osmanbhai out of his room. Osmanbhai was happy to lounge around in Suraj's room in nothing more than a towel. He gobbled a large pepperoni pizza, a medium four-cheese one in ten minutes. Suraj was happy to have one whole medium Hawaiian to himself. He wondered if he should save the pizza for later, but the thought of being discovered with Osmanbhai made him finish it. He felt greedy and full and sleepy. It was only when Suraj saw that Osmanbhai had fallen asleep on his bed (again!) with a pizza slice cheese side down on his hairy chest, that he felt the need to clean up a bit. He walked out of the house with the pizza boxes flattened and neatly wrapped to Sonny's house. Everyone went to work and hardly ever had any garbage. He quickly dumped the pizza boxes in their bin and walked back as nonchalantly as he could.

As soon as he entered the house, Suraj heard Osmanbhai snoring. He ran up the steps, thanking his stars that no one was home. He shut the door behind him. The room smelled of Pinesol and pizza. Since it was not drizzling outside, he opened the windows and let some fresh air in. He then gathered some clothes and showered, all the while thinking how he was going to ask Osmanbhai for money to make a bomb, or just buy a cool gun off eBay to kill the girl. When he emerged from the shower, the room began to smell of Pinesol, pizza, and bubblegum soap.

He trawled the Net for a cheap gun, but there were too many restrictions and he did not want to get noticed. The cops were forever ambushing unsuspecting people if they tried to buy any gun. He dare not call his super geek friend Joe and ask either. Joe would want to be a part of this adventure with a real live supari killer and Suraj wanted to be the toast of the family all alone, without anyone else's help.

It was afternoon when he heard Neeraj come in and walk up the stairs cursing. He banged on Suraj's door.

'Suraj! I want to use the Internet. Please let me in.'

'I'm downloading something. I cannot let you in. Go to Maya didi's computer. She's not here.'

There was no answer but it felt like Neeraj had walked off in a huff.

If everyone was going to come home one by one, Osmanbhai would surely be caught. Suraj called the taxi guy. The taxi guy was driving someone to Council Crest. He would take at least an hour to get here. Suraj told him to park the taxi by Sonny's house and walk.

Osmanbhai was ready for more tea when he woke

up. Suraj knew how to make tea with teabags in the microwave. It was not perfect but Osmanbhai liked it.

Suraj showed him a small PowerPoint presentation he had made while Osmanbhai was sleeping. It started with a picture of Supriya with a caption: The Enemy Chick.

Next was a slide of a sleeping Osmanbhai which had a caption: The Super Killer.

'I meant to write Supari, but...,' Suraj explained.

Osmanbhai swelled up with pride visibly. He didn't mind the title. He saw it as a sign of good times.

The third slide was that of the cab and the address of Supriya's home.

The fourth, fifth, sixth, and the other thirty slides were ideas on how to mutilate, sever, poison, blow up, asphyxiate, electrocute, drown, hang, garrotte, shoot dead, bake, freeze Supriya to death.

'Back, back, back!' Osmanbhai said.

Suraj looked at him thoroughly puzzled.

'Bake! You said bake? Like bread? Like cake? Who kills people by baking them?'

'You just put her in the oven, put the timer for three hours and she'll be toast!'

'Waah! Kya idea hai! Oi boy! I am not going to take some living person and put them in oven. I am not some bakerywala. I am Osmanbhai. I kill face to face. Not make people tandoori.'

Suraj winced. He was a loud man, this Osmanbhai. Neeraj would not have heard him, or did he?

'Arre Osmanbhai, these are just ideas. You don't get angry with me, okay. I gave you choice. That's all.'

'I give you one more choice: I will kill her with these two hands.'

Osmanbhai's eyes glazed. He wondered if he should wring her neck, or simply choke the life out of her. But Suraj did not give up.

'What if she has pepper spray?'

Before Osmanbhai could ask him what pepper spray was, his phone rang. The taxi guy! Osmanbhai scrambled to wear his clothes. There was no option but to wear the dandiya clothes. The stupid man had nothing else. Osmanbhai wore Suraj's jacket over the shiny dandiya clothes. He was ready to make his first kill in America.

Suraj was thankful for the interruption. He put his finger to his lips to shush Osmanbhai, bowed down to him to apologize and stepped out of his room. He peeped into Maya's room. Neeraj was at the computer with headphones over his ears. He would not notice or hear anything. Suraj tiptoed back to his room.

'Osmanbhai, the coast is clear. Let's go.'

Osman flexed his muscles, cracked his knuckles, and nodded. The two tiptoed downstairs and were out of the house in two minutes. Osman's dhoti and shirt flashed a thousand mirrors and Suraj hoped no one noticed them walking out. The taxi was parked by Sonny's house. Osmanbhai sat down at the back. Suraj handed a sheet with Supriya's address printed neatly.

'Where is his bag?' the taxi guy asked.

'Why you need to know? In time of work don't get in the way. Otherwise I will kill you also and her also.'

'Heyyyy dandiya! What you gonna kill with? Dandiya sticks? I have a gun, you fucker! Don't try anything funny with me.'

Suraj was stunned by their conversation. The taxi guy had a gun.

'You have a gun? Fantastic!' Suraj gave a little whoop of happiness. 'You really have a gun?'

The taxi guy was now confused.

'Why are you happy that I have a gun?'

Suraj was unstoppable. 'And bullets?'

The taxi guy answered, 'Of course it has bullets. Not much good without it, no?'

Osmanbhai was grinning like a wolf.

'Drive me to the gate.' Suraj was beginning to enjoy the way things were turning out.

He begged the taxi guy to allow Osmanbhai to use his gun. The taxi guy would not agree. He stopped the taxi at the gates and asked Suraj to get off.

'See, that gun is for my protection,' he told Suraj, 'not for some one-time use.'

Osmanbhai looked at Suraj and raised his palm up in a classic gesture of wait, stop.

'Arre Surajbhai, gun is for his use. My hands are good enough in India, and they are good enough for Amrika. Why you asking and begging? We not bhikhari, you know. No begging. I will manage.' Then looking at the taxi guy Osmanbhai asked, 'You take me to the address and bring me back here, okay?'

The taxi guy was not above making some more money. 'It will cost you a hundred dollars more.'

Osmanbhai looked at the greedy little weasel, and nodded. 'Yes, okay. Hundred.'

Suraj asked the taxi guy, 'You will call me from your phone when you come close to home?'

The taxi guy nodded, then pulled away from Winderly. Suraj walked home, pleased that he was the one who would save his family from ruin. All he had to do now, was to wait for the phone call from the taxi guy who would bring Osmanbhai back. Finally it was his turn to shine.

***

Saala this foreign country is very pretty, so clean. That's why all the peoples want to come here. The road had no potholes, the houses were neat and clean. Not like the Mumbai chawls. Saala itne log ki taking saans becomes difficult. Free clean air in Mumbai was only for rich people who lived in tall buildings. The taxi guy was driving so nicely. Saala no khitkhit, no asking what road to take. Address bataya, and he taking.

Osmanbhai liked the houses. Ekdum picture maafik. Picture mein kaise foreign mein jaakar hero and heroine sing songs, bilkul waise-ich. Chhota ghar, jhopdi ka maafik Angrez "A" wala chhat, bole toh roof, lekin style wala roof. Ghar ke saamne garden, aur har ghar ke darwaje ke saamne car. Foreign was good. Everyone had cars. Osmanbhai could picture himself in a Mercedes. Maybe he get driver also, eh? Idea was great.

Supriya's car was not in the driveway when the taxi reached the house. Osman asked the taxi to be parked right across the street. It was dark now. She should be getting home soon. People were returning home one by one. They waited for Supriya to come. Osmanbhai was used to waiting.

It felt like an eternity waiting across the street. The taxi guy had become fidgety waiting. And Osmanbhai had fallen asleep at the back. The pizzas were making a mockery of his digestive system. He had already farted more times than the taxi guy cared to count. The taxi guy had forgotten what had happened to him the last time he tried to wake Osmanbhai so he gingerly poked Osmanbhai.

Osmanbhai woke with a start, suddenly realizing that he was there to kill Supriya. And before the taxi guy could apologize for having startled the man mountain into waking up, he felt two hands choke every last ounce of air inside his lungs. The seatbelt gave him no space to struggle. When he twitched no more, Osmanbhai sighed. He opened the passenger-side door and stepped out. After reaching out through the window on the driver's side where the man was slumped dead, he reached into the glove compartment and took the gun. Then he went back to the passenger side of the taxi and sat down with the gun. This was his vigil.

When a car pulled into Supriya's driveway and a long-legged shadow walked towards the porch light, Osmanbhai sprang into action. He stepped out of the taxi and rushed towards the house across the street with a heart-stopping yell, aiming the gun at the shadow in the driveway.

At the very same time something large whizzed past behind him from right to left, taking the door of the taxi with it. Osmanbhai crossed the yellow line separating the north–south lanes still yelling at the frozen shadow when something equally large came from nowhere. Actually, came from his left and thwacked against his body. Osmanbhai was flung several feet in the air and landed on earth on the driveway, his head smashed against the kerb like a tender coconut.

The large SUV that bumped into the thousand glittering stars screeched to a halt, the man inside shocked at the object that looked like a swarm of fireflies from afar had turned out to be a person.

The shadow was now screaming hysterically.

The screams brought many neighbours into the street. When they discovered another dead man in Supriya's driveway, they called 911.

EIGHTEEN

Radhika had come back from Dr Patel's funeral quite shaken. She sat at the dining table furiously chopping vegetables and drinking chai. And Maya was subdued too. The cops were present at the funeral and they had casually asked everyone questions and had caught Maya and asked her if the good doctor was given to treating young women differently. Maya thankfully did not know the doctor, so she had escaped by saying she was there to be a support to her mother who knew Mrs Patel very well.

Radhika was giving Maya instructions on seasoning the spinach and daal curry. Chimanbhai had come back home with Elmore and Dean. The two had helped dust the entire store down and were cleaning up. Neeraj had carried a tray of tea and biscuits to Chimanbhai, and they were both watching TV. Chimanbhai was now obsessed with the progress of Dr Patel's story on TV. It had been relegated to one of the last mentions on the news stations already, but Chimanbhai was watching it fervently, hoping that they would not have unearthed Maya's car at the crime scene, zooming off right after

Dr Patel collapsed on his car. Just as the mustard seeds began popping in the hot oil, Radhika and Maya heard Chimanbhai scream.

He screamed so loudly that Radhika dropped the knife with a clatter on the floor, and Maya shrieked in reply. The oil for the seasoning spattered all over the floor. Both the women ran to where Chimanbhai was.

Suraj had also come downstairs hoping he would be able to announce his feat. He too was staring at the TV transfixed.

'Have you lost your mind, Chiman! How loudly you screamed! I almost died of fright,' Radhika complained.

Chimanbhai looked at Radhika, then pointed to the TV.

'What is it?' Maya asked.

Neeraj looked so shell, shocked that he too, like Chimanbhai, was visibly shaking with fright.

It was Suraj who pointed to the man they were showing on TV.

'Osmanbhai,' Suraj was saying.

'Osmanbhai?' All the tension in Radhika's head exploded in that one single question. 'Suraj! When will you stop making up stories? Go to your room!'

Suraj just stood there, his hands crossed, a mutinous expression on his face, furious at his mother and with life that was so unfair to him. But before he could tell all about Osmanbhai, he wanted to figure out what could have happened between the taxi guy and Osmanbhai. Where was the taxi guy? Why hadn't he called?

Elmore and Dean walked in to find everyone riveted to the TV. Supriya was incoherent, hysterical almost and the policemen were shooing the TV crew away. The anchor wanted his three minutes of fame, and was spinning yarns about South East Asian mafia wars in Hong Kong and how they were spilling over into San Francisco. Another channel that caught the story late was spinning the story quite differently. They had taken one look at Osmanbhai's clothes and had done a quick research on practitioners of witchcraft, Eastern witchcraft, and had inadvertently touched on the exchanging of betelnuts as a sign of contract in witchery ritual.

Unfortunately, a betelnut had spilled out of Osmanbhai's pocket when the forensic team had started their work. The nut gave the witchcraft story so much credibility that the second murder was relegated to an 'also found'. 'The man came out of nowhere, yelling something, waving a gun, and I turned around to see. Before I could scream, "Gun!" the man was sailing through the air and had landed on my driveway, dead!' Supriya in her statement had said. The police were so busy cordoning off Osmanbhai's body that the media had had a field day with the dead guy in the taxi. At first everyone thought he was asleep, but when a policeman knocked on his window to tell him to move along, that's when they noticed the missing door and the lifeless taxi guy.

The taxi guy looked as though life had been squeezed out of him. Something went hiss inside Suraj. Why had Osmanbhai killed the taxi guy? The police would find the paper with their telephone numbers and Supriya's address, for sure. Suraj knew Osmanbhai had stuck the paper in the inside front pocket of the jacket Suraj had loaned him. What then?

It was Maya who recovered first. She went back to the first channel. She knew they would speak with the police and be a little more logical than the one that sensationalized witchcraft and made a hit-and-run in front of Supriya's home seem like some conspiracy and coincidence that pointed to something more sinister...like a conspiracy to kill the Indian girl.

The TV channel had already moved on from the police investigation to a little probe on their own. They had googled Osmanbhai's outfit and had come to three possible conclusions. Either the dead guy was a Bolivian Morena dancer, or someone out for a costume party and was dressed in a flamenco costume, or he was a folk dancer from India. The question everyone was asking was, why did he choose to die in front of Supriya's house?

'He came out of nowhere,' the man who was driving the blue Nissan Sentra said. 'I thought they were a bunch of fireflies, and I did not think of slowing down. I admit I was a little drunk and may have been driving a little over the required thirty-five, but I am not a murderer. It was a mistake.'

The driver was arrested soon after this passionate confession on camera. The news then moved to Governor Kitzhaber's cat's birthday celebrations, Tonya Harding's bake sale, and other current affairs.

The Shah family returned to the dining table. It was not that the food was bad. Or that they were not hungry. It was just one thing that was swirling in the bowl like the spinach in the daal. Or was it the other way round? Who was the guy? Was he really out to get Supriya? Or was it a coincidence?

'I think you should kill her tonight. The cops would have all gone.' Radhika had finished her daal, and was demolishing the papad.

'What if she is spending the night at a friend's?' Dean said hopefully.

'I will drive you, Elmore, Dean is chicken,' Maya challenged.

'You going to drive your car, ne? You think you so smart? Waaidi chhe, Maya!'

Dean tried to reason. 'What if we kidnapped her?'

'You'd like that, wouldn't you? And where would we keep her? Here?' Elmore asked.

'And what would you feed her?' Maya added.

'Even if we get her here in the basement, it would be no good. The store cannot be ours unless she is dead.' Radhika was breaking a papad with a vengeance.

'Maybe we should sell the store to Supriya and

move back to India.' Chimanbhai was considering yet another option.

Radhika snarled only as a tigress would in a Nat Geo special. She wiggled her finger angrily at Chimanbhai, breathing hard so as to keep herself from throwing things at her husband.

'You...you...you, I...I know why you want to go back to India. That Meenakshi! She's what you are thinking about. I won't have it. I'm telling you. We won't go back!'

Chimanbhai pulled up his legs and put his hands to his ears, and started rocking himself. Nobody remembered Suraj. Not Chimanbhai. Not Radhika. Not even Maya. And definitely not the two guys at the table.

***

The neighbourhood was floodlit. The forensic team didn't look anything like they showed on TV. They were boring men plodding through every inch of the area surrounding Supriya's house. And they were eating doughnuts. The neighbours had been asked to stay indoors for fear of contaminating the crime scene. The team was confused by the strong smell of Pinesol that was emanating from the dead man. That and bubblegum soap. The forensic team found a folded sheet of paper in the pocket of the funny jacket the man was wearing under a cheap flannel-lined jacket that was so popular at Target last year. One of the detectives confirmed the price at $19.95 but they were foxed by a roll of banknotes in the inside pocket. Why would someone who had so much cash choose to be so badly dressed for the weather? The strange folded cotton trousers were completely inappropriate for the temperature. Nor did the shirt offer any resistance from the cold winds that blew across the state at that time of the year. The folded piece of paper had several telephone numbers and two addresses. One was written in a bizarre code and another was written in English. The address written in English was that of the hysterical Indian lady's house. Obviously there was a connection.

When a police officer rang the doorbell of Supriya's house, they were relieved to see a less hysterical person. In fact, she seemed like a different person. Supriya's forehead crinkled to see the lights and the dead body still outside her house but she let the officer come into the house.

The officer did not sit down, but sniffed. The air had a distinct smell of Pinesol. His eyes narrowed. But before he could ask, he saw the bucket and gloves. Supriya explained. 'When I am upset, I tend to clean up, OCD you know.'

The officer didn't care for explanations. He asked, 'You sure, miss, you don't know the man?'

'Never seen him in my life!' Supriya was quick in her denial.

Too quick, thought the officer.

'Then why does he have your address in your pocket?'

He allowed Supriya to look at the paper now encased in a ziplock bag.

Supriya looked at the paper. 'Yes, that's my address all right, the one written in English. But I don't recognize the first one. It's written in Hindi, and my Hindi is not good at all. And I don't recognize any of the cellphone numbers listed on the paper either.'

She was lying. The officer knew that. She was not looking at him directly. The officer grunted a non-committal 'Hmm'.

'Don't worry, ma'am, we have officers trained to read languages. We'll find out soon enough.'

Supriya quietly noted the address written in Hindi on her notepad in English. The officer who had left the house noted that the girl was writing from the open window.

The forensic team wrapped up their work quite late. The body of the taxi guy was easier to identify. The taxi network worked within strict rules. All cabbies had a state licence and were easy to trace. His papers seemed to be in order, but there was no record of him taking a legit passenger. Obviously this was personal business or simply greed. Two deputies with language skills were sent to his home to figure out if the dead guy across the road was related to him. The gun was registered to the taxi guy, but the bullets found in the gun were all blanks. If the dead guy was rushing across the street to kill the woman of that house, he would have been surprised to see her alive. Perhaps the taxi guy had lost his life over the gun. The police hoped the damned thing didn't get complicated.

Meanwhile, Theophilius Callaghan, the man who hit the swarm of fireflies turned out to be a God-fearing man who went to church every Sunday. He was so shook up that his wife had to take him to the priest for counselling. The deputy who accompanied him to the church had been witness to such great lament and remorse from the man that he had come back to the precinct with a yen to murdering anyone who laughed at his predicament.

Reverend Philip and his wife Maria Theresa accompanied the man with the deputy to the station. Just taking down Mr Callaghan's personal details was a headache-inducing effort. Every other minute the man in custody invoked the Lord's name in prayer and contrition, in a voice loud enough to reach the heavens themselves that there were sniggers all over the precinct.

'Lord! Forgive me, Lord! The fireflies are your creation. I should have stopped to admire their beauty, Lord!' The man fell down on his knees.

The deputy sighed again. This time he did not get around the table to help the man.

'Mr Callaghan, please get up and sit down on the chair. You can pray later.'

'Oh Lord! I am already surrounded by the minions of Beelzebub! Save me, Lord! I did not see the man, but I beseech you, look after me, look after me!'

The captain who happened to pass the deputy took

pity. He walked to the reverend. The reverend gave personal guarantee that neither Mr Callaghan nor his wonderful wife would leave town. The captain explained that they would need to keep the car and called the judge who expedited the bail proceedings in this accident case.

***

Morning came too late for Chimanbhai. He had spent a sleepless night, and had quietly showered at 5 am and was now standing in front of the altar of the gods by the dining table. His eyes were brimming with unshed tears and the result of a restless night. Chimanbhai lit the lamp and joined his hands in prayer.

'Hey, Ambe Ma! I need you more than ever in my life right now...give me strength, Ma!'

He listened. Was he loud? Did someone wake up? Chimanbhai could hear nothing except the beating of his heart. He looked at the goddess that was riding a tiger. He was not a god, and maybe he was not riding any tiger, but he certainly felt that he had grabbed hold of the tail of one. And this tiger sometimes looked like Radhika, sometimes the immigration officer and Elmorebhai and Deanbhai, sometimes the unknown, unseen Osmanbhai, and at other times Supriya. He shuddered. Then he remembered how doing kapaalbhati would drive all kinds of fears away and make him strong. Did he remember the sequence of pranayam? It had been ages since he had even sat down to watch his breath. Guruji would be so disappointed in him. He began to cry.

'Ma! I am so sorry! I will be a good son to you. I will start doing pranayam now. Forgive me, Guruji! Forgive me, Ma! Give me strength.'

Chimanbhai pulled a cushion from the chair and sat down for pranayam. First he knelt. Then he sat down on his butt. A searing ache ran down his ankles. This pain he remembered. What he did not remember were the breathing exercises, the pranayam. He uncrossed his legs and began to count slowly. The pranayam would come.

And then it happened. He remembered! He heaved a sigh of relief. He sat down once again in the... what was that again? Oh yes, the vajrasana. And he then did the anulom, vilom, the alternate nostril breathing and slowly, the fog from his brain lifted. He remembered how to do the kapaalbhati also known as the bellows breathing—whoosh, hiss, whoosh, hiss, whoosh, hiss. His breath came out with such a force that it could have launched him forward. But it didn't, because his legs were tucked in and all the blood had stopped flowing to his ageing ankles. He did the kapaalbhatis in all earnestness, because this was his prayer and he had better pray with his eyes closed to everything around him except the task of breathing.

It was a good thing that Chimanbhai was all twisted like a pretzel and his eyes were closed. Otherwise he would have seen Elmore coming stealthily down the steps from Maya's room.

At first Elmore was stunned to see Chimanbhai up so early, praying to the gods. He waited by the steps, holding his breath. Then he saw Chimanbhai sitting down and breathing in the weirdest manner. For a minute Elmore thought Chimanbhai had noticed him and was about to scream blue murder and rape. He also knew that if Chimanbhai screamed rape, Maya would not take his side, but say outrageous things just to annoy her father even further. The thought of Maya and her honeyed skin made Elmore sigh.

Chimanbhai heard a sigh. He stopped mid-breathing out. Did he really hear a sigh? Was someone there? Elmore could not breathe. He did not have an excuse to be inside the house so early. He did not want to hear Chimanbhai scream if he discovered Elmore skulking on the staircase.

Fortunately for Elmore, Chimanbhai was not used to so much exercise so early in the morning. His eyes began to droop as he waited with bated breath for the sigh to repeat itself. He decided to investigate, but the hurried unscrambling from vajrasana was disastrous. Chimanbhai felt a vicious attack of pins and needles in his legs with the blood rushing suddenly all over his legs. He yelped, and hobbled to the nearest Lazyboy and closed his eyes for just a minute.

When he opened his eyes, the house was bustling around him. Maya was cutting fruit as though she was making fruit salad for the whole neighbourhood. She looked like she had had a wrestling match with her cat. She was scratched and bruised on her neck. Chimanbhai rubbed his eyes, and then remembered the early morning tryst with the goddess. He felt a surge of strength from that knowledge alone. He walked towards Maya.

'Why do you allow that stupid cat to scratch you so much? Go put some ice on it or Kailas Jeevan. That cures everything.'

'Eww, Dad! Kailas Jeevan smells like hell.'

'You children! You know nothing! Kailas Jeevan is ancient remedy! But you children, staying in America has spoilt you. No values at all.'

Just then Radhika's scream came down the stairs, 'Suraaaaaaj! Feed Caligula!'

Chimanbhai hated the cat. Maya would earn many bad points in the big register of bad deeds because she named a cat after Goddess Kali. Maya looked at her father and anticipated the reprimand.

'Dad, Caligula was a Roman emperor. How can I name a tomcat after a goddess? He's a boy cat, Dad!'

Before the second scream made it downstairs, Suraj was at the microwave, warming the milk for the cat.

'Moron! You set it to "high" setting. Now Cali will have to wait,' Maya yelled at Suraj.

Suraj ignored his sister. 'Dad, Mom has turned your bedroom upside down. What is she searching for?'

It took a while before Suraj's words filtered through Chimanbhai's brain. When they did, they still did not make sense. What was Radhika searching for? He debated with himself. If he went upstairs and discovered that Radhika was looking for some odd earring that she wanted to wear right then, he would end up searching through miles of sarees for some bauble. But if he didn't go up to help (even when she hadn't called everyone for help), he would be the only one listening to her complaints afterwards. Chimanbhai sighed and went upstairs to find out.

***

Radhika looked fierce when determined. And oh yes, she was looking for evidence. Evidence to throw at Chimanbhai! All these years of living within a budget, and he was…cheating on her! Chimanbhai entered the room and as he was wont to do, almost offered help. But when he saw that it was *his* closet that was turned inside out, not hers, he was shocked.

'Whaa…Radhika? What are you doing?'

That Radhika was furious was evident, but he had never seen his wife so mad. She was glaring at him as though she was possessed with something.

'I am trying to find proof of why you want to pack up everything, our home, our children's future, the shop and move to India.'

'The reason is among my clothes?' Chimanbhai was genuinely puzzled.

Radhika's temper wasn't assuaged with that question at all. She wanted answers. She came at him like a hungry tigress. 'No? No? Then you tell me, na! I am asking for some time now. I am trying to save your business…' She dragged him inside the room. 'But you keep saying no to everything. All you want to do is go back to your mistress.'

'What mistress? What are you saying, Radhika?'

Radhika was desperate. She was holding on to Chimanbhai's kurta. His question disgusted her so much, she left the collar in sheer hatred. The force of her emotion made Chimanbhai fall down. Radhika's eyes widened. Chimanbhai's wallet had fallen out of his kurta pocket. It was lying there between them. An open case that proved Chimanbhai's lies and justified Radhika's anger. The wallet had a much-handled picture of a woman. Meenakshi.

'What is this, Chiman? This? This photo! She's the reason why you want to give up everything and go to India, no?' Radhika was angry. 'This? You were going to leave us all for this?'

Chimanbhai wanted to cower, but somehow he couldn't. He knew that this was a sign from the goddess. But he couldn't say anything to her. He just stood in one place, frozen.

Radhika was wailing now and tearing things. Paper, Chimanbhai's kurtas, whatever was in front of her. Chimanbhai slowly backed up to the door and in a flash fled downstairs.

'Puppa, I am going to save us all.' Suraj was mixing something in the kitchen. There was a FedEx packet with all kinds of powders on the dining table.

'What are you doing now, Suraj?' Chimanbhai asked, with one eye on the stairs, just in case Radhika came down accompanied by her foul temper.

'It's a bomb. You see, very effective. Looks like milk, doesn't it? Nitroglycerine! Just leave it on ice. As long as it is cool or even at room temperature, nothing happens, but away from ice, near any heat... Oh, boy! We hide this inside Supriya's shop and when the radiators are on, kaboom!'

'Suraj! Are you my son or the devil!'

'Some dead chap got a Nobel Prize for inventing this.'

'He's dead na? Why can't you be like Bapu?' Chimanbhai realized that Suraj wasn't listening.

Suraj was pouring the liquid into milk bottles. Chimanbhai just watched awestruck as Suraj filled in six bottles, and there was milky stuff left over enough to fill another six. He left them on the dumbwaiter on the dining table. As the bottles wobbled Chimanbhai's heart sank down to where his stomach was. His whole body began to shake uncontrollably and he reached for the edge of the table to support himself.

'Don't touch it,' Suraj warned. 'I'll get some more bottles. Now we will have twenty bottles in total.' And he ran up the stairs to his room.

Chimanbhai stared at the bottles in front of him with shock and awe. How long will the ice last he wondered, and shivered at the thought of more diabolical things that his son might have up his sleeve.

NINETEEN

Maya had climbed into Elmore's camp bed and the two of them were kissing noisily. Dean kept his eyes closed but his ears had had enough of the increasing passion. The room was not meant for a rough-and-tumble and the two lovebirds just did not care whether Dean watched them or no. Dean watched the tangled blankets and limbs dispassionately for no more than a minute or two and grunted. This was worse than Elmore sneaking into the house at night. 'You two! Keep it down! You mother will be yelling your name out any minute now!'

'No she won't.' Maya giggled. 'I told her Puppa was fucking some Indian chick, and now she's mad.'

'Your old man?' Elmore asked. 'Didn't think he had it in him. But Dean is right. We gotta keep this quiet.'

'That girl is a good person, Maya. I think we should drop the idea.'

'And go on living here and watch my dad's money slowly disappear? I don't want to be poor,' said Maya.

'Then what are you doing with Elmore?' Dean retorted. 'He isn't exactly Mr Moneybags, is he?'

Elmore's fist came at Dean so fast that Dean had no chance to duck. Elmore was punching him again and again, and all Dean could do was dodge as much as he could lying in bed.

'Elmore, enough, Elmore!' Maya was now afraid Dean's howls would have someone from the house come up there to investigate. She got off the bed and watched. Elmore was not about to stop. She spotted a jar of water, reached out for it and threw it on Elmore.

'You bitch!' Elmore reacted to having a jugful of water thrown at him.

'You're a moron, Elmore! Just see what you've done!'

Maya stormed out of the little room, and as she climbed down the ladder, she called out, 'Breakfast is ready! Come down!' for the benefit of everyone in the house.

With Maya gone, and water soaking his clothes, Elmore had sobered down. He got off Dean's bed and stripped off his tee. Dean lay in bed, bloodied and wet, groaning.

'You're such a sorry ass!' That was the closest to contrite Elmore felt.

Dean grunted something inaudible. Elmore ignored him and announced unnecessarily, 'I'm going now. We should finish this job now. Today.'

'You do it. I'm outta here.'

***

Maya spotted her dad alone at the dining table. She decided to shower before facing the scared old man staring at milk bottles. As she was going towards her bedroom, she crossed Suraj who was coming downstairs armed with six brown bottles.

'Hey, watch out!' Suraj shouted.

'Watch out yourself, smelly!' Maya retorted.

Suraj bought the six bottles downstairs and set them down on the floor.

'Puppa, I am going to show you chemistry magic.'

'What now?'

'Wait, let me get this out of the way, otherwise... kaboom!'

'Why are you doing this, Suraj? You are turning into a criminal, beta!'

'No, Dad, I'm not going to do anything on my own. I will send those two to plant this stuff at her house or maybe at her shop. You wait and see.'

Suraj began to pour vile-smelling purple liquid into a saucepan. He held the pan over the gas and soon the purple liquid began to smoke. The purple fumes alarmed Chimanbhai who sat rooted to his chair. Then like an expert Suraj strained the liquid over another saucepan he had covered with Radhika's thin kitchen towel.

Suraj was crowing over the black crud left on the kitchen towel. 'Puppa, Puppa! See what we have here! This stuff is so dangerous, even a feather landing on it will make it go kaboom!'

'Kaboom!' Chimanbhai repeated, dazed by the

turn of events, 'Why does everything have to go "kaboom"?'

'Puppa, really! You are the one who started this. We are doing this for your store. You're the one... wait, let me check this first...' Suraj went back to poring over some sort of instruction manual.

At that very moment Chimanbhai knew why the pranayams were not working, why Radhika had found Meenakshi's photo. Ambe Ma had deserted him. He knew only his Meenakshi would not fail him. Uncaring of Radhika's wrath, he picked up the home phone to dial Meenakshi's number.

'Save me, Meenakshi!' he blubbered over the phone.

'Who's ready for breakfast?' asked Maya as she entered the house only to hear her father confess.

'They've all gone mad, Meenakshi! No hope left. I have prayed and prayed...'

'I'm telling Mom,' said Maya calmly and went up the stairs.

Chimanbhai held on to the phone for dear life. Radhika, like everyone else in the house, had become unpredictable. She would start yelling.

'Chimaaaaaaaaannnnnnn!' came the angry yell from his bedroom. Radhika emerged, arms akimbo, at the top of the stairs, looking like some vengeful goddess herself. Chimanbhai dropped the phone.

***

Dean was throwing whatever clothes he could find

in his duffel bag when Elmore stepped out of the little washroom.

'What the fuck are you doing, Dean?'

'What does it look like?'

'You going somewhere?'

'Yes, because you won't listen to me. There is something obviously wrong here. I keep telling you that I have met the girl, and that she is not a bad person. So I am not going to be a part of this shit any more. I'm leaving.'

Dean threw the bag down and began climbing down the stepladder. Elmore followed.

'Why are you doing this? We are so close to finishing the job, Dean.'

'Yeah, you finish it. You keep the money. I like the woman and I am not about to be hanged for this.' Dean was adamant now. 'I am asking Mr Shah for just enough cash to cross stateside and I'll disappear in Chicago as we had planned earlier.'

Their battered car was parked inside the garage next to Maya's. Dean opened the garage and drove the car out. The duffel bag was still in the driveway. Elmore was standing over it looking sullen.

'Listen, buddy, I have nothing against you and Maya. I cannot do this. I'm going now.'

'What if I told you that you will not get a penny from Maya's mother if you leave, now.'

'Well then, so be it. But I am leaving, Elmore. I am going to help Supriya.'

Both men glowered at each other, with the duffel

bag between them lying like a bone. Elmore blinked first.

'Fine. Go.'

Dean picked up the duffel bag and opened the passenger door to dump the bag at the back.

'At least put the bag in the trunk so that the highway patrol don't get suspicious,' said Elmore.

Dean looked at his friend and partner in crime with a new respect. He did care!

He pulled out the duffel and went around to the trunk. He threw in the bag and turned around to shake hands with Elmore. Dean did not want to part bitterly. Suddenly Elmore pushed him and Dean fell clumsily inside the trunk. Elmore slammed the trunk shut. Dean couldn't believe what had just happened to him. The sudden push knocked the wind out of him. His eyes surrendered to the darkness that claimed him.

Elmore walked in to inform Maya about what he had just done. Only Caligula the cat watched the drama from the roof of the car, his tail swishing.

***

Chimanbhai stood shivering at the bottom of the steps and Radhika and Maya were standing poised to unleash thunderbolts on top of his head. If this weren't real life, it would be very bad high drama indeed. Chimanbhai looked like a man wronged, sad and shrivelled up, shaking like a leaf, his eyes pregnant with tears.

'Look at me, Chiman!'

Chimanbhai reacted like a startled doe. Radhika stood at the top of the stairs commanding Chiman's attention like some villainous Valkyrie in voile, ready to murder him by stuffing him with gor-papdi laced with the arsenic of her words. Beside her, stood her raven, the equally angry Maya, the fruit of his own loins, now betraying him shamelessly just so they could cling to some foreign culture, some foreign way of life.

Chimanbhai yearned for the smell of parathas and bhajias that he grew up with, but standing under the stairs, confronted by the women of his home, he could only remember the ugly warm smells emanating from the dark alleys of Ahamdavad's Mamu Nayak Ni Pol, not the chaat shared with Meenakshi at Manekbaag. He crumpled, and allowed the tears to fall.

'You coward! I cannot believe I am married to you! I don't know what my father saw in you! Hard-working he is, he said. He will keep you happy, he said. I should have married that Jignesh Mehta. He is having three motels now. King of New Jersey, he is! You! And you are just shopowner! Shop that we are trying to save, but noooooo...Mr Chimanbhai Shah is afraid. What do the Americans call it? Chicken! And on top of that you've been cheating on me with that...that woman. How dare you!'

She had taken every step with determination. Chimanbhai was rooted to the spot, with no courage to wipe away his tears and tell her off. Tell her that all she wanted was money not her husband, and this was what had made him think of Meenakshi again after so many years. He wanted to tell her that it was a wife's duty to stop her husband from thinking up dishonourable deeds, and then stopping him from setting those plans in motion. Not once had she stopped him. In fact, they had all revelled in plotting and planning against Supriya. Now that he wanted to stop it, they just wouldn't let him. And they were hating him because he did not want to be a part of something sinister.

Radhika was circling him now, reminding him of a National Geographic special on pack dogs.

'Maya, pack his bags. I don't want this man to be my husband or your father. Pack his bags. We let him go home. We will get him to sign the papers of the house to us and we will let him go home. To India, to someone he thinks still loves him. He is remembering that world, ne? We will push him there only. He will soon realize that India which he once lived in is not same. Where kootris like Meenakshi live. She married also, ne? Then why she calls you? Is that India's culture? Go, Maya, pack his clothes.'

Just then Elmore stepped into the house. He meant to tell Maya that he had Dean safely locked in the trunk of the car. He saw Radhika gesticulating wildly and circling Chimanbhai. He was crying, so obviously everything was not okay.

Radhika turned to see Elmore. 'Elmorebhai, go upstairs and help Maya pack clothes.'

'Who is travelling?'

'Don't ask questions. Why everyone asking questions? Go help Maya.'

Elmore raised his hands in mock surrender and took the steps two at a time to get to the bedroom. Maya was there.

Radhika rapidly found her anger lowering down to a slow simmer. But it was by no means gone. She was sitting down at the dining table where Suraj's strange concoctions that promised a big kaboom were brewing and some were on ice. Chimanbhai wanted to warn Radhika, and he even opened his mouth to tell her to be careful. But Radhika was in no mood to listen. She saw Chimanbhai open his mouth and then shut it. It was force of habit that made her pick up the serving spoon lying on the table. Then she looked at the table. It was dirty! There was some black crud on the table. She wondered what it was. Everything was so dirty ever since these two men came to stay with them that she had no rest. For one minute she sits down and there's stuff and dirt on the table! With a sigh she decided that she was going to clean up. She banged the serving spoon down.

Bang!

There was a small explosion on the table. Radhika jumped a step back. Chimanbhai almost jumped out of his skin. He ran towards the Lazyboy and cowered down behind it.

'I was telling you everyone has gone mad. That's Suraj's doing. He's building a bomb. God knows where he got money from. He had FedEx deliver him things. I am telling you, Radhika, we are doing wrong things...'

'Shut up, Chiman!' Radhika recovered quickly. Then she looked towards the bedrooms and yelled, 'Suraj!!! What have you done here! Come down now! Suraaaaaj! Suraaaajjjjj!'

Suraj came down wearing camouflage pants and a black vest, wearing three black stripes on each cheek.

'What do you think you are doing? What was that thing! The table is spoilt for ever.'

'Mom! I told Puppa to not allow anyone to touch it. It's iodine Mom! So simple! Even a feather can trigger off the bomb. Good, haan?'

'My brilliant boy! You are Rambo, ne?' Radhika said, hugging Suraj, 'See...see...see...Chiman! Who loves you? My boy or that kootri? Who will do so much for you? You go to that Meenakshi. Let us see what she will do for you!'

Radhika sat down to watch her desi Rambo clear the table slowly, picking up the crud and storing it in Ziploc bags, slowly.

When Chimanbhai's heart began to beat normally and his vision cleared slowly of tears, he decided to emerge from behind the Lazyboy.

Radhika was on the phone. She used her pointing finger to call him close to her. Chimanbhai walked slowly towards her. Would she hit him?

'Mr Benson, you listen to me first. He simply sign paper, and that will do or no? Say this now. We don't have time to come to your office. We think it through already...okay, okay, we will do that. Thank you...that's what I am saying first. Okay, okay. Thank you, have a nice day.'

She disconnected the phone and said, 'That I call Mr Benson. Chiman you write on paper that you leave house and shop to me. So when you go, you no come back greedy for what I gave up for you. We will make shop work and stay in this house only. You go to your Meenakshi or whatever. But you cannot take my life from my children and me. Come on, take paper. Write. Then you can go wherever you are going.'

There was a scratching at the door. The cat was mewing.

'Suraj! Get Kali inside. Otherwise the door will be spoilt more than it is already.'

Chimanbhai wrote furiously, sticking out his tongue at the corner of his mouth with the effort of forming words. He didn't think it would be so easy. He read it out to Radhika. 'I, Chimanbhai Himmatbhai Shah, is happy to sign the whole property in Winderly, Tigard and also my shop India World to my wife Radhika Chimanbhai Shah. I have no problems with her owning both home and shop fully. Nobody has forced me to say this. I am happy to give this to her. Thank you. God Bless America. I am going to India. Vande Mataram. Thank you. Bye bye.'

'What you saying bye bye?' Radhika was irritated, but then she had had enough, so she took the paper, read it again, and said, 'Sign it, ne. Put today's date also.'

Chimanbhai did as he was told. Kali the cat was sitting on the table looking at him with pity. Chimanbhai shooed the cat. It yelped and jumped off the low coffee table.

***

A blue Ford Fiesta slowly turned into Winderly. The girl had worn dark glasses that concealed most of her face and the scarf covered her hair. But she was biting her lower lip most attractively. She stopped by the sign that listed the owners of the different properties. Then turned into the lane where the Shahs lived. The car cruised the shady tree-lined lane, stopping every now and then while its passengers checked the numbers.

The car stopped outside the Shahs' home. The girl in the car wondered whether she should get off and find out why an unknown dead man had her address and theirs on a sheet of paper.

Supriya pondered for a minute, then stepped out of the car and on to the sidewalk next to the Shah home.

***

Caligula rubbed himself against Chimanbhai's legs and mewed balefully. Radhika had never liked the cat, but preferred it fed so that it wouldn't mew so consistently. She heard the cat and cursed.

'That Maya! Why name a cat after a goddess? Can't even curse it! Has anyone given it some milk?'

Suraj pointed to the table. 'The milk is hot still, Ma.'

'Feed the stupid cat, Suraj. Feed the cat. I cannot stand the mewing.' Radhika put her fingers to her temples and walked towards the stairs. 'I'm going to get your father's passport, and give him money to go to India. That girl Maya! Why is it taking her so long to pack the bags?' She then turned around and faced Chimanbhai once again. 'You have spoilt everything. You just be coward all your life. Coward.'

***

Chimanbhai was distraught. His heart was so heavy, he could not think straight any more. He decided to step out into the sunshine and wait. He was amazed that Radhika hadn't decided to throw him out of his own home with just the clothes he was wearing.

He looked at the hydrangeas. There was a time when Radhika would take so much care of the flowers. Now the plants looked a bit forlorn, just like he felt. When he looked up he came face to face with the girl who was responsible for the whole thing. Supriya! She was standing in his driveway looking like a ghost in a white shirt, white jacket, jeans, sunglasses, and white high heels.

'No, no, it cannot be...' Chimanbhai began to mutter. 'I am sure it is the cold. Yes, it must be the cold. I am feeling cold and that is why brain is conjuring up images to scare me. Go away girl! Shoo! When I am warm, I will not see you...don't look at me like that! No, no, please go away...I can do nothing any more...I am cold...the bomb is cold but the milk is hot...oh no, that Kali, she will be alone with the milk...oh no, the milk is on the same table...'

Supriya could not understand anything that Chimanbhai was saying, but he looked so disturbed, it alarmed Supriya. Chimanbhai stopped muttering. He heard a yowl. He stood right in front of Supriya not staring at her but listening hard. Supriya was undecided whether she should flee or stay.

Chimanbhai slapped the palm of his hand to his head in a classic gesture of despair.

'Milk! Kali! Oh no!'

He turned around and fled towards the house, yelling, 'Kaleeeeee! Kaleeeeee!'

***

Caligula was hungry and he could not hold off any more. He could smell the milk, but there was something acrid in the air that made him wary. But in the battle between his stomach and the brain, the stomach won.

The cat jumped up and sniffed. His tail was up, but he did not know why. So much milk! Caligula tentatively licked at the milk in the largish bowl. If cats could curse, it would sound like the tiny yowl that came out involuntarily. He licked his lips.

Just then he heard his name being called, 'Kaleeeee!'

He was not allowed up on the table. He decided to jump.

The dumbwaiter shook. The ice jangled against the milk bottles and the black crud kept in the Ziploc bags began to tumble. The milk in the bowl would surely scald him.

Elmore had managed to sneak into Maya's room. She was addictive. Even her giggling made him feel like Superman. He would kill that Supriya for her. But first, he needed to tell her about Dean's duplicity.

Radhika didn't know whether she should be packing Chimanbhai's suitcases to throw him out as planned, or pack hers, so she could run away to her sister's place in Birmingham. Maybe not Birmingham. England was not an option. She would have to tell her everything. And that would not do. Neeraj and Suraj were downloading more devious things from the net...when Caligula jumped off the table. And everything on the dumbwaiter and the table came tumbling down behind him and there was a deafening flash behind him.

***

As soon as Chimanbhai reached the front door

yelling, 'Kaleeeeee, Kaleeee!' he was thrown back by a powerful explosion. The windows shattered, and the very sidewalk that Supriya was standing on seemed to be jangled. She watched the house explode in front of her eyes.

With the explosion came the fire. There was so much smoke, Supriya started coughing. She was scared that Chimanbhai who was lying on the driveway would be dead. She whipped off the scarf that was tied to her hair and put it over her mouth. She ducked from at least three other explosions that shook the house when she heard knocking and a plea of 'Help! Somebody help!'

The voice sounded familiar. It was coming from the trunk of the car in the driveway. Somebody was stuck inside the car! The car keys were still in the lock on the trunk. Supriya unlocked the trunk and to her utter surprise, Dean untangled himself and stepped out. His legs were a bit wobbly from being locked inside, so Supriya helped him. The fire was now raging.

The neighbours started to gather now. Supriya screamed, 'Mr Shah!'

Dean spotted Chimanbhai lying down on the driveway. His clothes were torn and he had glass pieces stuck like shrapnel all over him. He looked a little scary in that bloody avatar. Both Dean and Supriya ran towards him and helped him to his feet. Chimanbhai looked dazed. He kept repeating, 'Kali, kaboom...Kali...kaboom...Kali...kaboom!'

Dean knew he had to take Supriya away quietly and quickly. Someone would have called 911 by now and neither of them wanted to answer any questions. Chimanbhai in the meantime spotted Supriya and yelled so loudly that both Dean and Supriya took to their feet. He got into the passenger side of the car and ducked low. She pulled a scarf over her face and drove out of there like a woman possessed, not looking back. When she was on the I-5, she heard the wailing of the police sirens and the fire trucks. Chimanbhai would be saved. She drove on and did not stop until she reached Rainier.

Chimanbhai knew he was being punished by the gods. In a flash he had lost his entire family. He had seen Supriya, and he knew that she knew. All of a sudden he saw that dreadful cat emerge from the smoke, his hair singed and lope off towards the woods. He knew his hair was singed and that Kali was all he had left now. He ran like a madman after the cat, 'Kali! Kali!'

TWENTY

Mr Shah had been of no help to Officer Wade. Even after being in the asylum for days, he had not uttered a word. Dr Anjali too had tried speaking in Hindi with the man. But it was of no use either.

Dr Anjali came in with a nurse. Mr Shah was sitting on the bed, staring blankly into space.

'Mr Shah, you have a visitor.'

Chimanbhai did not look up.

An elegant lady, wearing a beautiful apricot-coloured saree, entered the room and stood staring at Chimanbhai.

'Oh Chiman!' she said, exactly in the manner of Hindi heroines of yesteryears, and ran towards the bed. She sat down and held his hand. 'I have come to take you back to India.'

After days of having dealt with an unresponsive Chimanbhai, Anjali felt good to see him stand up, without letting go of the lady's hand.

Wade was waiting at the reception area of the asylum. The fire department had followed up with the courier who delivered many packages to the Shah house but every lead was a dead end. They had found human remains but everything was burnt beyond identification. There was no motive, no suspects. They had closed the casebook by marking it as an unfortunate accident.

The captain had asked Wade to work on a new case. And this case too would need Wade's newfound connections with Indians. The case was about something called 'kabootar'. Wade had not hesitated in accepting this case. He had already asked Anjali out for chai latte.

He saw Anjali beaming as she pushed Chimanbhai's wheelchair to the reception area. He was still holding the Indian lady's hand.

Wade and Anjali looked at the departing duo. 'Nice couple,' said Wade to Anjali.

Meenakshi looked back at the police officer and the doctor, then said softly to Chiman, 'Nice couple.'

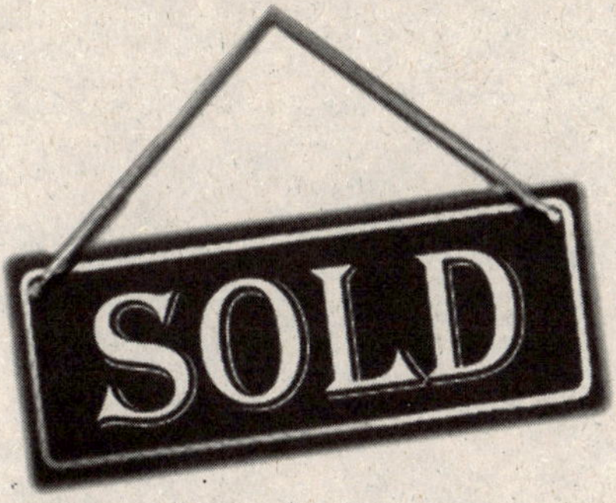
SOLD

ACKNOWLEDGEMENTS

The idea for this book had been simmering for a long time, and I am especially grateful to these marvelous people in my life who have made the book possible. Thank you.

To Mash and Agni, who gave me the space to write.

To Mash and Shashank Ghosh who loved the story first.

To Jugal Mody who allowed me to bully him into reading bits and paragraphs, without even asking what the whole was and for insisting I call Mita.

To Deepa Gahlot for Elmore Leonard.

To Mita Kapur at Siyahi for handling the details and all the paperwork like a fairy godmother.

To Milee Ashwarya at Random House and Mita for handholding and smoothening all hiccups.

And finally for SG for having blown my mind with Isha.

A NOTE ON THE AUTHOR

Manisha Lakhe is a writer and blogger (www.manishalakhe.blogspot.com and www.billiboli.blogspot.com). After a successful stint in advertising, she studied filmmaking at the Northwest Film Centre in Portland OR. She is currently based in Mumbai, where she runs an online writer's forum called Caferati (www.caferati.com). This is her debut novel.